OUR SHADOW SELVES

V.G. Lee

MUSWELL PRESS

First published by Muswell Press in 2026

Typeset in Bembo by M Rules
Printed and bound by CPI Group (UK) Ltd, Croydon CR0 4YY
A CIP record for this book is available from the British Library

ISBN: 9781068389382
eISBN: 9781068389399

Our authorised representative in the EU for product safety is
Easy Access System Europe, Mustamäe tee 50, 10621 Tallinn, Estonia
gpsr.requests@easproject.com

Muswell Press, London N6 5HQ
www.muswell-press.co.uk

MIX
Paper | Supporting responsible forestry
FSC® C013604

MUSWELL PRESS

2 4 6 8 10 9 7 5 3 1

OUR SHADOW SELVES

To dear Richie, the brother. My brother.

SONNY

Seven am. New Year's Day, 2015

Far below, vans and trucks arrive, men spilling out onto what once – some two decades earlier – had been a communal lawn. In the far distance, a weak sun hovers over the North Sea. On the balcony that encompasses the top storey of the Miller Building, Sonny re-positions his canvas chair so that he remains invisible. Through a small pair of binoculars, he continues to keep an eye on the busy scene below.

Clutching Styrofoam cups of tea and coffee, stamping their boots against the bitter cold, the men on the ground gather in small enthusiastic groups. He picks up a sense of their energy, as if a fresh project starting on the first day of a new year excites them. From the open door of one of the trucks, the sound of a radio is fading in and out. The song playing is *Millenium* but singer and title mean nothing to Sonny, however he likes some of the words: madness, hope, fate. They mirror his mood. The temperature remains just above freezing. Sonny draws the folds of his silk kimono closer to his bare skin before reaching for his own now stone-cold coffee.

The Miller Building might be considered ugly, even sinister – a decaying seven-storey cube marooned between sea and the resort town of Hawksbridge. But not to Sonny. On their first day, as his mother searched her handbag for the key, he'd stared up at the plaque above the front door: a worn carving of an ocean liner and under it the date, 1905. He'd taken several steps backwards to see the building better – counted six rows of small rectangular windows – apportioned a row for each deck. Two further steps and he could make out the red-brick balcony concealing the very top deck where even now, after all that has happened, he still likes to daydream of rich people asleep in their cabins having partied the night away.

There had been no taxi at the railway station, only a Co-Op van delivering to the nearby cafeteria. The van driver took pity on them. They looked forlorn: a small boy hanging on to his mother's hand. She with her lovely, tired face, shabbily dressed – bewildered? Their two flimsy suit-cases weighed next to nothing. The man had handed her into the passenger seat, let the boy sit on her lap. Dropping them off he'd watched from his cab as she searched in her handbag for a key. "God, give me strength," he heard her say. "Where the devil is it?" The boy, mouth hanging open, seemed in a world of his own. "Come on darling," she'd said. "This is it. Home."

An hour passes and then as if the time of eight am had been agreed, a steady stream of more lorries, vans and cars begin to arrive. Sonny counts seventeen men on the ground below. They start to pull on protective clothing. He particularly approves of their cherry-red hard hats. He wonders what they are talking about: the job, their weekend, or is it just that banter men indulge in? Banter is not a skill he excels at.

As the sun's rays breach the balcony wall, he glances

inland towards the damaged footbridge that spans the road leading out of Hawksbridge. Someone is attempting the perilous crossing. He continues to watch till he's reassured that they're out of danger although what would he do, what could he ever do to be of help? Placing the binoculars next to his empty cup he gets to his feet. He's ready now but is some form of prayer or eulogy required? In his head he hears his mother's voice full of affection, time and again: "You're a ruddy little show-off." He reaches for the chair to steady himself. The kimono falls open. The sun's faint warmth strokes across his pale, hairless chest and thighs.

From the open door behind him comes a small sound, maybe the clink of metal.

"I'm sorry," he says.

If anyone inside the room has heard him, they make no answer.

Approaching the parapet, he looks down. At first the tiny figures continue to go about their business: a builder's truck is being unloaded, orange cones set out to indicate an exit and an entrance and then someone looks up. In almost perfect synchronicity, heads lift and faces turn skywards. Arms are raised; hands point and wave . . . at him.

With care he climbs onto the balcony wall and sits. His legs now dangle in mid-air. He feels a moment of fear. All his life he's avoided physical pain but this isn't just his best option, it's the only one he has left. He is fifty years old with the unlined body and face of a much younger man and an unlined life to match: his own choice but on consideration the wrong one.

A chorus of voices rises up from the ground, the individual words indistinct. Sonny closes his eyes, imagining a swarm of benign bees. It will take at least an hour for anyone to gain access. Every window of the lower floors has been boarded up from the inside with thick plywood. Someone hits their car horn. His eyes flick open. Men are running to their own vehicles, hitting *their* horns: long notes, staccato notes, as they try to distract him, to make a connection.

Sonny slips the kimono from his shoulders and stretches his arms above his head. Pressing the palms of his hands together he salutes the morning sun. The sound of horns and bees grow louder. Sledgehammers attack the front door. There is the distant scream of splintering wood. He glances down. *What a long way to fall.*

"Five, four, three," Sonny counts. For the first time he is terrified.

He feels the lightest, tenderest touch as a hand cradles the back of his head. Gratefully he attempts to lean back – but meets resistance.

"Two, one," Shona says.

His body jack-knifes forwards.

Part 1

1

SHONA

New Year's Day, 2014

On several occasions recently you've observed, as if not guilty of pleasurably running your fingers through my hair countless times in the past, that long hair is unflattering on a woman (meaning me) over a certain age. Where I'm concerned, you adopt either a neutral or negative tone to your voice due to your poorly hidden embarrassment that you could have ever – well, it wasn't quite love and never sexual attraction, have adored me. *I adore her*, you told your friends.

Thoughtfully, I consider my reflection in the hall mirror. My smiling self looks back at me. I see a younger face, remembered from my teens and well into my twenties. *Happy New Year, Shona.* My hair is as thick and glossy as ever. It reaches almost to my waist. Fine streaks of gold from the previous summer working in your garden remain in the dark brown. It's not often that I take the time to stop and stare, in fact I try to avoid mirrors entirely; however, on this grey wintery afternoon, I'm alone in the house. You're not here to toss out an amused comment. The smile fades.

Even though I'm wearing baggy jeans and a shapeless t-shirt, long sleeves covering my wrists, it is obvious how unhealthily thin I've become. No longer 'fashionably thin', I am a woman in her mid-thirties who is *thin* from neglect.

In my wardrobe hang some of the clothes I wore before my breakdown. They haven't dated much but seem alien as if belonging to a woman I once knew slightly and never really came to like. If I were to slip into those skinny jeans, a fitted top, paint my face, Richard, what would you think? *Oh no, Shona starting another of her tortuous slides into manic depression.*

Yesterday, I walked to the seafront. It was cold but sunny and many of the cafés were open. The forecast had been for snow later on, but well wrapped up in layers, I chose an outside table to drink hot coffee and watch the world go by. Lazily I observed an elderly woman as she walked along the pavement towards me. I found myself admiring her straight back and perfect posture. The woman's face was unusual: gaunt yet full of animation, white hair pulled back from a severe middle parting. She wore dark colours, her clothes not at all 'age appropriate': a navy pea-jacket that once I would have worn myself, a skirt with movement, a length of cloth of a vibrant blue at her neck. It occurred to me that many decades earlier, she might have been an actress or a dancer.

I don't know what triggered my reaction but, as if we were old friends, I found myself on my feet, hands held out to greet her. Without a glance in my direction, she walked straight past. But as you well know, if I truly care about something or someone then I don't take 'no' for an answer. Burrowing in my coat pocket for sufficient coins to pay for the coffee, I tossed them on the table and followed.

Her thin legs tapering into black suede boots twinkled onwards like musical notes on a scale. She walked surprisingly fast. At the zebra crossing, although traffic was approaching from both directions, she stepped out into the road. To the right a van slowed, to the left, a car increased its speed. I seized her arm. She tried to shake me off but I yanked her backwards. The hem of her coat shivered as the car roared past. The driver yelled at us, "Stupid fucking women!"

We stood safe and unharmed on the pavement.

"I thought you were mugging me," she said, appearing a little shaken. Together we walked back to the coffee shop and I ordered tea and two almond slices.

Seated opposite each other, waiting for our order to arrive, she said, "My name is Mrs Gifford. And you are?"

I mentioned the encounter to you later that evening, told you that I'd invited my new friend to lunch in a few days' time. Richard – your face! You immediately looked concerned. "Oh, Shona!" you said. "I've seen these waifs and strays who wander around Hawksbridge. I might give them a quid but I wouldn't invite them into my home."

"She's neither a waif nor a stray. Her name is Irene Gifford and she lives with her son in the Miller Building."

"Nobody lives in the Miller Building."

"But *she* does," I insisted.

"Then she and her son are squatters. I rest my case."

"Does that matter? After all, I'm a sort of squatter."

You leant back in your chair. "I thought we were friends," you said.

That rattled me. Over the years you've called me many things but never 'friend'.

2

Throughout the preceding years spent in and out of various hospitals, Richard and I hadn't been in touch; my decision, not his. Just before my final discharge he rang. His voice on the public phone after such a long time sounded incredibly loud: "Shona, how are you?"

I'd held the receiver away from my ear. "I'm okay. Not bad."

"Listen—"

"I am listening."

"I wondered if you'd consider moving back in with me? No strings attached," he said. "I've rented out the London flat and moved north. Hawksbridge is by the sea – you'd like it. You can convalesce, grow stronger. Start to paint again."

"How did you know I was here?"

"Oh, the grapevine," he said breezily. "I still manage to keep tabs on you."

I was flustered. Even in a relatively medicated state I knew that the one choice I shouldn't make was to accept his offer, yet it was tempting. I was due to move into a half-way house near the hospital. I'd seen the accommodation: a second-floor room with a sink, a bathroom shared with five other people. A tiny window facing a brick wall.

"Only a stone's throw from the park," the social worker had said brightly as if she'd willingly house her own daughter, or mother, or self, there.

I reached a decision; surely it was better to go with the devil I knew.

"But I can't afford much in the way of rent," I said. I'd inherited an amount of money on the death of my adoptive parents but after two decades there was little of it left.

"Fifty quid a week. I earn more than enough to cover the two of us for the time being. Take it or leave it, Shona. No pressure."

"I don't want to be dependent on you."

Richard laughed, the laughter not quite genuine. "*Your* dependency wouldn't suit me either. Listen, during the week I'm away working in London. I get home late, fend for myself. I can offer you a pleasant room with a shared kitchen and bathroom. And there's a garden. You always wanted a garden. If you feel green-fingered then be my guest. Tidy it up, grow veg and flowers, dig a pond if you like. Horticultural therapy." He paused. I didn't fill the silence. When he spoke again, his tone of voice was gentle. "I know it won't be easy. Can't the two of us park our history for a while? Just come and get well."

To 'come and get well,' was such an easy and enticing option.

He collected me. It resembled a scene from a romantic comedy: perfect summer's day, a tanned and handsome man expensively suited, leaning against the passenger door of an open-topped sports car. Only I was miscast. In the many months since we'd last seen each other I'd added three stone in weight and my red-rimmed eyes peered myopically out at the world from a face become a ball of pallid dough. And carpet slippers! Men's, grandfathers', brown tartan provided by the hospital! As well as my face, my feet were swollen from the medication I was on; they wouldn't fit into the ridiculous satin slippers I'd worn when admitted.

"Shona," Richard said hurrying forward, his hand outstretched.

I had to admire the way his expression remained unchanged, that he had the sense not to say, *you look great.* He took my arm.

I shook him off. "I'm okay." As he opened the passenger door, I saw that the seat was narrow with almost no legroom. We looked at each other.

"You can let me help or try to manage on your own," he said. "Darling, I want whatever's best for you."

"Help me then," I said. "But no 'darlings' – all that is over."

"Fair enough. Lighten up." And that instruction was just so patently ridiculous given the situation that we both laughed. Just for a split second I found myself thinking, *if only.*

With some difficulty Richard managed to manoeuvre me into the front seat. Adjusting the seat belt proved even trickier but jokingly he blamed himself. "Typical me with that need to impress. I only hired the car a few hours ago. I thought you might like the wind in your hair."

That was the only time I saw uncertainty. His gaze swept over my dull and greasy plait and then away. A male nurse stowed my suitcase into the boot. Deep in conversation, Richard walked back with him towards the front entrance. My attention wandered. I almost slept but then Richard was getting into the car, throwing a bulky envelope and my bag of pills onto the back seat.

"Ready?"

"Yes."

"About an hour and a half drive. Let me know if you need to stop."

And so, I arrived at Richard's Victorian semi set in the shabby seaside town of Hawksbridge. I was surprised. Knowing Richard, I'd expected more, that at least we'd roll up in front of a modern detached house with a drive and double garage.

Helping me out of the car, he said, "Look, you can see the sea."

To please him, I looked. At the bottom of the road, there it was: an expanse of ominous dark grey. "Beautiful," I said.

He'd given me that familiar boyish grin: "Every day a different colour. Every hour. Sometimes the colour changes within a matter of seconds."

In those first few weeks in Richard's house, he was kind and caring. I concede that he pampered me back to life while keeping his distance. I didn't want cosy chats at his kitchen table; all I looked for was sleep and a measure of comfort, luxuries I'd been denied in a psychiatric ward. He'd prepared the bedroom at the back of the house, looking over the then neglected garden. There was a single bed.

"I wasn't sure if you were ready for a double after a hospital bed," he said. "But I can change it."

"It's fine." The bed faced a wide picture window. I could see trees and sky. Everything in the room right down to the paintwork looked brand new: pale calming colours. "Richard, it's all lovely. Thank you."

"Glad you like it. I'll leave you to settle in." He stepped out onto the landing, started to pull the door shut.

"No!" I was instantly in a state of panic. "Can you leave it open? Just till I get used to the idea of my own room. We were always locked in at night."

"No problem. I'm so sorry Shona." I still believe he meant it.

As Art Director of his own design studio in East London, Richard set off five days a week just after seven am but invariably he left a sandwich with a vegetable or fruit smoothie for my lunch. In the evenings, if he didn't go out, we ate 'take-aways' or ready meals he bought from Marks and Spencer on King's Cross Station. Generally, I ate in the kitchen while he'd arrange his food on a tray and carry it into his front room.

Having the house to myself day after day, I was able to enjoy showering and washing my hair again. In hospital, there were no locks on the bathroom doors, not even a plug in the bath or hand basin for fear that we inmates might try to drown ourselves. A bathroom to myself in an empty house was a luxury.

I remained vigilant. In the past our relationship had been weighted in his favour; this time I was determined – as vulnerable as my position was – to retain my sense of self. I took on the tasks of his washing and ironing, ferrying his suits to the dry cleaners, (I must admit that any loose change I found in his pockets, I kept.) I cleaned the house, made a start on his overgrown garden. Our relationship settled, became ordered; my role was one of housekeeper. Yes, the power lay with Richard, owner of the roof over my head, provider of food and utilities but at least instead of entirely paying my way I was providing an invaluable service. It seems extraordinary how limited my memory was. Ten years earlier I'd made this very same assumption.

Richard loved food but in small quantities. He had always been self-conscious about his weight. As a schoolboy, even well into his teens, the other boys teased him, gave him the nickname of 'Fat Dick'. That was the reason he insisted on being called Richard – abbreviations not allowed. He told me once, early in our relationship, that ideally he'd like to be addressed by his full name of Richard Christopher Maplin. At the time I'd laughed because I'd known that laughter was what he wanted rather than understanding. After that I did sometimes call him Richard Christopher Maplin in a fond teasing fashion. He'd liked it and then I must have used the name once too often. 'Not funny, Shona,' he'd said, his expression darkening. "End of."

One evening when I'd been out of hospital for almost a month, I decided to surprise him. So far cooking had been something I'd avoided, but I would prepare a modest cooked dinner. The freezer was well stocked and I managed to produce lamb cutlets, potatoes and mint from the garden, broccoli and gravy. No pudding required. I laid the kitchen table, even discovering some paper napkins in one of the drawers. I found candles too but ignored them. This wasn't intended to be a romantic dinner – I was thanking him for his care and kindness because what would have become of me otherwise?

The energy and concentration required did me good. All went well. I found myself listening out for his key turning in the front door. When finally, I heard Richard's footsteps in the hall, I tried to appear normal, as if cooking a meal was no big deal. At the sink I washed some pans. No further sound came from the hallway. Were both of us listening out for the other, unsure what our reactions should be?

I broke first. "Is that you, Richard?" I called out.

"Who else would it be?" he answered. "Something smells good."

Once in the kitchen, he said all the right things: *Shona, this is great, fantastic. Love the lamb cutlets. So proud of you.* But there was no pleasure in the gaze sweeping the room, absorbing the tidy work surfaces, the shining hob and carefully laid table. Not even relief that his house guest was finally starting to stand on her own two feet.

In total silence we ate. At the end of the meal, he said, "Mm, delicious. Can I help stack the dishwasher?" He'd already picked up his half-full wine glass and taken a couple of steps towards the hall.

"No problem. I'll do it."

"Well, if you're sure?"

"I am." I began to clear away the dishes.

He left the kitchen.

I heard the door of the living room closing, a few minutes later the sound of his TV.

While in hospital the very first time during my teens, it was explained to me that I was insensitive to the feelings of others. I accept that this is true, however I *am* hypersensitive to atmosphere. That evening I knew that my efforts in preparing a meal had caused a misalignment between the two of us. Was it happening again, that switch from care to coerce? Richard, seeing my ability to function as some kind of threat? I pushed the thought away because ... I didn't want it to be true.

3

2014

Mrs Gifford came and went. As at our first meeting she was dressed in a distinct style – I'll call it 'elderly theatrical person style'. Her fur coat (possibly lynx) with padded shoulders was initially impressive, but as she sauntered past me in the hallway, I definitely picked up the whiff of moth balls.

"Nineteen-fifties," she said then as if reading my mind. "This cat has seen better days."

I caught the coat as it slipped from her thin shoulders.

Underneath she was dressed for warmth: a calf-length skirt, bright-blue pullover that matched her knitted hat. She was half-an-hour late, I'd given up hope but now I was ridiculously pleased to see her. I fought the urge to bombard her with trivial questions: had she knitted the hat and pullover, was blue her favourite colour, was the coat a gift from a long-ago admirer? Instead, with a friendly smile and gentle touch to her elbow, I ushered her into the kitchen.

My initial thought that Mrs Gifford might once have been a professional ballet dancer was proved correct but not Saddlers Wells or the Royal Ballet as I'd grandly imagined.

During the 1960s she'd been part of a minor troupe touring the north of England. Seated at the kitchen table she told me that she'd had a son by a man who was desperate to marry her. "But only to get my boy. He didn't love me." To raise her child, she made a career move into teaching, first ballet but then as it became increasingly popular, ballroom and Latin-American. Her tone became flat and lifeless which I took to signify that this later career was a disappointment or even perhaps a failure.

As she revealed a quite sad life of unfulfilled dreams, I began to relax a little in her company. What could be more calming than to sit with a view over the garden and some early daffodils, while someone else expressed dissatisfaction with *their* life?

Half an hour passed. I began to prepare our lunch. I poured us both a glass of elderflower cordial.

"Did you make this yourself?"

I was tempted to say yes but feared Mrs Gifford was sharp enough to recognise a lie. "I bought the cordial and just added chilled tap water."

"Very refreshing," she said. "And you, Shona, what do you do all day?"

"I used to be an artist."

"Used to be?"

"I've been ill, but I'm almost fully recovered." Instantly I regretted talking about illness so early in the friendship. I leapt to my feet, "Just home-made vegetable soup. Last autumn's harvest. I hope you'll like it."

Earlier I'd washed my hair. It hung loose and damp down my back. I turned on the heat beneath the saucepan and began to stir the soup while with my free hand, I stroked a brush through the tangles. In the gloom of the kitchen, I could see the electricity sparking as I brushed. Dreamily I imagined how I must look: a Pre-Raphaelite beauty, Jane Burden, artists' model, wife of William Morris, lover of Rossetti. I possessed the same rippling waves, same swooping eyebrows. Once Richard had likened my eyebrows to 'two glossy swallows'. He'd hate to be reminded of *that*. First, he'd deny having ever said it and then insist he'd been joking. Or drunk. But no, I clearly remembered the expression on his face as he'd made the comment – as if unable to believe his good luck.

Mrs Gifford's voice cut through my thoughts like the crack of a whip. "Not over the saucepan, Shona."

"Sorry." I stumbled awkwardly out of my daydream.

"If you must brush your hair, do it in the hall. I'll keep an eye on the soup."

From the hallway I watched as she turned down the heat, then as if this was her own kitchen, she reached for the fresh loaf of bread I'd taken out and began slicing it into far neater and more regular slices than I could have achieved. Here was a woman with an innate knowledge of small domestic tasks, who had cooked and cut bread possibly most of her life as she fended for herself and her son.

"Butter?" she called out.

"In the fridge."

She opened the fridge door and took out the tub of butter. "Your fridge needs cleaning," she said.

"I know." I was smiling. It didn't embarrass me in the least to be reproved; in fact it made me feel . . . visible.

"Perhaps a clean tea-towel?"

Knotting my hair at the back of my neck I pulled open a kitchen drawer. I tried to make a choice, the tea towel that would most please her. I chose a flower print in Irish linen. If she was pleased – and really why should she be? – she didn't show it!

"Soup's ready," she said. "I'm surprised. It's rather tasty."

"I'm a reasonable cook."

There was humour in her eyes. "I'll have to take your word for that, for now." She began to pour soup into our bowls. This role reversal seemed perfectly natural. Placing the saucepan back on the hob she joined me at the table, unfolding her paper serviette. Instead of placing it on her lap she tucked the corner into the neck of her cardigan. "Shaky hands," she said. "This soup could land anywhere."

She helped herself to a slice of bread while I topped up our glasses with fresh cordial. I held up my glass. "New friends," I said.

Before responding she hesitated, assessing me. "New friends." Our glasses touched.

She tasted the soup. "Hot," she said.

"There are no spices in it."

"I mean 'too hot'." She waved her hand in front of her mouth then leaned back in her chair. "Shona, do you know who Margot Fonteyn was?" Mrs Gifford's eyes were as bright as a bird as she searched my face for some reaction.

"Of course. A famous ballerina."

"Oh, she was much more than that." She began to crumble bread over the soup. I sensed she was taking her time waiting till she was sure that my interest was captured before leaning forward, taking a deep breath and then, "I met her once. At that time, I was nothing or almost invariably believed myself to be nothing."

I understood that belief very well.

"Margot Fonteyn was the guest of honour when I danced the dual role of Odette-Odile in the ballet *Swan Lake* for a Charity Gala – the only time our troupe ever appeared in London. Fonteyn was still considered to be at the height of her powers." Mrs Gifford smiled at the memory. "She was incredibly beautiful. In 1962 when she danced the same role, Nureyev said of Fonteyn, 'when she left the stage in her great white tutu, I would have followed her to the end of the world.' Has anyone ever felt like that about you, Shona?"

"I thought they did but I was mistaken."

"You're still young – there's time." She sat back in her chair, folding her arms across her stomach. "After the gala, Fonteyn came backstage to my dressing room. That was the only time in my entire career when I was given a room for myself. In the mirror, I saw the door slowly open and she walked in as if she was a normal human being like you or me. But of course, she wasn't. She was perfection in every way it is possible to be perfect. In the mirror, our eyes met."

As she spoke, I pictured the scene: Fonteyn with diamonds in her dark hair, at her ears and around her neck, an ermine stole falling away from her bare shoulders, the lights, their two lovely faces reflected in the mirror.

"As if she knew me and my work well, as if she'd followed my career path for years and believed us to be old friends, Fonteyn said, 'Irene, if you could dance as consistently well as you did this evening, you would be one of the great ballerinas.' She placed rose-tipped fingers on my shoulder and pressed down – I was twenty-two years old and four months pregnant. That night I went home happy and yet suicidal. Have you ever felt suicidal?"

"Yes," I said.

"Then you might understand that being noticed by Fonteyn, having her few words of praise to remember, were going to have to last me for a lifetime and anyway . . ." Mrs Gifford's voice became harsh. "Even then, I knew that I wasn't capable of doing anything 'consistently well'."

Rhythmically she began to spoon the mush of soup and bread into her mouth. It wasn't a pretty sight.

"My poor son knows these stories of mine by heart."

"I look forward to hearing more of them." I said this lightly while inside thinking, *Is her Margot Fonteyn story even true? Perhaps Richard is right – this woman is going to disappoint me. I've started something that will prove awkward to withdraw from.*

Her soup finished, mine almost untouched, Mrs Gifford carefully wiped her mouth with the serviette. Turning away from the table she took a powder compact from her handbag and studied her face. Satisfied, she snapped the compact shut. "Excuse me," she said. "That was impolite but I feel comfortable enough with you to forget my manners. Believe me Shona, that doesn't happen often."

Despite my misgivings, I was flattered.

She continued. "Perhaps you'd be interested in visiting the Miller Building. My son's about your age, maybe a few years older. He's very much alone. I'd like him to have some company other than his mother and her elderly friends. I'm sure the two of you will get on well. He's interested in so many subjects."

I told my first and only lie that day, "You do know that I have a partner? Richard. The man I share this house with."

Her response didn't skip a beat. "I've no doubt my son would like to meet Richard too. Do you have a car?"

I shook my head.

"Then I'm afraid it's shank's pony. It is something of a hike but I manage to walk to the town and back at least twice a week."

"We – I," no way was I including Richard in any future visit, "could get a taxi."

"Cab firms refuse to collect or drop customers off in such

a remote area." She pushed her plate aside. "Any Tuesday or Friday if the weather's good. Come for tea. After two-thirty. The view as you approach the building from the sea alone is worth the walk." A smile transformed her face and instantly won me over.

I had made no friends in Hawksbridge. Her son was lonely. For now, loneliness could be as strong a bond as any.

"I'll watch from the window for you. There's no doorbell, no phone line, no way of contacting us but if for some reason the front door's locked come in by the underground carpark. In the hallway you'll find a lift. It looks intimidating but has never broken down."

"But where is the underground carpark?"

"Left hand side of the block as you approach, push through the shrubbery."

"It sounds like something from Alice in Wonderland."

"Far better."

By the time you came in that evening, I'd found a map of the area. The Miller Building was listed as an historic landmark. It was almost two miles away from Canberra Road where we lived.

"Glass of wine, Shona?" you asked.

"No thanks."

From the wine rack you took a bottle of red wine. You opened a cupboard, your back to me as you reached inside for a glass. "So, how did your lunch go?"

"Not bad. Interesting. I've been invited to meet Mrs Gifford's son."

"Surely not a date?" Turning around you started to laugh. "I don't know which one of you will be the most appalled. I mean, honestly Shona, look at yourself."

I should be inured to your comments about my

appearance by now, only they invariably arrive out of the blue when I'm almost convinced that we're getting on better.

"It's not a date," I said. "He's lonely. Living where they do, I think he's quite cut off from people of his own age."

You slopped wine into the glass. Several drops splashed on the tiled floor. "Lonely. Cut off." Echoing my own thoughts, you added, "Sounds as if you're made for each other." Your mobile rang. You took it from your pocket and flipped it open. Your gaze shifted to me. "Privacy Shona?"

Dismissed, I stumbled out of the room. I am not normally clumsy. I am capable of grace. It is only with you, when I react to your chilling tone of voice – then I'm reduced into becoming a lesser creature.

4

MRS GIFFORD

Drawing the duvet closer, Mrs Gifford is thinking that tonight there'll be a hard frost. She closes her eyes again but sleep eludes her; instead, she finds herself puzzling over the name of the young woman she'd had lunch with. This also eludes her. It was nothing obvious like Helen or Cathy. Something Nordic? Was that what the waist-length hair was all about? Helga, Gudrun? Mrs Gifford quietly chuckles. Everyone's age she judges in relation to that of her son. Someone over sixteen but under thirty is still classed as 'boy' or 'girl'. 'Young' she applies to the in-betweens: over thirty but under fifty. Privately, at fifty, she's set Sonny forever in early middle age. For much of his life he's defied her age rule in looks and behaviour, remaining in the 'boy' category. She would never apprise him of the change of status. The knowledge would be a wound impossible to heal; he must remain forever – boy.

Mrs Gifford's worries over her son are engrained, but this morning she's content to let the small incipient anxiety that she's caught a cold take over. Her throat hurts, her bones ache a little, but the need to cough she'd fought since the night before has subsided. There is just a faint crackle of congestion coming from her chest.

Shona! That was her name. The first time they'd met, walking past the outside café table, she'd vaguely been aware of someone getting to their feet, intending to greet her. There was an impression of a smiling smooth young face: an un-expressive face that suddenly prompted a childhood memory.

Save any emotion. Poised in front of half a dozen six-year-old girls, the dance teacher – Miss Campbell – raising one elegant hand towards her eyes. *Deliver them only when performing. Over-use will render your emotions stale.*

Seventy years on, Mrs Gifford can still hear the rolling sound on the 'r' of 'render'. Not that *this* young woman could ever have been a dancer. Large feet, ugly hands, she would be an inveterate butterfingers.

That was how my cold started – sitting outside that café with the temperature only just above freezing.

Mrs Gifford switches on the bedside lamp. At the window the rectangle of sky immediately changes to purple. Her cold will pass. It is of no consequence. She must keep her mind focused on the immediate tasks, keep moving, sleep enough, fight the inevitable rundown. Spring will come; in summer she thrives. Mrs Gifford is confident her strength will carry her through another year. Why not another five years?

From outside in the corridor she recognises the sound of Sonny's door noisily opening and closing. He intends for her to hear, if asleep, to be woken up. Now he is in her living room, no doubt peering into the kitchen in the hope of finding a small sweet treat. He scratches at her bedroom door.

"Ma, it's gone seven."

"Ten minutes," she calls back.

"That long?"

"Put the kettle on."

"It doesn't suit me."

She obliges with a hollow laugh. "Just ten more minutes."

Mrs Gifford receives a state pension which she collects monthly from a post office in Hawksbridge. For over twenty years she's kept five hundred pounds worth of Premium Bonds under her vests in the dressing-table drawer. It's been a long time since she's found herself a winner, but they represent a nest egg, something to fall back on should times become tight.

Living in the Miller Building she pays no rent, rates or utility bills. Electricity for lighting and cooking is nowadays supplied by a small generator. She uses this sparingly. Heat is provided by the two small fireplaces: one in her lounge, the other in Sonny's bedroom. The chimney vents are to one side of the building, which means their thin streams of white smoke in the winter months are not visible from either the road nearby or the town.

Hawksbridge Council, owner of the block, believe that the building lies empty, that in the twenty-first century it would be considered uninhabitable for even the poorest tenants to contemplate given the state of its dereliction. Mrs Gifford chooses to rarely think about the council. When she does, she imagines a gigantic well-fed cat of a person, perfectly satisfied overseeing the paving of the town's streets in a herringbone pattern of smart blue-grey bricks, building a plate glass, state of the art, cubism inspired college, creating stone fountains and wrought iron benches – all good, all admirable – while ignoring the decaying Miller Building and the nearby rows of empty houses. She is grateful for their omission and hopes the incompetence will continue at least during her lifetime.

The isolation of where they live suited her son. Imperceptibly over many years, his affection for the building's interior has created a distrust of Hawksbridge town sprawling like a hazy threat, visible from some of the eastward-facing windows. Sonny rarely leaves the apartment now and never during daylight hours. The opportunity has long passed when Mrs Gifford felt able to discuss this subject. What could she say when she knows that Sonny's vision of a hostile world for him would be true? She can't envisage her son moving with ease among the many students.

'Ah well, snow tomorrow," Mrs Gifford says. She is still hungry for the bliss of a deep, dreamless sleep; for the release from fear and the unfamiliar version of her face in the mirror, from the old woman's hands spread over her bony knees. She closes her eyes but only for a moment: then she is throwing back the cover, crossing the room to where an exercise barre has been fitted along one wall. Hand resting on the barre she goes through the exercises she has done almost every morning for more than seven decades. Of course, her body has changed but she remains strong, retains muscle tone. Back straight, chin held high, she imagines herself young and oh so beautiful.

5

SONNY

When Sonny was a child, they'd rented a flat in St. Albans. It was his first day of the summer term at a new school and he hadn't wanted to go. His uniform was all wrong, bought six months earlier for his last school.

"I'm not made of money" She said.

"That's not the point," he said. "I'll be the odd one out."

"You'll be an even odder one out if you're late." And then to get him to go she used an old ploy that he always fell for. "Darling, if you decide you hate the school, come home at lunchtime, but just give it a try. For Mummy?"

By the time Sonny arrived at the school gates it was already nine-thirty. Another five minutes were wasted before he felt brave enough to cross the deserted playground. Finally, he entered the building. As if to herald his arrival, somewhere ahead of him, a piano struck up the opening bars of 'All things bright and beautiful'.

"The school day begins at nine am." A teacher emerging from one of the classrooms impatiently tapped his wristwatch. "I presume you have enrolled?"

Sonny shook his head.

"Never mind. You're not the only one. You need the gymnasium." Through thick lensed spectacles he peered down at the silent boy. "Okay, I'll take you. You look petrified. The first day anywhere can be intimidating."

The teacher's hand grasping his felt enormous. Sonny was dragged forwards, forced to run to keep up.

"Here we are. Queue up with the other newbies."

"But," Sonny said.

"Your name is?"

"But."

"Your name!"

"Sonny Gifford."

"Jennifer," the teacher waved his hand towards a woman seated at a long table, "I have a Sonny Gifford for you."

"We're not ready for you yet, dear." Her voice was friendly as she pointed towards the back of the room where at least twenty boys stood in a straggling line. Already, they seemed to know each other. As Sonny approached, they turned to stare at him with hostile curiosity.

After five minutes the name 'James Gifford' was called. Sonny didn't move. The boy in front of him stepped on his foot. "You're Gifford, aren't you?"

Watched by the entire queue, Sonny approached the table. The woman indicated to a wooden chair. He sat down.

"James or Sonny, which do you prefer?"

He didn't answer.

"Well, I think we'll stick with James then." Reaching for a fresh enrolment form, she gave him a tired smile. "I'm Mrs Bradshaw. I have a note about you from your mother. You suffer from asthma?"

Eyes fixed on the sheet of notepaper she was studying, he inclined his head.

"Your father passed away some years ago?"

Again, he nodded.

"I'm sorry. That must have been very hard for you to deal with." She leant back in her chair. "James, talk to me. I won't bite. I'm on your side."

Sonny took a deep breath and then in a strangely adult voice replied, "First I stole jam, and more jars than we could ever eat. I opened every lid and let in the flies."

"Oh dear," the woman said. She touched her forehead as if she feared the onset of a migraine. "I think it might be best if—"

Sonny leant across the table, an eager expression on his face. "Mrs Bradshaw?"

"Yes dear. Yes James."

"I heated lard in a pan, mixed it with bread and rat poison."

She shook her head. "I think that's enough now."

"The sparrows were used to me. After all, mine was the hand that fed them. They flew down. Forty minutes from first peck to final twitch."

The noise in the gymnasium abated. There was a moment of absolute silence.

"May I use the toilet please?" He got to his feet. "I need to go right away."

That day, a prefect took Sonny to the toilet. "Don't wait," Sonny said. "I have constipation."

"Gross," the prefect said and left him to it.

A few minutes later, Sonny made his way back across the playground and through the wrought iron gates. Arriving home, he met his mother on her way out.

"What happened?" she asked.

"They didn't want me."

He never returned to the school. Within a week they were on a train, destination Hawksbridge.

Forty years later, he's still adding to his story.

"His name was Terence Rogers," he'd said only a week or so ago.

"You've never mentioned a Terence Rogers before."

"He was the boy who took me to the toilet. He tried to kiss me."

She'd nodded, said something like, "Cheeky so-and-so."

Even in the dark, Sonny prides himself on knowing every centimetre of the Miller Building: the wide oak staircase that opens up onto spacious landings, the windowless corridors and where the doors to the three apartments in each fall, every service entrance and fire exit – all now blocked to make the building secure from intruders. Sonny knows if there is a change in the air, a door left open, a window broken, a rat or mouse scuttling across the basement floor – not quite where and when a spider weaves its web. Were he blindfolded and bound – sometimes he imagines himself in this exact scenario – he could pinpoint his location in any part of the building by pressing his cheek or forehead against the wood of a panelled door, inhaling the smell of a peeling, plastered wall.

In Sonny's imagination his home remains a set of rooms on Deck Four of a vast ocean liner. At an historical level he has researched all he can about the building's history: that it was one of the very first housing developments to be built from an amalgam of concrete and steel. That Boyd Steven Berwick, the renowned London architect, had been influenced by the French engineer François Hennebique. The shell was modernistic, the interior made up of high-ceilinged square rooms linked by wide corridors. The windows that appeared so mean and narrow from the outside suited the building's concept: that a construction so close to the North Sea should present as similarly powerful. Sonny had copied down one of Berwick's quote's when later the architect had been forced to defend his design:

> 'Let the most violent of high tides sweep away all in its path, be it men, women and their kin. Come the bright new morning as folk weep for their losses, the Miller Building, in defiance of the sea, shall remain unscathed.'

On completion in 1905 the lower floors were rented out by the room, at peppercorn rents, to artists and craftsmen. Those above housed a floating population of refugees, travellers and the genteel homeless. No rich people lived on the seventh floor. Up till the 1950s the one huge apartment had been split in two and reserved for families of ten or more.

New materials, new ideas of social welfare, from the very beginning the Miller Building was unpopular, its philanthropic ethos controversial. *The Times* – foremost of many critical voices – dubbed it, 'a no doubt indestructible blot on an otherwise perfect landscape.'

More than a century later and the 'perfect landscape' had acquired the reputation of an area to be avoided. The nearby tenements emptied, although random lights continued to shine after dark through the splintered woodwork of boarded-up doors and windows. The tenants remaining in the Miller Building were offered alternative accommodation with central heating and double-glazed windows on estates close to the modernised town centre. Only Sonny and his mother, content in their three rooms plus kitchen and bathroom, ignored the offer. With satisfaction they'd watched as the last occupants piled their belongings into ramshackle cars and vans and drove away. It appeared they were forgotten or that somewhere, someone in the local council was waiting them out.

Months of quiet passed and then one morning a solitary van pulled up. Two men spent a week boarding up the window of the lower floors. They sealed the imposing front door with a criss-cross of battens. That was it. Job done. The Giffords let another month go by. Sonny's mother came and went via the cellar entrance that led through to a dark, airless carpark beneath the building. On another New Year's Day – the best New Year's Day either could remember – they felt confident enough to call the Miller Building their own.

Behind each door on every floor are rooms that, over the years, he and his mother have reduced to empty carcasses. Their clearance has been the source of much shared pleasure. For both it seemed extraordinary, the treasures people were willing to leave behind. Sonny still has delicious dreams where he discovers yet another set of rooms: a secret door that has always been there but gone unnoticed.

Their biggest haul was discovered one freezing cold January in the late 1990s, the year electricity was finally switched off throughout the building leaving only the lift working. "A different circuit board," Mrs Gifford had explained as if she knew all about electricity.

The top floor apartment, the one they called The Penthouse was the last to be cleared. It stretched the entire width of the block. Often over the years they'd discussed what they'd find on the other side of the quite grand entrance.

"Probably empty," he'd said, spurring on his mother's flight of fancy.

"Decaying luxury. Gilt furniture and glass table tops

resting on marble dolphins. Sonny, I think we've saved the best till last."

She was wrong about the contents but yes, they had saved the best till last.

"Come on, slowcoach," his mother said.

Having taken the stairs, she was waiting for him outside the lift gates. He remembers smiling to himself, because she was still fast on her feet, still able to beat the elderly lift as it wheezed and clanked its way upwards. She had the key. Between them they had bundles of keys, keys to every room, storeroom and cupboard. The lock turned. They exchanged glances, then pushed. The door gave but only fractionally.

"Will it be good?" he asked.

She grinned. "Who knows. Let's find out."

They used their shoulders against the woodwork opening up a gap wide enough to individually squeeze through.

Once before, on a lower floor they'd found a young woman in a sleeping bag, sitting upright against a wall. A paperback of Harper Lee's *To Kill a Mockingbird* lay face down next to her. She had obviously been dead for some days. Now, Sonny half-expects that awful, remembered smell of decay to waft out, at least a gust of stale air – but no, the air from the apartment was fresh. Squeezing through the gap, he took a step forward but found he could go no further; his face was only inches away from a wall of carpets piled one on top of the other.

Grabbing a fold of thick woollen fabric, he hauled himself upwards. He felt her hands flapping against his legs. "I can manage. Leave me alone," he called back to her. The heaped carpets formed a strange, undulating terrain stretching out in front of him. They reached to the windowsills; some obscured the glass but the room was still full of light.

"What can you see?" his mother cried out.

"Another world." Laughing, he'd reached down and gripped her hands.

"You're hurting," she wailed but she let him pull her up. At the top, she lay on her stomach, leaning on her elbows. "You're right. This is another world," Mrs Gifford said.

Over time they tallied up their spoils: fifty room-sized Eastern and Oriental carpets; thirty smaller rugs, dhurries and ikats in vibrant colours and patterns; and a predominantly scarlet Bokhara runner, over twelve feet in length that Sonny immediately acquisitioned for his own bedroom.

Her fingers pressed into the pile of a small rug, turning over a corner to inspect the weave. "This is good Kashmiri. Hand-woven. Quality."

"Why would someone leave all this?" he'd asked her.

"Maybe wherever they were moving to didn't have the storage space."

"Won't the owners come back for them?"

She shook her head. "I wouldn't think so. These rooms have been empty for years now. If anyone wanted to clear the stock, they'd have done it."

Like a pale spider, on hands and knees Sonny skittered away from her into the adjoining room, stopped then dropped out of sight. "French doors to the balcony!" he called back.

More slowly, his mother followed, easing herself down from the high step of layered rugs. This second room was almost empty apart from a Victorian wrought-iron double bed and mattress plus two rickety chairs. In the kitchen she ran a tap. At first the water was rusty brown and then it cleared. In the bathroom, she tugged at the old-fashioned toilet chain. The cistern flushed. Everywhere was filthy. Through the glass door, Sonny could see the balcony, its grey concrete floor. "You could have plants. We could sit outside."

"Someone would see us. Even from the seafront this top floor is visible." She read the disappointment in his eyes. "I'm sorry, but we'll take the best stuff downstairs with us."

"Are we capable of doing that?" He'd sounded doubtful.

"Oh, I think so. What about the bed?"

"Let's leave it here," he said.

It took them a fortnight of concentrated effort to drag everything they wanted into the lift and down three flights of stairs. They left the spoils heaped in the corridor outside their rooms until space was made. Then they covered floors and walls – even some of the windows – with rugs, sometimes to a depth of three or four layers. By the end of that year neither could recall their original flooring. Mrs Gifford had a memory of walnut parquet – Sonny thought navy-blue linoleum.

6

SHONA

2004

I met Richard when I was twenty-five and in the first year of a Fine Arts degree course at a London college. Richard was also a student but coming to the end of his final year in Media and Design Illustration. There was a buzz around him. Already he was being tipped as the student most likely to succeed. It wasn't just that he was good-looking, he was charismatic as well and slickly (my initial opinion of his work) talented. In the refectory, in the neighbouring pub popular with the students, he was always at the centre of an admiring crowd. I, the observer, sitting in a dark corner, hunched over a fruit juice, covertly observed him. I could pick out no particular individual, man or woman and think, 'Ah, so you are one of his close friends'. Richard inspired admiration, respect, definitely desire in others, but he shunned intimacy. It was as if he operated from within an unbreakable glass bubble of his own creation. The two of us were strangers but even then, I knew we were worlds apart except for this one thing: the shunning of intimacy.

Not that I saw him often, maybe once every ten days or so at most and usually from a distance. As I've said, it was his final year and he was busy preparing his degree show while already taking on work outside the college at a semi-professional level. On the rare occasions I spotted him walking towards me in the corridor, I'd somehow 'slope' past, head lowered, grazing the wall with my shoulder.

My college experience was proving very different. Most of the students in my year were younger, straight out of school. I felt no connection with the lives they appeared to take for granted, doting on mildly annoying parents, holidays abroad, their laptops, their phones, conversations about food consumed and what expensive brand of toiletries they used.

At the start I was questioned. "How about you, Shona? Do you get on with your mum and dad?"

"They're dead."

"Oh, bad luck. Brothers, sisters?"

"No."

"And you're from?"

On that one, I'd close up.

Most of my days were spent in the studio up on the top floor of the art block. I was invariably the first to arrive as the college was under a mile away from my flat. By the time the other students began to roll in, my paints and brushes would be laid out on a stool next to my easel and I'd be hard at work. Nobody bothered to greet me. Not because they were unfriendly – I think the way I was always so engrossed in my painting made them awkward, as if only I was the adult.

One morning, the studio empty, I found a small white envelope resting on my easel. It wasn't sealed. I opened it. Scrawled on a thin piece of card were the words, 'Meet to talk? RCM', followed by a mobile number. It was 2005, few students had mobile phones. I had to head out of the college to a phone box. I had no idea who RCM might be but I rang the number.

"Hi there, Richard Maplin speaking." I recognised his voice. His tone was warm, very adult.

"This is Shona," I said.

There was silence. *Oh God,* I thought. *The message isn't meant for me.* In the studio there were at least twenty other easels.

"Shona, can we meet right now? In the refectory before it gets busy?"

"Are you sure I'm the right person?"

"Tall, wears too many clothes, has scars on her neck, possibly also shoulders and arms – just guessing here."

I stopped breathing. My mouth dried. "But—" I croaked.

He'd gone.

It took me ten minutes to reach the refectory. On the way I stopped off in the student washroom to soak my face in cold water. My reflection in the smeared mirror above the sink looked terrified. *Come on Shona, have courage,* I told myself. *He doesn't know you, doesn't know your history. But your scars? A lucky guess.*

He was seated at a table facing the swing doors, arms folded, head lowered so I couldn't read his expression. I remember he wore a blue denim shirt, neck open with a string tie loosely knotted. Even then, in the relaxed art college environment he dressed quite formally, standing out from the casual ripped jeans and sweatshirts of the other students.

I pulled out a chair and sat down. On the table in front of him lay a black leather zipped file.

"So?" I said, making the word sound hostile.

He looked up. His eyes were friendly. "I'm not a stalker, nor a blackmailer, you intrigue me, that's all. Nothing too intimidating about someone finding you intriguing, is there?"

"I'm not intimidated."

"Perhaps not." He tilted his head to one side, "I wonder what it would take—"

I cut across him, "What do you want? Just tell me."

Instead, his hand shot out towards my face.

I jerked my upper body away from him. "Don't!"

Hastily, he withdrew his hand. "Your face is so perfect." He laughed shakily. "I wanted to touch it. I'm sorry. Inappropriate." Weeks later I discovered that he'd been embarrassed by his own action. Richard so rarely allowed himself to make a spontaneous move.

An awkward silence fell between us, neither knowing quite how to proceed and then someone sauntered across to our table, laid *his* hand on Richard's shoulder. "Hey man, how you doing?"

"Busy. Fuck off." Without glancing up, Richard shrugged him away.

"Sorree!"

So, you don't like physical familiarity either, I thought.

"What did you want to talk about?" I asked.

"I wondered – I don't suppose you'll agree – but I'd like to take some photographs of you." And there it was breaking through: Richard's first boyish smile.

"What sort of photographs?" I kept my expression blank.

He unzipped the file and drew out a black and white image, yellowing at the edges. He slid it towards me. A young girl, maybe fifteen years old, sat on a thin mattress, on a narrow iron bed, her back to the camera. All she wore was a towelling dressing gown. It had slipped off her shoulders, the material lying pooled around her waist and hips. She held up her hair so that her slender neck was partially revealed.

"Where did you get this?"

"During my late teens I had a holiday job in a psychiatric hospital. Mostly I worked outside in the grounds, but on one occasion a cleaner was ill and I was asked to empty the office wastepaper bins. There was no-one about. This photograph was lying on a desk. I tucked it into my overall," he looked up at me. "It is you, isn't it?"

"You can't see her face."

"I recognised the formation of scars on the back of your neck. One day in the summer I sat behind you in the lecture theatre. I'd seen you around the college. You stand out – chiefly because it's so obvious that you want to be invisible. It was hot in the theatre. The windows wouldn't open. Just for a second you lifted up your hair. I made a sketch and then later I began using my imagination." He pulled out a sheaf of pencil drawings. With a flick of his wrist, like a magician, he turned the pages into a fan before placing them in front of me. The central drawing was a stylised reproduction of my face, the others showed my back, arms and neck. Beneath my hairline was the neat zig-zag of small circular scars from burns inflicted on me in early childhood. On the rest of my body were Richard's accurate imaginings; scars, the puckered skin picked out in minute detail, scars looking as fresh and painful as the day they were caused. "Will you let me draw and photograph you? Please Shona, name a price."

I don't know why I agreed but I did. Perhaps something about Richard's chilly, withdrawn personality and yet his apparent warmth towards me was flattering, whatever, I was willing to trust him. Not in every way, but in this one request. I didn't accept his money. My one stipulation was that my name wouldn't appear as his model.

"I promise. By the time I've worked on your photographs you'll be unrecognisable."

And he did make me unrecognisable: digitally enhanced, transformed into a serpentine metallic monster, scars turned into scales. Only my eyes he left alone.

Later he told me, "I tried to change them, but nothing I came up with seemed right. Shona, you do have the eyes of a monster." He meant this as a compliment. He had no idea how close to the truth it was.

His degree show, with the truly extraordinary photo-realistic female creation as a centrepiece, was an outstanding success. For me it was a disturbing experience, recognising something of myself, but a self turned inside out? Made other?

His tutors were bursting with pride, that this insignificant, small college in a dead-end area of London had produced such a talented artist. I watched as people queued up to shake Richard's hand and have their photos taken with him and his artwork. I moved around the room, looking at the displays of other students. I felt sorry for them: the projects they'd laboured over for three and four years were eclipsed. All the excitement came from Richard's corner of the room. Only once he caught my eye. He winked. The person he'd been talking to followed his gaze. I sank back, let the tide of his many admirers conceal me.

Within a week of leaving college Richard was commissioned by a leading advertising agency to produce a series of graphic illustrations: a contemporary interpretation of the Swiss painter H.R. Giger's iconic work which had blended human physiques with machines for the highly successful

1980s film *Alien*. He took fresh photos of me, naked, face partly concealed behind my long hair. Unrecognisable as myself, I became the face of a high-tech, luxury German make of car that year. My face and body unwound on television screens, I appeared on the side of London buses, probably German buses as well, on a billboard in Piccadilly Circus. The campaign won awards. Richard won awards. Suddenly in the particular artistic sea he now swam in, he was becoming mildly famous: feted, interviewed on television and radio arts programmes. He cropped up in the social pages of tabloid newspapers, attractively dishevelled, each time a different beautiful woman hanging on his arm. But never me. He didn't want the link to be made between us, attention to shift away from him. If anyone asked who his model was, he used a stock reply. "Classified information, mate." His voice slightly cockney-fied, aping the film star Michael Caine.

I continued to paint, continued with my own degree course, but now each evening I crossed London by bus to Richard's three-bedroomed apartment at the top of a renovated factory building in East London. There was a roof terrace which I loved and every room was filled with light from floor to ceiling windows. We never shared a bedroom, never had sex. With wonder he'd stroke my face and scarred body. I found his touch – soporific. With Richard, I knew that physically I was safe. It was a curious relationship. Hand on heart I wasn't in love with him. I may have said before, what he felt for me was a form of adoration that by its very nature kept intimacy at bay. He didn't want to know what made me tick. He preferred his own interpretation. For those few brief years, I chose to believe that we were good together, dove-tailed – although neither bore any resemblance to a creature as gentle as a dove.

7

2014

We are in the kitchen. You are making fresh coffee. "The usual rules apply," you say turning to face me, holding one of your recent purchases of white fine china latte mugs to your lips. In your eyes I read affection for both the coffee, the mug and myself. "I'll be back some time on Monday. I hate these trade fairs but I do love Edinburgh. If it wasn't so cold, I think I'd move the studio up there."

I say, "I don't understand – what usual rules apply?"

"The television. You're welcome to watch it, but . . ."

"Oh, those rules: no food or drink to be taken out of the kitchen." Anger bubbles in my chest. "Richard, you don't have to keep telling me."

"But Shona darling, I think I do."

I let the anger fizzle out. I want no confrontation. Fair enough: your house, your rules.

By late afternoon as you set off for the train station wheeling your smart Prada suitcase, I am feeling foolishly happy at the thought of being on my own for forty-eight hours. Returning to the kitchen I make myself a sandwich and open a bottle of white wine. Nothing expensive, bought from the supermarket by me and for me, specifically for a possibility of this evening. I prefer red but as I intend to break one of your rules and take both wine and sandwiches into your precious front room, red would be tempting fate! It is still early, just gone six. *Shona, take your time. No need to rush.*

Richard, I may have issues with *you* but your taste remains impeccable. You've furnished every room with well-designed pieces that were eye-wateringly expensive and yet, they don't scream *MONEY*!

"Hand-crafted," you said when your two Italian leather sofas arrived. "Don't ask me how much they cost." It hadn't occurred to me to ask. They have sleek lines and are more comfortable than they look. There is a modern coffee table of beech, chrome and glass, linen blinds at the bay window, flanked by floor-length curtains in a Designers Guild fabric that are for show and rarely drawn. In the alcoves are shelves – also made of beech. Beech is your wood of choice: conservative, a little bland yet on trend. Again, your words.

I choose the sofa that you rarely use. Squeamish maybe, but I dislike the idea of my buttocks resting on the upholstery where yours have rested. My bottle and glass I place on the slate coasters protecting the coffee table. I allow myself to relax into the leather cushions. On the rare occasions I get to spend time in this room, I'm always surprised at how incredibly 'giving' they are for my shoulders and back. My scars are twenty years old yet each one still makes itself known if I'm leaning against a firm surface for any length of time.

Daydreaming during the early evening news I almost fall asleep. Although I don't exactly covet your wealth, I have become susceptible to the comfort it affords. Re-filling my glass I watch an unsatisfying two-hour documentary on 'women who kill'. The women involved are dismissed as 'evil, ice-cold psychopaths'. There's little reference to their childhoods, their back stories, any interior devastation. I find myself thinking about my birth mother Dorothy, the woman I lived with up till the age of eight. At some point in almost every day, I'd wished her dead or just gone; pushed from a high window, in front of a train, off a cliff. Always 'pushed'. As a thirty-five-year-old adult, I still understand the attraction of that concept. Pushing hardly seems like violence, more accidental, uncomplicated – a relief.

While in hospital the first time and still in my teens – even then I was drawing. All I was allowed were sticks of conté crayon. I pressed so hard the sticks often snapped. I remember my need to transfer some of the emotional pain in my head and heart into my fingers, and then onto a page. I rarely drew the Kirkpatrick's – my memories around them were still too fresh, but my mother was a different matter. I could always access vignettes from our life together. Dorothy in repose, lightly sleeping in her chair, whisky glass hanging between thumb and two fingers – with dread I'd watch that glass, wait for it to finally slip from her hand and drop to the carpet. The slight sound would trigger the raising of my mother's eyelids. I would be the first thought in her head on awakening. She was capable of humour, could be carefree but never for long. The need to hurt someone other than herself lived just below the surface of any good mood.

The room spins a little as I get to my feet. I'll clear away all signs of my evening tomorrow. Halfway up the stairs, I realise I've left the television switched on. Back down I go.

Unplug. Smooth leather upholstery. Carry glass, bottle and plate back to the kitchen. *Bed now Shona.*

An hour later, I wake choking from a nightmare. In my head I hear Dorothy: *'Don't breathe, Shona. Will you just stop breathing?'* My hair is soaked with sweat, my heart pumping. My mother still has the power to terrify me. Even a dream can yank me backwards. I tell myself that she is dead, long gone. Yet how would it be if, with great relief as my life closes, I discover that yes, there is some form of heaven, but instead of angels there to greet me stands Dorothy, her hand extended, eyes like grey marbles?

I remember Dorothy's armchair is pulled up close to the gas fire. She is a neat, curvy figure, leaning forwards to warm her hands, the heat mottling her legs through sheer tan tights. On the mantelpiece above her head is a cut-glass tumbler of neat whisky. She takes out a menthol cigarette from a packet on the arm of her chair.

A man carrying a leather briefcase enters the room. This room also serves as the bedroom Dorothy shares with me. She has the double. I have a Z bed that is folded up during the day. At the moment, I'm sitting on the floor near the folded bed. Dorothy has told me to face the wall, but during the course of the man's visit, I often turn my head to watch.

"Hello there," Dorothy calls out to the man. "I'm relieved. I was expecting some tight-arsed female do-gooder."

He places a business card on the coffee table before settling on the one other chair in the room, crossing his legs, adjusting the material of his trousers, unclipping a pen from the inside pocket of his jacket.

Dorothy looks faintly amused. "Is this really necessary?"

"I do need to make a few notes, Mrs Blake."

"Then, ready when you are." She reaches for her glass. "Shoot," she says.

"Do you perhaps have any female family members you can rely on?"

The question surprises her. "I don't quite see the relevance."

"This will no doubt be a difficult time. You say you've been ill. Once Shona leaves," he glances in my direction and then back to Dorothy. "You'll be on your own. Isn't that the case?"

Her lip curls. "Why assume that 'female family members' might be of any support?"

"You don't like women?"

She sniggers. "As far as I'm concerned, they're irrelevant."

"And why is that?"

"Parent, sister, cousin." Dorothy looks again in my direction. "Child – they're all out to get you."

"And are your relationships with men any more successful?"

"You must be joking?" She drains her glass. "Shona, top me up." Her eyes when she looks at me are like truly like cold grey marbles.

By the time I return from the kitchenette with a fresh glass, Dorothy has embarked on one of her monologues.

"I did intend to assert that very little frightens me but . . . I have always been fearful of embarrassing myself, exposing my true feelings to others and receiving a negative or . . . unwelcome reaction. I live alone apart from." She nods in my direction. "My decision. I'm not unattractive." Sends him a quick look. "I've been told I have Candice Bergen's bone structure." Raises her hand to touch her cheekbone. "The film star?"

The man looks blankly at her and then starts to write.

"Obviously, there have been countless sexual encounters. It's how I make a living. That is why you're here, isn't it, to assess what kind of mother I am?" She laughs nervously. "I hope I'm not sounding old-fashioned – not raunchy enough."

He breaks in, "I do need an idea of the exact nature of your relationships with men."

"How long have you got?"

"Were they ever violent? Where was your daughter when men came to the house?"

"I'll take the fifth amendment." She smiles at him.

His face remains impassive. There is silence in the room. Finally, she says, again with that same brief laugh, "Well, where else would my daughter be? As you can see, we share a bedroom. Apart from kitchen and bathroom, this is what there is." She spreads out her hands indicating that the room is her entire universe.

"So, your daughter is where when your . . . clients come here?"

Dorothy's eyes are full of laughter. The fresh whisky has gone. She is drunk, her mood moving towards playful. "Well, sometimes she sits on the stairs outside, sometimes I send her to McDonald's for a Big Mac, and sometimes . . ." She pauses before saying, the words coming out in a rush, "she has to sit behind an armchair and read a book while I get on with my job. She's a great one for reading."

The man's pen stops moving forward. "But she's not a part of the sexual act?"

"Very rarely."

His head jerks up.

"Only joking! My clients aren't interested in children."

"And so?"

"I require them to be . . . suppliant. Relaxed. Almost

narcoleptic. I'm sorry I know this must sound hilarious to you . . ."

"It doesn't."

"Almost to the point of losing consciousness? You'd be surprised how many men find that a turn-on."

"I'm sure they do." There is an element of distaste in his voice.

"Oh, how young you are!" Suddenly Dorothy is enjoying herself. "I offer a service, satisfy a particular need."

The interviewer changes tack. "You were married once. Shona's father?"

She shakes her head. "Never married. We spent a week in a boarding house in Shoreham on the south coast and that was enough for both of us. We never saw each other again after that. I assume he's her father but it could easily have been any number of men."

"How did you feel about your pregnancy?"

"I didn't mind the pregnancy. I wasn't happy with the result."

"And how does your daughter feel about you?"

"Guess?" She shrugs.

He resumes writing.

She stares at his bowed head. "Cup of tea? Coffee? Something stronger?"

"No thanks. Almost finished." He removes a sheet of paper from the clipboard. "I'd like a few words with Shona in private, if that's okay with you?"

"It isn't."

"Then, can I speak to her in your presence?"

"By all means. Shona, come over here."

My gaze remains fixed on the floor as I cross the room.

Gently the man turns me around and lifts up my hair. I feel the light touch of his fingers on the back of my neck.

"Shona, how did this happen?" he asks.

"She plays with matches. The child's a pyromaniac," Dorothy says. "If it isn't matches, it's my cigarette lighter."

"Shona, will you answer my question?"

Dorothy exhales a stream of smoke from her cigarette – her gaze is fixed on Shona's face. "You won't get any sense out of that one."

The man appears to take a moment to think. Finally, he asks Dorothy, "And are you satisfied with our decision?"

"If some childless couple wants to take her on, I'm relieved. Shona," she calls out. "What do you think? Will you miss me?"

8

MARTIN

He'd been terrified. He'd just bedded down in a shelter on a deserted section of the sea front. The temperature was below freezing but he had half a bottle of whisky in his sleeping bag for company. Almost, he'd felt cheerful. Safe and dry for the night. And then came the banging on the window behind his head. Really loud as if a fist was trying to smash the glass. He'd shot upright expecting someone huge, threatening and male to appear. Instead he stared at a small figure – sex concealed by hat, scarf and overcoat, holding out a packet of peppermints.

"Take two," they'd said. "I'm Mrs Gifford."

While he sucked the sweets, she stood facing the sea, her hands clasped behind her back. She turned. "Want another?"

"No." He'd regretted eating them. They'd spoil the taste of the whisky.

She came closer. Her breath smelt of peppermint. "I live in the Miller Building with my son. You're welcome to stay for a few days."

He hadn't leapt at the offer. He knew this area and its reputation.

"We have plenty of room, food and heat. You will die if you spend many more nights outside." She said this with such certainty that he'd almost believed her.

"Forecast is for snow, maybe a blizzard." She put the peppermints into her coat pocket. "Do you like bacon?"

She waited while he rolled up the sleeping bag and gathered together his few possessions.

"It's closer than it looks," she said.

"How far?"

"Over there. Directly in front of us."

He hadn't noticed the black square against the navy sky. No lights shone.

"It looks deserted."

"We live there. Watch where you step, there are rabbit burrows. You could break an ankle."

He'd kept a couple of paces behind her to give himself time to think. The closer they came to the building, the more uneasy he felt. As if sensing his anxiety, the woman slipped her gloved hand into his. "Almost there," she said. "We have pizza too."

Inside, he hadn't felt any more reassured. It was like stepping from a cold bath into a freezer. He smelt the damp and dirt. She lit an oil lamp. It was unbelievable, the twenty-first century yet no electricity. He was relieved she avoided the lift – it resembled a cage out of a gothic horror movie. Following her up three flights of stairs he'd wanted to turn and run and keep running till he reached the light and warmth of the town. She kept chatting on about the history of the building; someone had been found dead on the second floor, families of twelve and more used to live in some of the two-roomed apartments.

"Unbelievably cramped," she said looking back over her shoulder at him. "Wouldn't be allowed now."

And then after what seemed a half-mile walk down a narrow corridor she stopped and threw open a door – dramatically, as if she was revealing something precious. The heat hit him, bathed him. His shoulders relaxed. The room in front of him smelt nice. He stepped inside.

At first, he *was* impressed: one old woman and her middle-aged agoraphobic son had taken over an entire building, created a home that was luxurious compared to the places he'd dossed down in. And Sonny: he was like some science fiction character with that strange pale hair, skin looking as if it had never seen daylight. He wore an ankle-length kimono. It was clear he was naked underneath. He'd brought out a bottle of wine. His mother without pausing to take off her coat went into the kitchen, slipped two large pizzas into the oven. Made him a delicious sandwich of fresh bread, bacon and ketchup while the pizza cooked.

"I'll leave you two boys to get acquainted," she'd said, placing another wine bottle in front of them.

Had he been sober, Martin might have queried the 'two boys'. He was in his mid-twenties. The son must be at least twice that. But stomach full and happily drunk, what was not to like about taking his first bath in weeks and sprawling on a soft rug in front of an open fire with someone who was that pleased to see him?

It was days later that he began to feel like a fly in a spider's web, just a few silken threads holding him in place, but every caress and compliment Sonny gave him, every delicious meal Mrs Gifford prepared, every comfort he enjoyed, added to the ties tightening around him.

9

SHONA

2004

Following Richard's initial success, money and projects poured in. Each week seemed to bring a new, highly paid commission. He was euphoric. Often late into the night we'd sit together while he'd tell me of meetings and the exciting clients he'd met. He'd discuss ideas, always looking for feedback. "You have a unique view of the world," he told me. "That's what I need, someone whose ideas are totally fresh." Not that every client wanted 'fresh ideas'. Richard was inundated with requests to re-configure the work from earlier decades of other graphic artists: the airbrush king, Philip Castle; the fantasy work of Frank Frazetta; Warhol and Hockney. At first each project excited him – and then they didn't. He'd expected to show the world what *he* was capable of in his own right, expected to become an art world superstar but instead he was (and no doubt still is) a brilliant copyist. Did it really matter not being an innovator? Well yes, for Richard it mattered horribly.

I remember Richard, having finished one bottle of wine

and in the process of opening another, saying, "More than anything I want to be acknowledged as a major talent, a front-runner in my field. The work I did around those photographs of you was my best. I can't look at the preliminary drawings now. They've set the bar too high." He'd pulled that lopsided grin that always fooled me.

"You're young. Who Knows what you'll achieve?"

"To be creative you need to take risks or be . . . brilliantly deranged in some way. Money and lasting talent rarely go together. Look to yourself, Shona – virtually penniless but still blindly blundering your way forward." A mean gleam had shone in his eyes. It died. "Take that as a back-handed compliment."

At *my* degree show, a couple of years after Richard's, nobody was queuing up to commission me for anything. My tiny paintings depicting uncomfortable dramas played out within meticulously rendered inanimate objects didn't draw any crowds. During the afternoon I counted no more than three people: two men, one woman, stopping in front of the set of a dozen canvases. Their expressions were unfathomable. I hovered in the hope that one of them might want a word with the artist but as the light faded outside, I slipped away. Rain was falling steadily. The vibrant London streets were reduced to shades of black and grey. I pulled up the hood of my raincoat and instead of taking the bus I walked back to Richard's. Standing outside the building I didn't really want to go in, but what alternative was there?

Richard's overcoat lay across the hall table. He must have only just arrived home, because drops of rain still clung to the fabric, but it wasn't soaked through as my jacket was.

"How did it go?" he called from the kitchen.

"Okay," I said.

"What's up?" He appeared in the kitchen doorway, bottle in one hand, glass in the other.

"I wish you'd been there today."

"I wish I had but it's been one hellish week."

"I would have liked your support. Nobody showed the slightest interest in my work."

He rubbed his face with both hands. "Darling, I'm not sure what you expected."

"If you'd showed up, others would have come."

"You wanted me to endorse your work? Is that what you're saying?"

I didn't answer.

"Well, I couldn't. I'd be lying. I don't get your little … what do you call them? Interiors. Never have. They're not my bag." He saw the shocked expression on my face. "Come on Shona, you're not a fan of anything I've ever produced. The world and its fucking wife can think I'm great, but you hold back, that reserve you have for anything you don't consider 'real art'." He tipped half a glass of wine down his throat. "Anything in mind for dinner or shall I order a take-away?"

A week later, the two of us seated under a striped canvas awning outside a patisserie in Covent Garden, I discovered that *The Guardian* had singled me out in an arts review of college degree shows. Just two lines but they meant everything to me. *In her absence, Shona Blake's unsettling still-life paintings offer an insight into a strange and macabre world. Stunning imagery.*

"Richard," I said, excitedly holding the newspaper out to him. "Look at this."

"I read it earlier. Meant to tell you. Amazing. So, what

do I know about the art world? But well done." He glanced at his watch. "Early meeting. Got to rush."

That afternoon the Beatrice Salmon Agency telephoned offering to represent my work.

I was so excited, I rang him at his studio. "Can you believe it? They're a major agency."

"Shona, calm down. What did you tell them?"

"I said I had to speak to you before I made any decisions."

"Good girl."

"So tomorrow I'll say 'yes please'?"

"Tomorrow, you'll turn them down." I could imagine him giving advice to clients in the same measured tone. "Don't jump at the first offer. It would be better if initially you completed a strong body of work rather than burden yourself with *their* expectations. That was the mistake I made."

All excitement crushed I said, "But what if I never get another offer?"

"Christ Shona, have some backbone!"

Richard's advice proved correct. Refusing the offer gave me two years to concentrate on painting, developing ideas and experimenting with different mediums, gave me time to visit galleries, time to just look and absorb. He supported me financially. Maybe I should be ashamed of taking his money while giving so little back. I'm not. I don't do shame. What's done has to be done. I cooked and cleaned for him, made the roof terrace bright with planters full of flowers and herbs. I validated his heterosexuality – that must have been worth a lot to him.

Had we been lovers the relationship would never have lasted. Neither of us looked for the comfort of familiarity. We didn't spend time reminiscing over meals, sharing our life histories. Richard still had parents living in South Africa. He'd fallen out with them after they'd given him the money to set up his own studio. Eventually he'd severed all ties.

"They imagined I was bought and paid for," he'd told me. "Wrong."

We kept conversations in the present, a little in the future. He shared his hopes and dreams but sometimes I knew he lied or at the very least, fabricated. I was mainly silent, the mute muse which suited both of us. He insisted I intrigued him: "Will you ever let me in to your past?"

"You know enough."

"But your arms and shoulders – those aren't cigarette burns. You left Dorothy when you were eight years old. You were in your teens when I discovered that photograph of you. Remember?"

"I don't want to remember."

"It would do you good."

"No, it would do *you* good."

"Please your fucking self." Richard never liked those rare occasions when I stood up for myself.

10

2014

Weekday mornings are peaceful apart from the muffled sounds of your radio as you get ready for work. But today you surprise me, padding silently into the kitchen as I'm quartering an apple to accompany my recent 'healthy eating' of oats and yoghurt. With a clatter I drop the knife. It ricochets off the porcelain floor tiles.

You pick up the knife and rinse it under the tap, thoroughly dry it before returning it to me. "That could have sliced your foot," you say.

I notice that you're wearing an un-ironed t-shirt and jeans.

"Aren't you going to the studio? Are you ill?" In all the years I've known you the only illness you've ever suffered has been a virtually annual bout of bronchitis.

"Nope." You pull out a kitchen chair and flop, long legs sprawling between the table and where I'm busy next to the sink. In the centre of the table is a bowl of narcissi I'd planted up in late autumn. The creamy yellow blooms are fragile, almost transparent. This is the only room in the house where my choice of flowers is allowed. You pat the chair seat next to you. "Sit down Shona. I've some news that might surprise you."

I take my time, place breakfast bowl, yoghurt and jar of honey on a tray. Ignoring your chosen chair, I slide into the seat opposite. From under lowered lids I observe you. Today your body language seems somehow different. I'm just thinking, wonderingly: *your reserve's down. This is more like the Richard I knew in our twenties*, when you announce, "I'm selling the design studio. No more commuting. I'll be a free man."

I add two scoops of yoghurt to my bowl and reach for the honey jar. "Surely selling the studio won't be easy. It will take some time?"

You grin at me, "Actually, the sale went through last Friday. Completion's this week."

My head is a jumble. The possibility of now having you in the house all day is an appalling one. What I'd like to do is take my thoughts and breakfast away to somewhere warm and quiet and Richard-free. I've recently begun to paint again. I need quiet and calm, not you with your no doubt fresh plans and projects. And I'm bewildered and more than a little irritated that you failed to mention something as huge as selling the business you've built up from scratch.

"Nothing to say? No congratulations? No well done, Richard, I knew you'd been dissatisfied for years – this is great news?"

I answer, "I don't know what to say. You've rather sprung this news on me."

"Look at me, Shona."

"I'm eating my breakfast." I sound like a sulky child. What I should have said was, 'I need time to process this. You know I'm not good with surprises.' But that would have implied an intimacy between us that hadn't been in place for years.

"You're unbelievable. Everything's always about keeping Shona happy."

"I'm sorry if it seems like that to you."

"But aren't I right? I'd lay money that the main worry in your selfish little head is what am I going to do if Richard's in the house all day? You're going red. I'm spot on, aren't I?"

My face may have reddened but so had yours. You look not only angry but upset. Leaning forward, you demand, "When in your life have you ever earned money apart from that brief flash in the pan when you sold a few paintings?"

"More than a few. If it hadn't been for my breakdown—"

"And who was there waiting to pick up the pieces?" you snarl.

"I picked up my own pieces," I snarl back.

You take a deep breath, tilt your chair so it's balanced on the two rear legs.

I push my bowl away. I'd choke if I tried to eat. "Can we stop now? I don't want to argue. I'm sorry. It is brilliant news and yes, you're right, I was thinking of myself." I try to smile, aware that my mouth has a life of its own: from smile to grimace to my lower lip trembling uncontrollably.

You see this and the anger fades from your eyes. "I'm making myself a coffee – would you like one?"

"Yes please. Thank you."

Every sound you make as you switch on your coffee machine, cupboard doors opening and shutting, all are like pin pricks on my skin. I'm aware of the glances you throw in my direction. Finally, you burst out, "Shona, it is a new beginning for me. Surely, I'm not too old to start again, maybe try something new?"

I get it right this time, give you my full attention, "Of course you're not. But will the money from the studio give you enough to live on while you're deciding on a future?"

My question proves a hilarious one. You start to laugh, "Shona darling, I'm loaded. Over the years I've made an absolute fortune. I've only recently sold the London flat. It went for well over a million."

"I didn't know you'd kept the flat."

"Why would I tell you? I'm not forty yet but if I wanted to – which I don't – I could retire – right now – in comfort."

I'm astonished. I'd somehow imagined that your income had fallen drastically. The Italian sofas in the front room, much of the furniture are beginning to show their age.

You continue. "In September, I plan to start with a year at Hawksbridge College bringing my computer design skills up to par, also a photography course if there's one available. As you know, I'm good but probably rusty. Long term, I'll try for a PhD in London. Maybe even the USA."

"But why? If you have money why not travel?" I look around the fairly utilitarian kitchen. "Or you could move to a better house, a better road. Relax, enjoy life."

Your eyes narrow. "This house has suited you."

"I'm not talking about me."

"No, we weren't." He sniggers, "You had great abilities yet didn't make the most of them. I had a tiny, tiny skill," you demonstrate the smallness of your talent between finger and thumb, "And I exploited it to the full. Now I'm able to do what I want. I may move eventually but it isn't a priority. Enjoy life? Relax? Do either sound like something I'd be interested in?"

There is no point my responding and really, I know I'm being an unreasonable bitch. I remind myself of how kind you were in the months following my discharge from hospital. But you're not kind anymore. But then I'm a 'guest' who has overstayed her welcome.

"Would you like me to find somewhere else to live? I'm sorry; I should have sorted myself out ages ago."

"Shona, I despair of you." You slap your forehead. "The two of us – I thought we were a team. We've got each other's backs. Isn't that how we are?"

I nod in agreement that we have each other's backs while knowing this is rubbish. Between us there remains something toxic; a poisonous snake that lies sleeping underground to emerge just when I'm reassured that it's moved elsewhere. *Please God, don't make me be the snake's driving force.*

"Don't worry," you say. "I promise I won't be under your feet all day. To re-acquaint myself with student life, I'm starting a six-week adult-ed course on Architecture and Interior Design. I did consider Fine Art but the two of us would end up in that old competitive thing we used to have going."

"I don't recall being competitive."

"Oh, I think it was six of one, half a dozen of the other." You reach for your coffee. "Just teasing! It was all male ego on my part."

"I think it was," I say quietly.

"And what about you?" You are breezy now as you carry your cup over to the sink. "You seem to be broadening your horizons. I've noticed the sketch book in your bag. Do you think you're finally getting back on track?"

With a tentative smile I say, "I've been back on track for a few weeks now – most days, I'm feeling positive."

You look surprised. Almost humble. "I'm sorry. I should have noticed."

"It's okay. We live separate lives. Honestly Richard, I'm very grateful that you've let me stay here."

"I wanted you to get better, to be happy. We do want the best for each other, don't we?" In a crowded room you have a way of looking into my eyes as if only the two of us existed. You give me this look now.

I break eye contact. "I think we do."

"I'm going into town," you say. "Is there anything you want?"

"I'm fine. Will you be gone long?"

"Home, early evening. I thought I'd call into the college. There's a 'meet the tutors' event." You pause. There's something else you want to share. "Do you remember Raoul?"

I nod. How could I forget? The only time I'd ever witnessed Richard in tears had been over Raoul.

"He's teaching at the college."

Once the house is empty, I reclaim the kitchen table. Opening my portfolio, I flick through some recent sketches. There is one of Mrs Gifford drawn from memory. She has a small, neat head and I've given her strong dancer's legs. In this drawing she is old but not diminished. My thoughts wander and I'm thinking of Richard and Raoul and how Raoul always had the upper hand. Richard in love had been fascinating to observe, for once every ounce of vulnerability on display. My thoughts turn inwards and there is Bea and the few precious years I spent as an artist with her agency. She has hold of my hair as she tells me she won't wait forever. I'd imagined the power in that relationship lay with me. How wrong I'd been.

I find myself staring at the narcissi. Close up I can see the flowers are fading. One petal falls onto the table. As if it retains a life of its own, the petal drifts towards me. Getting to my feet, I go upstairs to my bedroom. I keep the room meticulously tidy. I turn to the bookshelves. I have only one memento of Bea, from our last day together: a cosmos flower pressed inside a copy of Edna St. Vincent Millay's poems. I know the page, the poem is 'Wild Swans'. I flip through the pages. Shake the book. Somehow, I'm not surprised that the flower is gone.

11

2007

Eighteen months following the mention in *The Guardian*, I was invited to display three paintings in an exhibition at a gallery in Exeter. I'd waved the letter in front of Richard. "I can't believe that I'm one of the 'Ten Young British Artists to Watch Out For'."

Hardly glancing at it, he said, "Exeter, darling. Not Europe or even England. My advice would be to send in the artwork but make an excuse not to go. Such a schlep and you won't sell anything. Trust me, you'll come home discouraged."

"It's my first exhibition. I think I will go."

"Then I'll come with you."

I shook my head. "I'd like to do this on my own."

"But we could rent a cottage. Make it a long weekend away. I could surf. You could sit on the beach and sketch. Get a bit of colour. You're so pale."

At the time I didn't show it but I was angry with him, that Richard wanted to take over my special moment, make the weekend about the two of us. By then we'd been together almost three years. While knowing nothing about 'relationships' I was beginning to question ours. Moving into my late twenties, so far my life had fallen into two separate sections; the lost years leading up to the deaths of my adoptive parents and the decade spent between hospitals, an assessment centre, a remand home for a while, college and Richard. No friendships formed, just me working a way through guilt, finding a small voice, discovering I had a talent . . . and again Richard.

"Please Richard, let me do this."

He held up his hands. "I'm not stopping you, it was just an idea I thought you might like."

"It's a great idea but not in this instance."

"Please yourself." He'd turned his back on me. "But I guarantee you won't enjoy being on your own."

I booked a room in a small, expensive hotel on the outskirts of Exeter and yes, Richard paid for it, and yes, the money in my shoulder bag was Richard's as well. In those days I had no credit card, no bank account. Contrary to his prediction from the moment I boarded the Exeter train I felt happy. It was an amazing feeling. I couldn't stop smiling. The hotel bedroom was decorated in creamy colours, creamy bed linen, a few nice pieces of furniture painted white. I think I responded to the femininity of it, because Richard's London flat was minimalist: white walls, with everything else black or shades of dark grey. His taste has mellowed since but then I wasn't allowed to introduce any colour, not even a vase of pink tulips.

After a surprisingly good night's sleep – I've rarely managed more than a few hours at a time without waking – I enjoyed a late breakfast. I was the only person in the dining room. It was a beautiful summer's day and my plan was to walk the short distance to the gallery to arrive around mid-day. I was a little intimidated at the thought of meeting fellow artists but I reassured myself that I'd been chosen for a good reason. I prepared with care, taking Richard's advice: "Don't dress like a loser. Dress as if you're not only a critical success, you're a financial success as well."

I wore a long-sleeved silk dress of navy-blue, knee length and with a dramatically high neckline. It wasn't overly expensive. Could have been Zara. Richard used to say I could make a rag look like a designer piece. As I write this, I'm thoughtful, because obviously no matter how dysfunctional I've painted our relationship, Richard *was* capable of giving compliments. My hair I wore in one long burnished plait hanging over my breast. I *am* tall, I *was* pale and slender. I had a perfect face that gave little away. No one would have known that there was a wicked bone in my body.

The exhibition was gratifyingly busy. Several of the artists lived in Devon and they'd brought along friends and family. There were tourists probably just looking for a refuge from the hot sun but also people who seemed to be genuinely interested in the paintings. I introduced myself to Bill, the gallery owner.

"So, you are Shona Blake," he said as if I were someone important.

In the middle of the room was a line of banquette seating. Having taken my time studying the artwork on show, I sat quietly, my hands clasped in my lap, keeping an eye on my own three small pictures. I didn't feel lonely at all. I felt as if I were quietly waiting – for nothing big – some throwaway positive observation would be enough. People did stop and peer at my work. They made comments to each other although I couldn't hear what they were saying. The expressions on their faces were not disagreeable. I noticed a woman – rather elegant – in a pale grey trouser suit who kept returning to my small space on the wall, studying each image closely, her nose almost touching the paint. I watched as she approached Bill. Again, I couldn't hear what was said, but both of them looked across at me.

Bill called out, "Shona, could we have a word please?"

As I got to my feet, the woman held out her hand.

"Beatrice Salmon," she said. "I came to Exeter just to see your work. I was at your degree show a few years back, but you'd already left the college. I couldn't discover any contact details and then a friend on *The Guardian* told me you had work in this exhibition."

We both turned slightly as Bill placed a red dot next to one of my paintings. And then next to another. And then the final picture.

She smiled. "I'm getting in on the ground floor. In a few years they'll be worth ten times as much. Ring me as soon as you're back in London. I wish I could stay longer but—" she hesitated. "What about dinner this evening?"

"Don't you have to be somewhere else?"

She laid her hand lightly on my arm. "Yes or no, Shona?"

That day proved to be a brilliant day. Beatrice promised to pick me up from my hotel at seven. The remainder of the afternoon I spent at the exhibition. Those three red dots next to my paintings gave me confidence. Like some of the other artists, I now hovered near my work. I was asked questions about art, being an artist. I was included in conversations. I found I shared much common ground with the other exhibitors: hopes for the future, what we liked, what we loved. Richard had absorbed me into *his* life and *his* friends and activities and I'd been grateful. But people liking *me*, finding *me* of interest in my own right – this was new. At one point during the afternoon as I sat sharing a platter of sandwiches, laughing at a joke someone made, I thought: *this is how my future could be.*

Richard would never understand the pleasure I was getting from the day. I well knew the rearing back of his head so that his chin tucked into his neck: 'Really? My Shona engaged in chit-chat with total strangers? Doesn't sound like you at all.'

Quite late that evening, he rang me at the hotel. "So, how did it go?"

"Not bad," I said. "I'll tell you all my news tomorrow?"

"Oh, come on Shona, don't play games. Did you sell anything?"

"Yes."

"So, it wasn't a complete waste of time?"

"On the contrary," I said again – playfully. "The day exceeded my expectations."

"Exceeded your expectations?" he mimicked. "So, what happened?"

"Tomorrow," I said.

"But why not tell me today?"

"Because I'm tired."

"I rang earlier. Where were you?"

"We all went for a meal."

"So, you weren't too tired then?"

"I'm putting the phone down."

He was still annoyed when I arrived back in London. His tone was sneering, "Ah, so the wanderer returns."

I told him about Beatrice Salmon travelling all the way to Exeter to see my work. I genuinely wanted him to be happy for me.

"Beatrice Salmon rears her ugly head. Smells fishy, my darling," he said.

A few days later, while he was out, I rang her agency.

That afternoon, she emailed an interim contract which I signed and sent back.

Richard was furious. "If you choose to swim with the fishes."

"What does that mean?"

"Dead in the water."

12

SONNY

From under lowered lids Sonny watches Martin. "You're losing your stems,' he can't resist calling out.

Martin has spent the afternoon trying to assemble three paper Oriental Poppies that Sonny's mother had recently discovered in a box outside a charity shop. His thin nicotined fingers seem to possess a life of their own as they riffle through streamers of emerald-green and scarlet crepe paper. From the arm of his chair a long twist of green ribbon unfurls slowly towards the floor.

"I don't think the whole kit's here," Martin says thoughtfully.

"Then don't waste your time with it."

"Your mum asked me to sort it out." He doesn't look up.

"So what? Sort it out later." Sonny pats one of the cushions he's stretched out on. "Come and talk to me."

"No thanks." Martin says. "You talk, I'll listen."

Abruptly, Sonny sits up. When the roads are wet, his mother's footsteps are easily recognisable, as her boots splash along the pot-holed tarmac. He gets to his feet and stretches. Parting the heavy curtains, he's just in time to see her scurry into the building. Martin joins him at the window. Their shoulders are touching, Martin turns his head towards him, presses his lips hard against Sonny's mouth.

"Why now?" Sonny asks. "When she'll be back at any minute."

"Why not now?" He strokes Sonny's cheek with the tip of his tongue.

Sonny hears her footsteps pattering down the corridor. He is unable to breathe. The key is inserted in the door lock. The two men break apart as she enters the room stamping energetically on the mat. Water drips from her plastic raincoat and the telescopic umbrella hanging from her wrist.

"You're making puddles," he says.

Martin relieves her of her shopping trolley and the umbrella. "Bought my ciggies?"

"Of course." She counters, "Finished my Papavers yet?"

"Not possible Mrs G. The wire's missing for the stalks."

"Plenty of wire. Try the kitchen drawer." She drops her umbrella into the coal scuttle and turns back to face Sonny. "What's the matter?"

"Nothing. Miserable day outside. Depressing."

"Be glad you're in the dry then." She takes off her raincoat and drapes it over the padded footstool. "Fetch my slippers, dear heart." There is tension in the room but she seems unaware of it.

"Fetch them yourself." A moment passes, before Sonny retrieves the slippers from under her armchair and places them in front of her.

Boots kicked off, slippers on, she shuffles out to the kitchen. There is a *whoosh* of water into the electric kettle.

Deeply Sonny sighs.

"I heard that," she calls out.

Martin follows her. "Any cake, Mrs G? I need a sugar hit."

Sonny hears his mother's indulgent laughter. Within a few short weeks Martin has forged a bond with her. They are how he's imagined a mother and son would be with each other, familiar, joking, affectionate – nothing like their own uncomfortable parry and thrust: complaint (his) and anxious reassurance (hers). He is jealous. Why can't he and Martin at least be as brothers? He'd settle for that. For a while. Against the windows, the rain spatters heavily. He reaches a decision.

"No tea for me," he calls out.

Before he can reach the door, his mother – tea towel in one hand appears. "Where are you off to?" she asks. "Bored with our company?"

"I'm going to read my book."

"Let me light the fire in your room. It will be chilly."

"Don't fuss."

"It won't take a moment."

"For once in your life just leave me alone."

She looks shocked. Martin appears beside her. "Don't yell at your mum."

"At least take a mug of tea," she wheedles. "The kettle's on."

By the time he makes his escape, both has a paper flower on their lap and are absorbed in winding crepe paper around pieces of wire. Sonny mumbles something but neither look up as, carrying his drink, he slips from the room. He doesn't turn right towards his room, instead takes the stairs leading up to the seventh floor. As he pushes open the door of the apartment, his resolve faulters. The space is vast. Light streams in through the French windows, through the six narrow windows on the adjacent wall. It is merciless, emphasising the damp spreading like continents across the walls. There are entire cities of black mould. But the bedroom is better. No damp although actual chunks of plaster lie on the floor. The iron bed dominates the room. An old khaki blanket – an army blanket his mother had told him many years ago – has been thrown over the mattress. In her bedroom three floors below are soft blankets in pastel colours, quite clearly female. This one, the almost felt-like quality to the material, is definitely male. He imagines a soldier squatting in front of a campfire, a tin mug of tea laced with brandy in his hand, the blanket wrapped around his shoulders keeping out the cold of a night spent under the stars.

Against one wall is a paraffin heater. No paraffin. He'd used it up the day after Martin's arrival. There was more downstairs. He must fill the tank, check the wick. There is at least two more months of cold. Such an expanse of floor. He must bring up some rugs. From a child he has always wanted to dance. But she is the dancer. She claims the title. He opens the balcony door. Icy but clean air sweeps in. Sometime in the future there will be the sound of music, voices, laughter – the murmur of conversation, these rooms will come alive.

He touches the side of his face that Martin had licked. Did Martin care? It was always Martin who made a move. And then withdrew. Was it a game that Sonny didn't understand? Blanket across his knees, mug warming against his stomach, he leans back against the wrought-iron headboard. He recreates that first evening: the firelight making shadows dance on every wall. His mother, in the background, supplying him with much needed confidence.

Martin had been at ease. He'd kicked off his trainers and left them out in the corridor. Padding into the room, the first thing he'd said was, 'I'm sorry. My socks are filthy and my feet stink.' Sonny admired the way this was an assertion not an apology.

'Would you like a hot bath?" his mother had asked. "Our bathroom's lovely and warm, isn't it, Sonny? '

'Warmest room in the house.'

'I've no clean clothes.'

'I'll find some. You and Sonny are about the same size, you're a bit thinner, but they'll fit after a fashion. My son doesn't always wear,' she'd smiled gently, 'robes.'

'Can I eat first? I'm starving."

'Of course.'

Right from the start she'd always managed to hit the right note with Martin. Later on, towels over her arm, she'd led Martin away, chatting in her most beguiling fashion. As she'd passed Sonny, she'd laid her hand on the back of his head and immediately he'd felt calmer. 'Appreciate,' she murmured. He'd understood and was grateful. His mother had presented him with the finest, least expected gift. All would be well. And it had been.

She'd provided them with bottles of beer, San Miguel. Martin's thin face had broken into an incredible smile. And then a bottle of red wine. Sonny wanted to remain sober but Martin kept on drinking. The alcohol seemed to have no effect on him at all.. The following morning when they'd come up here to the top floor the room had been full of sunshine. 'This is amazing,' Martin said – that smile again. Out on the balcony they'd both gone quiet, Sonny holding back his words not to spoil Martin's sense of wonder. He'd allowed himself to hope that this was how the future could be, the two of them living together up above a world he had no part in. Their own fire in their own grate, their own soft rug to lie on, for Sonny to slip out of his kimono, Martin to peel off his shirt and jeans.

On this bed they'd lain together, at first separately and on their backs, talking. Sonny told him the story of annexing the building, the dead woman they'd found, the treasures they'd discovered. How they'd utilised those treasures.

'But the woman? What did you do with her? Was she decomposing? Fucking hell, Sonny.'

'The building was freezing cold, middle of winter. I don't think the body had started decomposing. We wrapped the woman in a sheet and between us, carried her to the lift. She didn't weigh that much. There's an underground garage. She's buried in the dirt floor. Mum read out a poem. The first two lines were, *because I could not stop for Death—he kindly stopped for me*. That's all I remember.'

And then they'd grown sleepy and climbed under the blanket. And then they'd grown hot and stripped off their clothes but stayed under the blanket. Later when the temperature in the room dropped to around freezing, he'd lit the paraffin heater. Pulling on his kimono, he'd gone downstairs to get some food. There was no sign of his mother. He'd crept back into the room. Nicely warm, he'd thought. Martin was asleep. He'd pushed back the blanket. Martin's arms and legs were spread wide across the mattress like a starfish. Sonny set down the carrier bag containing left-over pizza, fruit cake and a flask of tea. He'd bent forward and kissed Martin's forehead.

'Don't.' Martin's eyes were open.

'You're awake.'

'What time is it?' Leaning on his elbows, he sat up, turned his head towards the darkness outside.

'Almost seven. We've been here most of the day. I've brought pizza left over from last night and some tea to warm us up.'

'I'm warm enough.' Even so Martin pulled the blanket up to his armpits.

They both drank the tea. Martin consumed the pizza and cake while Sonny watched him.

'Don't watch me while I'm eating.'

'I like watching you.'

'I won't tell you again.'

'What's the matter? Have I done something wrong?'

Holding the blanket at his waist, Martin got off the bed. 'Could you go away, while I get some clothes on?'

'But why?' He'd tried to laugh, laugh Martin out of his altered mood.

'Because I say so.'

Sonny gets off the bed. He closes the French windows, turning to assess the room. One day he will make this his home.

13

SHONA

2014

I leave the house clean and tidy, a ready meal from Marks and Spencer in the fridge for you should you arrive home before me. Even though Mrs Gifford came here empty handed, I feel compelled to take a gift. Some days ago, I bought an orchid. It was in bud, today it's in bloom. I want to make a positive impact on both of them: Shona sweeping in with her flying mane of hair carrying an exotic offering. The orchid *is* exotic, almost shockingly white petals veined with purple, the blossoms dancing along one slender stem.

Some would wonder what appeal an elderly second-rate ballet dancer might have to a woman four decades younger. Maybe those people grew up with options to pick and choose their friends, work colleagues? To discard the odd and the 'awkward brigade' – one of your phrases Richard when quizzing me about the Gifford's. I started too late to absorb the mores required. Within the circumscribed life I lead, the Miller Building and its occupants offer an opportunity where the odd and awkward might feel comfortable, or that is what I desperately hope for.

I'm taking your torch. It's heavy duty, encased in thick rubber. If the afternoon proves a success it will already be dark before I start for home. "Useful as a weapon," you said and I am grateful for it because a shadow of your mistrust of the unknown has transmitted itself to me. I've done some research into the Miller Building – although derelict, it's considered of major historic importance with links to the Arts and Crafts Movement of the early nineteen-hundreds. There is an entire Wikipedia page on the construction's social and architectural relevance. But reading further I discovered less impressive facts: newspaper accounts of multiple arrests for drug offences and a near fatal stabbing all within half a mile of the block. A family had been killed when part of the footbridge collapsed onto their car and less than a year ago the decomposed body of a young man was found in the cellar of one of the nearby empty houses. All valid reasons why the cab firms I'd rung refused to drive me.

Canberra Road dips down in a straight line to the promenade. Each time I step onto the pavement outside this house I'm aware of a strange optical illusion; the horizon appears level with my gaze, the sea a high, threatening wall of water poised at that very moment before it crashes down and floods the beach, shops, the seafront. I set off at a brisk pace and soon the wall of water falls back, reverts to being a sparkling expanse. There is the sun already half-way towards the horizon although it's only just after two o'clock.

It is mild for late February but I'm taking no risks. I've dressed for warmth in woollen trousers, walking boots, a pullover and a fleece jacket. At the promenade I turn right. Hawksbridge is busy but the further I walk, the fewer people I pass. After a mile, the well-maintained paving disappears replaced by uneven ground. I discover the remains of a municipal swimming bath: some faded blue tiling, a cracked mosaic of dolphins swimming in the few inches of dirty water pooled at the bottom.

To my left the tide has begun to creep up the shingle – green-blue, edged with froth like delicate white lace. I pause to get my breath back; shading my eyes with one hand, I scan the sea line. Bobbing on the water like children's toys are several yachts with brightly coloured sails. How foolish of me not to at least bring a sketchbook.

Half a mile further on and Mrs Gifford's beach shelter comes into view. Unlike the smart glass and concrete shelters closer to the town, this is made of wood, the paint so eroded it's impossible to determine the original colour. Facing me is one small grimy window. I can't see if anyone is sitting inside. My heart beats faster, but it is okay. The shelter is empty.

I turn to face inland. About half a mile away the Miller building rises like an ancient monolith out of a bleak, flat landscape. And yet there's also something reptilian about the way it straddles across my direct line of vision, as if it waits for me. For the first time I feel apprehensive. I'm completely alone. There is not a single soul anywhere. Clambering onto a fallen branch, I look for a path through the overgrown vegetation and see the zig-zag flattening of the grass, the track a cat or small animal might make. Which Mrs Gifford – on her journeys back and forth to the town – must have helped to make.

The walk has taken longer than I expected. I try to increase my pace but it's difficult to go fast on such uneven terrain. As yet there are no signs of fresh spring growth, just the unhealthy yellow, brown and black vegetation from the previous autumn. Even so, my spirits rise. I welcome that itch in the fingers of my drawing hand to close around an implement, to make a start. I count the windows in the building ahead of me; six on each floor. It's difficult to make out those at the top, the balcony impedes my view.

The following morning, you are already in the kitchen tipping muesli into a bowl when I come downstairs. You look up and grin, "Those nightmares of yours are becoming a habit. When you weren't shouting, I could still hear you muttering away. I was tempted to bang on the wall."

"I'm glad you didn't."

You pull out a chair and sprawl. "Can you make my coffee? I've a hell of a hangover. I'd forgotten how much alcohol students like to put away."

"I don't know how to use the coffee machine."

"Instant will have to do then." You sigh as if unused to anything that comes out of a bog-standard jar.

Coffee made, I carry mine to the back door.

"Surely you're not going outside. It's fucking freezing. Your feet are bare. Have you no sense at all?"

"Richard, all I intended to do was stand on the step. I want to see if the spring bulbs are showing yet."

"Can't that wait till I've left the house?"

"Yes, of course it can."

"Hallelujah!" In a friendlier tone you ask, "So how was it? Did your would-be surrogate family welcome you with open arms?"

"I only saw Mrs Gifford. She said her son was having a difficult day."

"How old is he?"

"I'm not sure. It didn't matter that he wasn't there. We talked. I probably said too much but she didn't seem to mind." And then I just can't help myself, I burst out with all the enthusiasm I'm desperate to share. "Richard, she was so . . . nice. Her home, the entire interior of the building is extraordinary. It's like entering a cross between a fairy tale and," I start to laugh, "a gothic horror story!"

You hold up your hand like a traffic cop. "Shona, you've spent your life searching for fairy tales and horror stories to insert yourself into. All fine, till they go wrong. And they do go wrong. Ours certainly went wrong."

My positive mood is swept away. Shoulders sagging, I stand with my back against the door staring at you, aware that my mouth is hanging open repulsively but somehow, I'm incapable of closing it.

"I don't mean to be unkind," you say.

"Then why are you?"

Taking a gulp of coffee, you pull a face of pure disgust. As you tip the contents of your mug into the sink, I walk quickly out of the room.

The front door of the Miller Building was battered and huge as if created for giants. There was a snarling lion's head of a doorknob, black with age and dirt, that must once have been polished brass. It turned easily in my hand. I pushed and the door reluctantly opened, clicking shut behind me as I stepped inside. The temperature dropped by at least ten degrees. If it wasn't for the flickering oil lamp hanging from a hook next to the staircase I'd have been plunged into total darkness. Even so, I took out the torch and switched it on. I shivered, not only from the cold but the eeriness of the cavernous hallway. My torch beam skittered across walls and ceiling. There were cracks like the skeletal branches of ancient trees winding upwards from the splintering skirting boards. Above me, the once grand ceiling rose looked diseased, with dangling mis-shapes of peeling and carbuncular plaster. Breathing in, my nostrils filled with the smell of damp and something inherently rotten. 'Nothing sinister," Mrs Gifford told me later. "Years of blocked drains."

I rejected the staircase, which would demand a trek up several flights of stairs. The Victorian lift. little more than an iron cage was preferable. I yanked back the safety gate, then the inner grille. Under my feet the flooring seemed to give slightly. A yellowed enamel sign informed me that the lift could carry up to four people. I didn't believe it. Two would have been a squeeze. A rusted ladder was attached to the concrete wall of the lift shaft, no doubt used for maintenance. Or escape? I pushed that thought away and pressed the button for the fourth floor. The lift juddered into life. As it moved upwards, my imagination took over. The opening to each floor presented an unknown threat. Were there others hiding in the darkness? Ghosts, monsters; rats would be bad enough! And then from somewhere above I heard the faint sound of music. Concentrating, I recognised the 'Blue Danube Waltz', Sheila Kirkpatrick's favourite; the music they'd danced to in their living room on the eve of my fifteenth birthday. In my imagination, I could see Sheila clearly, her head tilted forward brushing Brian's shoulder as she concentrated on the waltz steps. Brian supremely confident. He'd been taught to dance as a boy at boarding school. His face was full of love for her.

"Oh," I gasped because the memory even from so long ago had the power to hurt me.

The lift stopped. The music stopped. The pain disappeared.

Opening the gates, I stepped out into a corridor. Halfway along, light was streaming from an open doorway. Here, there was no decaying ornate plasterwork to admire and the parquet flooring was made up of smaller blocks of splintering wood. Bare walls, once white, now dirty and mottled, whole sections of mortar traced with spider webs of fine cracks.

I walked quickly, rustling the carrier bag containing the orchid to give whoever waited for me some notice of my arrival. But supposing there were no Sonny and Mrs Gifford, supposing this was a trap? I'd set off on a whim. I was on my own in a vast empty building in the middle of nowhere on the strength of an invitation from a woman I hardly knew. My only defence was the torch and a ceramic pot. I could be raped, murdered. And then as I paused in the doorway I moved from cold and fearful to their polar opposites. Heat from a roaring fire reached me and colour, rich jewel shades, almost too vivid for my eyes to tolerate! I'm an artist, in my work I use colour sparingly, but in life, I love it!

The room I stepped into was beautiful, even luxurious: high ceiling, every inch of wall covered with Eastern and Oriental rugs, tapestries in vivid shades of red, blue and jade green. There was little in the way of conventional furniture apart from an old-fashioned armchair pulled up close to the fire and some sort of day-bed – later Mrs Gifford called it a chaise longue – placed in front of velvet curtains. The thickly carpeted floor was scattered with plump embroidered leather bolsters. From the armchair, Mrs Gifford hauled herself to her feet. She took a couple of steps towards me. She didn't seem quite focused and I wondered if she'd been asleep.

"Shona, come in. I expect you're perished. Let's get this door shut."

Shyly I placed the orchid on a small table at a distance from the fire and looked round. Had the cruel winter light been allowed in, it might all have looked shabby and worn.

To me, smiling like a dazzled fool, it seemed magical. The following day, you would be right about my preference for fairy tale over reality. When you've had nothing at all, you – I don't set my sights on some dull happy medium, no I yearn for the stuff that dreams are made of.

She found me a stool. The cushioned seat was of faded pink velvet, something one might find in a junk shop and yet again, it charmed me. I felt young because I felt Mrs Gifford saw me as 'young', of an age to comfortably perch on a stool, my face level with her knees!

"I hoped you'd come today. Shall I be mother?" She indicated the tea tray resting on a brass coal scuttle and set with two cups on matching saucers, pretty plates edged with a pattern of yellow roses. "Kettle, pot and cake are in the kitchen. Would you be a dear?"

I was more than happy to be 'a dear'.

Over the course of the next two hours, I was surprised to find us both with much to say. Conversation was far easier than when she'd come to Canberra Road. She plied me with questions: why had I chosen to be an artist? Did I like Hawksbridge? She showed an interest in you, Richard. I was in a generous mood and so described you at your very best, from a time when we'd suited each other better.

When I ran out of steam, she said, "You talk about Richard as if you love him."

It was as if icy water had been thrown in my face. Tortoise-like I withdrew. My voice that I'd tried so hard to make pleasing, grew cool. "I never loved Richard. If he ever loved me it was as a prized possession." I managed a shaky laugh aware that even the flames in the grate seemed to have ducked down in response to the chill of my tone.

"Shona, you're lovely. Why wouldn't he love you for yourself?"

"Our relationship is complicated."

She placed her hand over mine. "Then that gives us some mutual ground to work from. The relationship I have with my son is also complicated."

It was after five. By now outside the curtained windows night would have fallen. She seemed to read my thoughts.

"Well Shona, time I think for you to go. But first your lovely orchid. Thank you so much." With care she picked up the pot and carried it into what I could see was her bedroom. "Come in," she called.

Again, the room was beautiful but very different: pastel colours, blues and creams and coral pink. I thought of my bedroom in Canberra Road, everything shades of beige and none of it chosen by me.

I joined her at the window. The view surprised me. Mistakenly, I'd imagined every window would have a sea view. I looked out over barren fields, a few trees.

"Your orchid will do better here. The fire next door sucks the oxygen from the air." The white orchid in its white ceramic pot looked perfect on the windowsill. "Now, I'll walk you to the lift."

She left the living room door open to shed light into the corridor.

"Is there no electricity?" I asked.

"As you saw, the lift still works – probably for maintaining the upper floors, not that anyone does. We have a generator but we use it sparingly. Power in the rest of the building was switched off some years ago."

After the warmth of the room, the corridor felt doubly cold. I had to steel myself from shivering but Mrs Gifford seemed unaware of the icy temperature. I noticed a band of red light showing under one of the neighbouring doors. "Someone's home," I said.

If she heard me, she didn't answer.

Once outside, I secured the front door with the key she'd given me, then as instructed dropped it back through the letterbox. With the beam of my torch to guide me, I crossed the tarmac and found the narrow path at the point where it disappeared into long grass. I looked back. The Miller Building appeared to be in darkness. Suddenly from the top floor balcony, a single spot of yellow light appeared moving from side to side. It streaked across the path and settled at my feet. I began to laugh. How thoughtful of Mrs Gifford to watch over my progress.

I turned my torch upwards so that our two beams met and then her torch was extinguished. I raked the balcony but there was no sign of her.

14

1988

My surname is no longer Blake, it is Kirkpatrick and I am nine years old. For the following I move into third person. It is too painful to own this child, this shadow self.

Ten months earlier a childless couple in their mid-forties, Brian and Sheila, had agreed to foster Shona with a view – if all went well – to adopt. Initially the girl's change of circumstances represented a temporary cessation while she waited (with dread) for her mother to reclaim her. As time passed however, the change destabilised, cast her adrift, there were aspects of her old life that she missed.

When Shona lived with Dorothy, (never mum, mummy, mother) together they'd watch old cowboy movies and series on TV – little else. The news, comedy programmes, games shows were of no interest. The dynamic of 'the cowboy', the good and bad, white Stetson versus black Stetson, tall, rangy men adored by fragile but feisty women dressed in bonnets and gowns that swept dirt roads took Shona's mother out of the reality that was her life. They were her passion from her own childhood in the 1950s: videos of Rio Bravo, High Noon, Shane, Laramie. Into this passion, Shona inserted herself, made herself a companion of sorts.

Shona knew little of spelling or how to add up, where Scotland or Wales or Ireland might be, but she could read and draw a horse and a cowboy hat, she knew all about the Wild West and Matt Dillon and Jessie James. Any moments of kindness from Dorothy, any glimmer of affection materialised during the fifty minutes or hour and a half, when they sat each side of the gas fire, their faces lit by the flickering television screen.

It is the beginning of September. Sunlight filters through the foliage of three elderly apple trees, making patterns on the grass. The week before, Brian had dismantled the child's swing hanging from one of the lower tree branches, intending to replace the rotten wooden seat. The swing's rope supports lie in two thick coils under the trees.

There is another girl with Shona, Lynda Wilson. Lynda lives across the road in a house with a far larger garden but they always play in this garden because Lynda's mother, Sarah suffers from depression.

"Play nicely," Sheila instructs. "Lynda has no father."

"But I hate her."

"Darling, you're too young to even know what hate is."

Beneath the trees, three wooden crates lie on their sides. Brian has asked the girls to fill them with windfalls and any apples within reach on the branches. Instead, they are using the crates and fruit to play shop. On a makeshift counter, the apples have been divided into green and red, ripe and unripe, bruised and perfect.

Shona is the shopkeeper, Lynda her customer. After a time, Lynda decides that it is her turn to be the shopkeeper. "We agreed," she says.

"No, we didn't. Look, you can have three apples for the price of two."

Lynda pushes out her lower lip. "I'm going to tell your mummy that you won't let me have my turn." Lynda has told tales before.

She will cry and snivel and say, "It isn't fair. Why is Shona so mean to me?"

Shona sweeps the apples off the counter, forcing Lynda to jump out of the way, fearful of getting juice from the rotting fruit on her white ankle socks.

"What are you doing?" Lynda demands.

"Wait and see."

One balanced on top of the other, Shona replaces the crates arranging them on the grass directly beneath the branch that held the swing. Dissatisfied, she removes the top crate, placing it next to the other two, so they form a simple staircase. Pleased with her creation, she leaps from the grass to the first crate and then goes one crate higher. She grabs hold of the branch and swings from it.

Lynda is unimpressed. "Now what? I'm bored," she says. "Can't we go indoors and watch TV?"

Shona shakes her head. They're definitely not going back indoors. She knows that Lynda envies her having Brian and Sheila, that she'd like to swap her own mother and home for them. Lynda would like to sleep in Shona's bed, play with Shona's toys. She drops back onto the ground, grabbing the end of one of the coils of rope. It snakes across the grass taking on a life of its own. "Yee-hah!" Shona yells making it crack like a whip.

Lynda tries to pull the rope away from her. They wrestle. Lynda loses the fight and starts to cry.

"Have patience." Shona adopts Sheila's soothing tone of voice. It works. Lynda settles cross legged in front of the crates.

After several attempts Shona manages to toss one end of the rope up and over the branch. Brian has taught her about knots. This was one of the few subjects that had secured her full attention since coming to live with them. Standing on the top crate, she ties the rope to the branch using a double reef. "Another name is a 'Hercules' knot," he'd said. "Because it's strong. Invincible."

To form the loop at the other end of the rope, a slip knot is required. The loop grazes the ground. She winds the rope round and round the branch until the loop is level with her head.

Lynda eyes are bright and curious. "What are you doing? What is it?"

Shona puts her head through the loop and smiles down at Lynda. "We have a noose and a scaffold."

"What's a scaffold?"

"I'm standing on it. The sheriff and the townsfolk march the killer up onto the scaffold and hang him."

"Oh cowboys," Linda sneers. "They're boring."

"No, they're not." Shona stands with her hands linked behind her back as if they're tied or handcuffed. "Lynda, you're the sheriff. Your job is to sentence me to death."

Uneasy, Lynda gets to her feet. She looks back in the direction of the Kirkpatrick's house. At any moment she will start to run.

Throwing off the noose, Shona leaps down. "Okay. You go first and I'll make the pronouncement. Listen very carefully and then when it's your turn, repeat what I've said." She takes hold of Lynda's elbow and guides her up onto the first crate.

"But it wobbles," Lynda says.

"Not much. You're not scared, are you?"

"Of course not." She shrugs Shona's hand away and steps onto the topmost crate. "I can see your house," she says distracted. "Can I stay for tea?"

"Yes, but let's finish the game first."

"I wish we were sisters. I could live here forever. We could share a bedroom. Would you like that? Someone to talk to when the lights are out?"

Shona would hate it. She tries to smile but her teeth are bared. "The game," she says.

"I don't like it."

"Then you can't be my sister. Look, place the noose over your head and afterwards we can play at being sisters."

Reluctantly, Lynda takes the noose and drops it over her head. It settles loosely on her shoulders. "Ready."

"Lynda Wilson, I sentence you to death by hanging," Shona says.

"Is that all?"

"Have patience." Again, the words have a calming effect. Shona approaches the scaffold. "Reach down and take my hand, then I will give you the final benediction."

Shona holds out her hand. Their fingers intertwine.

"Lynda, Lynda, Lynda," The words are a chant. Shona's fingers tighten and she tugs just enough for Linda's body to tilt forward and the second crate to shift.

"Jump," she tells her. "I'll catch you."

Lynda shakes her head. Her eyes are wide with fear.

"Jump!" Shona kicks the side of the lower crate.

Lynda makes a yelping sound and launches herself into the air.

Shona drops her hand and steps back.

Suspended only a few feet from the ground Linda claws at the noose. Her legs and feet paddle furiously. The sounds she makes are horrible.

Shona turns away, walks back towards the house. In the kitchen she finds Sheila folding laundry.

"There's been an accident." Her tone is matter of fact.

"What sort of accident?"

"Lynda. She might be dead."

A towel drops silently to the kitchen floor. "Oh my god." Sheila is already moving towards the back door. "Get Brian. He's in the garage."

Inside the garage, Brian is cutting wood with an electric saw. HE waves her away. "Not when I'm working," he shouts above the noise.

"Sheila says you're to come now: to the apple trees."

He switches off the saw and carefully lays it down on the work bench. "What's happened, child? Is it serious?"

Shona nods her head. "I think so."

Roughly he moves her aside and heads out of the door, calling back over his shoulder.

"Touch nothing!"

The saw lying on the workbench is horrifyingly fascinating. Even silent it has a threatening power. Following the electric cable back to a plug point Shona flicks the switch to 'OFF'

15

2014

Usually if the weather's fine I prefer to sit at one of the metal tables outside the café but today, because it is so warm and sunny, all of them are taken. As I wait for my coffee to cool, I make quick sketches in my notepad of the clientele, their body language and facial expressions. Next to each image I write a one-word assessment of their mood: bored, absorbed, happy, sad, engrossed. Only half my attention is engaged. The remaining half is thinking how your good mood has continued. Since your college course started, you're out most of the day and several evenings during the week. You're more like the Richard I remember, brash and self-absorbed but still capable of kindness.

My gaze is drawn to the café window. A middle-aged couple are making a production of gathering up jackets and shopping bags. Hastily I grab my pad and coffee so I can lay claim to their table. As I rise from my chair, I see that two men have beaten me to it.

The woman looks up at one of the newcomers, smiling in recognition. "My son enjoyed your lecture at the college last weekend."

I can't see the man's face but he makes her a small bow.

Her husband nods agreement. "You were excellent. Now come on Marge. Shopping centre."

Arm in arm the couple walk away. The men sit down. A waitress goes outside and begins to clear the table. I hear them ordering: *cappuccino* and a *latte*. They settle with their backs to me, legs stretched out, faces turned towards the sea view.

Sketch forgotten, I study their body language, trying to work out the dynamic between them. When the waitress returns with their drinks one of them looks up and says, "Sorry, I should have said, a KitKat as well." His companion holds up his hand. "Not for me." It's infuriating, I can hear them quite clearly but the waitress is blocking my view.

A group of students stop to read the menu hanging in the window and the entire scene outside is obscured. One of the students presses his head against the glass to see inside. His nose and mouth become flattened and ugly. Seeing me, his expression changes to a ghoulish grin.

I turn away and count to ten. When I glance back, the students have gone and the two men outside have turned their chairs to face each other. It's a shock seeing you out of context. And Raoul looking not a day older than in the handful of times we met pre-breakdown. Once his name was mentioned incessantly – at first came denial: *A waiter? Give me credit for better taste, Shona, one-night stand material only* – changing to, *Raoul this, Raoul that, Raoul's the love of my fucking life!*

Your arms are folded defensively across your chest, legs are crossed at the ankle. Are you uneasy in your ex-lover's company or fighting a desire to just relax with this man you once knew well?

The waitress places a KitKat in front of Raoul. He squints

up at her, a little dazzled by the sun and makes an inaudible comment. All three of them burst out laughing. In mock admonition the waitress gently bats the top of Raoul's head with her tray. It is clear he is a regular customer. Raoul picks up the KitKat and begins to peel back the wrapper. He does this slowly as if enjoying the process. You're mesmerised, mouth hanging open. Then suddenly as if you're aware of behaving like a hungry voyeur of some intimate act, you force your eyes away, towards the window and me.

To give myself some time to gather my thoughts I go to the counter and pay the bill. As I wait for a further coffee to take out, I decide to adopt a casual approach. 'Hi Richard,' I'll say with a friendly nod before walking away. As I step outside, I find just the waitress loading their crockery and half of the KitKat onto her tray.

"Those two were in a hurry," she says. "They hardly touched their drinks."

Later that evening I expect you to make some acknowledgement that you'd seen me, but in the common ground of the kitchen both of us behave self-consciously and keep conversation to a minimum. That hackneyed phrase – the elephant in the room – is never more appropriate.

As we're about to have dinner, you receive a phone call. Answering it, all you say is, "Fifteen minutes," before hanging up. You race upstairs. I hear you pulling open drawers and taking stuff out of the bathroom. I remain in the kitchen waiting for some explanation but no, you head straight for the front door. "Back tomorrow afternoon," you call out. "TV's all yours. Usual rules apply." And then you are gone.

The oven timer buzzes. I take our two ready-made lasagnes out and leave them to cool for a few minutes. I hear a car slowing down in front of the house. Quietly I slip into the front room and peer through the narrow gap between the blind and window frame. A car, black and gleaming has pulled in outside the house, the engine is running, a deep expensive purr. Raoul climbs out, takes your rucksack and throws it onto the back seat. He slams the door shut. The two of you stand in the road facing each other. I'd always thought of Raoul as being shorter, slighter in build, but no, he is a few inches taller than you. He grips your elbow in a playful greeting as if it's a preliminary to some horse-play. And then he draws you towards him, your faces almost touch– and you – hater of intimacy – look delighted.

It must be ten years at least since Richard first met Raoul: a summer's evening, close to midnight in north London. We were with several of Richard's male work colleagues and their girlfriends. The men in the party all told me I looked stunning. My jeans were skintight. I wore a long-sleeved black leotard – I used to love wearing leotards, they made me feel remote and beautiful, concealing my scars while revealing my shape – good breasts with not an ounce of extra flesh on the rest of my body. Oh, and chrome-yellow incredibly high-heeled shoes, a birthday present from Richard. The shoes were painful to walk in but he loved them, loved the way I towered above most of the women he knew. "You're my super-heroine, my Amazon," he said.

None of Richard's friends took me seriously though. As an artist I wasn't yet rich and/or famous. Several of them would have liked to fuck me. A couple of times I'd overheard myself referred to as 'the dumb, shaggable brunette'. The women saw me as a failure – a strange creature – because in the first decade of the twenty-first century, I was an anomaly – a kept woman. An artist? What kind of artist? Yeah, yeah, yeah – who is she kidding?

The talk was loud: of clothes and careers and upcoming holidays abroad. I searched around inside my head for anything to contribute, but just one of my revelations would have killed the conversation. They'd look at me with horror. Or – equally likely – think I was lying in an attempt to gain attention.

Earlier we'd been to a Turkish restaurant in Dalston. At the end of the meal I'd wanted to go home, but no, Richard insisted on one more round of drinks at a local wine bar. Several people he'd worked with on a project in Brighton the previous summer would be there. It would be good for him to network.

The bar was already crowded. We were forced to take our drinks onto the pavement. Just before midnight a waiter came outside and deferentially asked us all to keep the noise down. The wine bar was in a semi-residential area and neighbours had complained.

"Fair enough." Richard's tone to the waiter was amiable. "One more bottle of Pinot and we'll head off home."

"The bar's closed," the waiter answered.

"Oh, come on now." Richard put his hand on the man's shoulder. They were very different: Richard tanned and polished, the waiter pale and a little haggard looking.

"Richard, can't we go? I'm tired," I said.

He ignored me.

The waiter didn't shrug Richard's hand away. Instead, the two men exchanged glances, not hostile – combative.

"Okay." It was the waiter who finally gave in.

"Great mate." And Richard followed him back into the bar.

Furious, paying no attention to the conversations around me, I sipped my now warm cocktail. Through the bar window, I could see Richard deep in conversation with the waiter. The waiter shrugged and then smiled at him. I tapped on the glass. Without looking in my direction, Richard held up his hand, the fingers spread: five minutes.

I tapped harder. "Come now," I mouthed frowning. "I want to go home."

He took no notice, turning his attention back to the waiter. 'Maybe later?' was easy enough to lip read. I had my own key to the flat. I could hail a cab. But insecurity kept me hanging about until Richard finally left the bar.

"Shona, darling." His eyes appeared slightly glazed. "I'm so sorry."

"You're not sorry. You couldn't care less about anyone except yourself. You're a selfish bastard."

We had the attention of all his friends. Smilingly, Richard stretched out one hand to stroke my shoulder. I slapped it away. "Fuck off!" I shouted.

"Excuse us." Richard smiled at his audience. Fingers closing tightly around my arm he steered me out into the road where we stood between two parked cars. "Just cool it, Shona," he said.

No way could I 'cool it'. Literally I was seeing red. "Don't patronise me!"

"Darling, I'm impressed. I don't think I've ever seen you in a strop before." He pulled me closer. His grinning face was only inches from mine. "I can see it in your eyes. Just for a moment you wanted to kill me. Didn't you?" His hand slipped under the silk of my shirt. His fingers traced old scars.

I remained rigid in his arms until finally his grip loosened and he stepped away. From the inside pocket of his jacket, he drew out his wallet. "Get a cab home. I'll be back in the morning." A twenty-pound note fluttered to the pavement. Richard turned on his heel. His friends had been watching.

The group parted, slapping his shoulders to welcome him back as if he was a conquering hero.

I picked up the money. I had no pride. Heading towards the busy Kingsland Road, I passed a mix of shops, cafés and wine bars. Most were closed and in darkness but lights still shone in the flats above. I can't recall a time when I'd been out alone that late at night. There were still plenty of people about but I was fearful. A young woman, no more than twenty and staggering slightly asked me for money. I shook my head.

"Bitch," she spat out.

On the other side of the road a man put his key into a front door lock. He winked at me. "Fuck you," I muttered. For a moment I had no idea where I was. I turned my head and there was the Kingsland Road, cars and vans waiting for the lights to change. I breathed deeply. Took a step forward. The heel of my shoe snapped and in an ugly, awkward movement I fell sideways, my elbow hitting the pavement with a crack. Pain shot up my arm.

A woman stepped out of a doorway. She glanced in my direction. Frowning, she walked towards me. "Shona? It is you." She started to laugh, "Christ almighty, you scrubbed up well!"

I'd been nine years old when I'd last heard that voice. Horrified I stared up at my worst nightmare: my mother. Dorothy. Rougher now, but still familiar. In the half-light of the street she appeared hardly altered, only thinner, smarter, but the inevitable cigarette in one hand.

She bent over me, studying my face. "Do you know how I recognised you? No? Cat got your tongue? Your eyes. Still the same." She took a drag of her cigarette and the tip glowed. "Terrified."

I shrank away from her.

"I'll take over," Richard squatted down next to me. "Too much to drink, darling. We need to get you home."

"I think she's broken her arm."

"Thank you," Richard said. "You may be right."

"Are you, her bloke?"

"None of your business." He got to his feet. "And whoever you are, this isn't a good time for a chat. You can see the state she's in."

"Okay, but—"

"Just piss off."

Her gaze flicked from him to me. "You'd like me to do that, wouldn't you, dear?"

"Yes," I answered.

Smiling, she tossed the cigarette into the gutter. "Should have given these up years ago," she said. "Lung cancer. Eighteen months left if I'm lucky."

Ignoring her Richard walked out into the road and hailed a cab. We spent two hours in Accident and Emergency.

The following morning the pain from my broken arm woke me early. My body ached but at least my mind was clear. With difficulty I rolled out of bed and went to Richard's room.

I scratched at his door. "Are you awake?"

"Just about," he mumbled. "Coming to terms with a god-awful hangover and lack of sleep." His eyes opened. "How's the arm?"

I pulled a face. "It hurts."

"You were away with the fairies last night."

"Was I?"

"You do know that you ruined my evening?"

"The waiter?"

"Poor guy was dead on his feet anyway. Might hook

up at the weekend. Go back to bed. I'll bring you tea and painkillers." Richard threw off the duvet and padded past me heading for the kitchen.

I complied.

"So, who was she? That woman seemed to know you." He placed the tray down on the bedside table.

"A tutor from college."

"I don't think so."

I stayed silent.

"Not going to come clean? One of your secrets? Please yourself." He stretched, "I'm feeling better now I'm up. Might go to the gym."

"Can you open my blinds, please?"

"For Christ's sake, Shona, you've broken your arm, you're not dying."

It was so peaceful once he'd gone. I closed my eyes and tried to let the memory of my mother slip away.

16

SONNY

Outside Martin's door Sonny pauses to listen. He hears the regular sound of breathing. It's seven am. Martin won't wake before eleven if left undisturbed.

In the distant past this particular windowless room was used by successive janitors to store ladders, tools and cleaning materials. Sonny and his mother had enjoyed discussing turning it into a walk-in wardrobe or an ensuite shower room or even knocking down the intervening wall and enlarging his bedroom. But these were daydreams that passed the time on a dark winter's day and nothing practical ever came of them. And then one morning they had found themselves galvanised, inspired to create a guest bedroom. The floor was now carpeted with strips of green and purple felt, pock-marked plastered walls concealed behind leopard-skin patterned wrapping paper. (Both materials discovered in a builder's skip by his mother.) That had been a good day, a good week. For once they had done something other than talk.

There are two divan beds with storage underneath, a rail (painted matt black) for clothes and a scratched G-Plan nest of tables on which stands a lamp with a red bulb and no shade. When Martin is in the lamp remains switched on day and night. Martin has lived with them for over almost two months now, yet Sonny still experiences a rush of happiness, welcoming that line of red at the foot of the door seeping out into the darkness of the corridor.

Martin's reaction to the room hadn't been the one he'd hoped for. "It's a cupboard. Where's the window?"

"A spacious cupboard."

"I'll feel trapped in here."

"But you're not. Trust me."

"Why should I?"

Sonny had shrugged. "No reason. Trust my mother if you like."

Martin had taken the few steps needed to cross the room, run his hand over the wall before picking at a corner of the wrapping wallpaper. Bewildered, Sonny watched him peel off a long uneven strip.

"Don't you like it? It was a choice of leopard-skin or balloons and Happy Birthday."

"Would it be okay if I painted the walls white?"

"Does that mean you intend to stay?"

Martin hadn't answered.

Sonny reaches a decision. He'll risk Martin's anger. "Martin, are you awake?"

The sound of breathing stops.

This time he knocks, quite loudly. "Martin, I'm coming in." Under his breath he counts down from five to one before pushing open the door. It takes a moment for his eyes to attune to the red light and then he sees that Martin is pulling on his clothes. A pair of pyjama bottoms lie crumpled on the floor.

"There was no need for you to get up. I thought we might have a chat."

Ignoring him, Martin throws on a sweatshirt.

Sonny moves across to the bed and sits in the warmth Martin's body has left on the mattress. "These days, we seem to be like ships passing in the night."

Martin looks up from tying the laces of his trainers. "Sonny, I'd rather you didn't just walk in here." He frowns. "Don't you ever dress properly? It's the middle of fucking winter and you're wandering around in a silk dressing gown."

"Kimono. My mother wears dressing gowns. I'm used to the cold and anyway I can't bear zips and belts and buttons. I don't like feeling constricted." He sits on the bed, eyes bright, youthful, he hopes. "You once said—"

Martin is on his feet. "That's enough. Whatever I said when drunk, I'd rather not know about." The expression on Martin's thin face softens. "I'm the lodger, not your boyfriend – that is what we agreed, isn't it?"

"Of course. But we can still be friends, can't we?"

"In my own time, Sonny."

"You keep saying that."

"And you keep pushing."

"Because there *was* a spark on our first night and the following day, I didn't imagine it."

"If you say that one more time, I'll go and I won't come back."

"I'm sorry."

"Don't keep saying 'sorry'. It's annoying."

"I'm sor-," Sonny slaps his forehead. "Martin, really, I can be whatever you want. I'm not used to company. Give me time to adapt. Now, what about breakfast?" Sonny turns away to face the rail holding Martin's few clothes. He must not display any eagerness.

After a few moments, Martin says, "Will your mum have the fire going?"

"Of course."

"Okay. I'll meet you there in half an hour. I need to make some calls."

"Perfect," Sonny says. "Friends?"

"Yeah. Why not?" He rumples Sonny's hair.

Back in his own room Sonny counts their exchange as something of a success. Humming under his breath, he unrolls the thick rug that serves as a mattress. Seated cross-legged, hands on thighs, he admires his reflection in the heavily framed mirror leaning against the wall. For once he doesn't worry about his age. The image is of a wise man – ageless – someone a younger man might turn to for guidance. That will do for the moment.

From his mother's room comes fresh sounds of movement. She will be boiling the kettle and making good any untidiness from the night before. He acknowledges that she is the real thing, a truly wise woman, with the ability to weave a life so delightful and seductive and playful, till now he's found it unbearable to contemplate any other. He recalls some scrap of her advice that he keeps coming back to: *'It's easy to imagine we see our needs reflected in the eyes of those we love. Darling, believing that a connection has been made may be no more than a matter of our own wishful thoughts.'*

This morning Sonny is convinced that for once she is mistaken. There is nothing wrong with his memory. On that first night Martin was impressed: by the flames leaping in the fireplace, a mother bringing in pizza, Spanish beer and wine. Surely the very strangeness of mother and son comfortably tucked away in this huge silent building was intriguing. 'Sonny, I love it here,' Martin had insisted.

"Love your old mum. Love it all.' Over and over, Martin the same mantra, *love, love, love.*

Sonny is half asleep, in that daydreaming state when the impossible becomes a possibility. How would it be if . . . ?

17

MRS GIFFORD

Today the town is crowded. There is the weekly street market with traders travelling from France bringing with them varieties of bread and cheeses, wine and bric-a-brac. Heading for the library Mrs Gifford stops to buy a baton and a wedge of Camembert. As she strolls between the stalls, she watches out for couples who walk hand in hand, the older the better. There is a story to be imagined, enduring love made plausible. Any smiles she saves for the dogs she meets. If she could live her life again, Mrs Gifford would choose a dog over any child of her own.

On such a pleasant day the Victorian library offers a dark unwelcome interior, but this is her set routine. The library card she uses for both herself and Sonny is in the name of Julia Steele, a name adopted by Mrs Gifford when she'd first moved to the area. Nobody has ever queried the diversity of books Julia Steele orders: crime, the bloodier the better for her son; biography and historical non-fiction for herself. Books chosen and stamped, she climbs the two further flights of stairs up to the reference library.

The 'daily reference library users' maintain a hierarchy

that she is excluded from. They have their preferred seats and first choice of the newspapers. Mrs Gifford is happy to just fit in with everyone. Due to her age, regulars have at least allotted her a chair, one with a narrow seat and unsteady chair legs that nobody else risks testing. Mrs Gifford weighs next to nothing and possesses perfect balance and posture. In the unlikely event of the seat collapsing under her she would rise from its wreckage like a graceful phoenix.

For an hour, she works her way through the newspapers as they become available. She's on the look-out for book reviews, making a note of titles to discuss with Sonny when she gets home. The local paper is tossed onto her table. She reaches for it greedily, turning to the pull-out property section. Her dream is that one day she will live in a bungalow, in the area on Hawksbridge outskirts she has christened Bungalow City. Mrs Gifford has a list of all four local estate agents and visits them on a regular basis. They humour her. When business is slow, some agents have even taken her to view a particular property. There's nothing today that catches her eye. Reluctantly she draws *The Sun* and *The Mirror* towards her. Not her favourites, she prefers text to photographs.

She finds herself thinking about the situation developing between her son and Martin. When she'd first brought Martin home, her hopes had been high. Leading, luring really; him back to the Miller Building. Hurrying him through the dark corridors, fearing that at any moment he'd turn and run. All in all, the evening had eventually exceeded her expectations. That night, she'd gone to bed actually feeling happy.

Over on the other side of the table, someone pulls out a newly vacant chair and sits down. A mobile phone is laid in front of him. Mrs Gifford glances at the man. She would guess him to be in his mid-thirties. In her eyes still a young man. He wears a brown leather jacket over a black polo neck.

The man inclines his head towards her. "If you've finished with *The Mirror*, could I take a look at it?"

She meets his gaze. His eyes are friendly.

"Of course." She hands over the newspaper.

"Thank you."

Obliquely she continues to watch as he skips through the pages.

Ten minutes pass then, bored with *The Sun,* she pushes that paper towards him.

He shakes his head. "I'm only marking time." The screen of his phone lights up. He turns away from her to answer. "Hi Shona," he says quietly, then, "No, I don't know what my plans are for later. Look, I'm in the library. Shona, this isn't a good time for a chat." Slipping his phone into his jacket pocket, he grins across at Mrs Gifford. "Sorry about that. Got to go."

"Me too," she replies. gathering up her shopping bags, she follows, making sure to keep a few paces behind. She understands how easy it would be for him to pigeon-hole her as some batty old woman; the type to be found in libraries and hard to shake off once they start to talk.

By the time she reaches the lobby, he is already pushing open one of the glass doors. He holds it for her to go first.

"Thank you," she says. So, this must be Richard because surely there can't be another Shona in such a small town. She desperately wants to claim some valid intimacy with him. *I think I know your girlfriend. I've been to your house. We're great friends.*

He is already striding across the square towards the college.

"Richard," someone calls out.

A taller man grips his arm. Their faces are almost touching. She thinks they are quite unique: not young and careless like the students. Both are well dressed, polished, well turned out – far younger than her own son yet they are men. Together they disappear into the college. Mrs Gifford stands on the library steps, hands clasped, eyes shut. She makes a wish.

18

SHONA

2014

Intending to try my luck with Mrs Gifford again being home, I walked as far as the shelter that faces the sea, its back to the Miller Building. The morning had been grey and overcast; by mid-afternoon a sea mist had started to roll in, the temperature dropping by about five degrees. The distant building looked horribly forbidding. I could hear your voice in my head: "Really Shona? You only saw the woman ten days ago. What will the two of you have to talk about?" I knew you were right. There *would* be disappointment probably on both sides: the son would decide not to show himself, leaving me and Mrs Gifford trying to come up with some mutual topic of interest and failing. She would want me to go. I'd be desperate to stay.

So instead I chose to sit in the shelter, resolving to head for home once the cold started to creep inside my coat. I took out my sketchbook and began to draw – silly doodles really. I was half asleep lulled by the constant lapping of the waves. Slowly I became conscious of someone approaching across the shingle. I lifted my head. Was it Mrs Gifford? But no, it was a young man, flapping towards me like a human scarecrow, shouting again and again, "I'm free to do what I want any old time!"

I huddled into the corner, hoping he'd continue up the beach. He continued to make straight for the shelter, coming to rest in the opening, bending himself double, head touching his knees, hands holding his ankles. He panted, almost like a dog might. There was no one about, no way I could get past him. My hand closed over the scalpel I kept in my charcoal tin.

"Sorry. Did I frighten you?" With grace his body uncoiled. He was maybe in his mid-twenties. Rough looking, stubble and not designer on his chin, hair long and unkempt. "You're Shona?"

Still clutching the scalpel, I nodded.

"Sonny's mum described you. Your plait. Don't see many plaits in Hawksbridge."

I put the scalpel back in the box. Closed my sketchbook. He sat down next to me, too close for comfort. I edged away.

"Were you drawing? Can I look at your book?"

"No."

"Why not?"

"It's private."

"If I wanted, I could take it off you."

Suddenly I wasn't intimidated. My temper was beginning to kick in. But I said nothing, kept my lips pressed together. He subsided next to me on the seat and began to roll a cigarette.

"Are you Martin?" I asked.

"Yes." He lit his cigarette. "Want a puff?"

"Don't smoke."

"Didn't think you did."

I noticed his watch. It looked expensive.

He caught my curious glance and grinned. "Rolex – fake," he said. "Sonny thinks it's real. He keeps borrowing it. He's a fucking kleptomaniac."

"Is he? I've only met his mother."

His grin widened. "Lucky you. I like her. Not so sure about him."

It was so rare that I had a conversation with anyone, I had no idea what response was required. Weakly I said, "But the two of you have become friends?"

The grin disappeared. "We're not friends. For the moment, it suits me to be there. How about you?"

"I live with someone."

"Proper house?"

"Yes."

"Got a spare bedroom?"

"No."

We talked for a bit. I asked him what he'd been shouting. He said, 'The lyrics from a Stones number.'

"And the Stones are?"

"You've never heard of the Rolling Stones? My dad's favourite band. Not mine but the words suited my mood. Okay?" He'd sounded almost aggressive.

I tried to draw the conversation back to the Giffords.

Surprisingly skilfully he diverted me away.

The mist coming off the sea had almost reached the shelter. It was quite eerie, very cold. I was glad I'd worn a thick coat. "Aren't you cold?" I asked.

He took my hand and placed it on his forehead. He was sweating, his skin hot.

"Time for me to go home," I said.

"I thought you were visiting the old lady."

"Not today. Not in the mood."

"I'll walk with you as far as the town centre."

"Martin, most of the shops will be closed by now."

"I'm not shopping."

I preferred my own company but there was no alternative. We walked in silence till we reached the turn-off for Canberra Road.

"Actually, this is where I live," I said.

I allowed him to hug me, my body rigid. This was the closest I'd been to another human being in years.

"You're thin," he said.

I tried to pull away but he held me fast.

"Mrs G tries to force feed me. I resist." Martin's silent laughter stirred my hair. He let me go. "See you, Shona."

He started to run cutting in between the dog-walkers and skateboarders. In no time at all he'd disappeared from sight. I didn't mention Martin to you, Richard. You'd classify him as one of 'Shona's waifs and strays'. You might be right. You often are. I wasn't sure if I actually liked Martin, but there'd been some connection.

Are men always like that? Like you Richard? While the man smoked, in the silence, I had a *déjà vu* moment, of a time when you and I were still living together in London. Both working in the big living room, you were at your desk hunched over your laptop. I'd finally finished a portrait, something I'd never attempted before. I was excited and cautiously satisfied with what I'd produced: what to my mind was an iconic image of Dorothy, sprawled in her armchair, the whisky glass dangling, waiting to fall. One of the self-same dresses she wore, her work uniform, always grey, (high) OUT button-through, three-quarter-length sleeves. I believed I'd captured her air of slumbering menace, but also something else. I can only call it turmoil: within her, passed on to me. I lifted the picture off the easel and rested it against the wall. Without thinking I hummed one line of a song that was often in my head, a song played constantly by one of the nurses during hospital spells in my teens, *I can see clearly now.*

"Shona, I'm working. Can't you do anything without making some intrusive sound?"

"I'm sorry." I'd given you an appeasing smile.

"You never stop, when you're unpacking groceries, having a bath, taking out the recycling."

"Okay. I said I'm sorry. I'm just satisfied with a picture. That doesn't happen every day."

You sighed before closing your laptop. "Can I see it?"

"Actually yes, I'd appreciate an opinion."

Yawning, you pushed back your chair. I remember that I'd positioned myself in front of the canvas, inexplicably protective.

You took me by my shoulders, almost raised me off my feet, as you set me to one side. "Thank you," you said. You moved closer to the painting and then took a couple of steps backwards. "And this is?"

"Someone from childhood," I said.

"Does she have a name?"

"No."

"Or you don't want to tell me?"

"Does it matter?"

You shrugged. "She looks like the woman we met that time you broke your arm."

I shrugged. "As I said, just someone out of childhood."

"What, someone in an armchair with a whisky glass? It's your mother, isn't it? Or some alcoholic aunt?" He turned back to the painting. "What to say, Shona: it's well executed, but it does nothing for me. Although what do I know? I'm just a jobbing graphic designer."

"I'm pleased with it." I sounded defensive.

"Well, that's all that matters." He smiled, "However, once the paint dries could you turn the picture to face the wall? There's something about the face I find disturbing and not in a good way."

19

The doorbell rings as I'm about to make a salad for my lunch. Almost every day books and DVDs arrive for you so I assume it is yet another delivery. I hurry down, throw open the door. There is Mrs Gifford, the blue knitted hat perched at a chic angle on top of her smooth French pleat.

"I was in the neighbourhood." She executes some balletic movement that transports her and her shopping bag from the step, past me and into the hall. "Kitchen, Shona?" Her tone is imperious.

"Not garden?"

"Not warm enough."

I am obliged to follow *her*!

She picks up the kettle and waves it at me. "Tea?"

"*I'll* make the drinks. I prefer an infusion of fresh lemon and ginger."

She pulls a face as if the idea mildly disgusts her.

"Would you like a biscuit?" I ask.

"Just tea."

One of your art books lies open on the table and she begins to flick through it.

"Mrs Gifford, please sit down. You've probably had quite a walk today."

"Oh, I'm used to walking ... but yes, it is nice to be waited on." She sits at the table with her back to me, pulling the book in front of her.

"And how's your son?"

She shrugs but doesn't turn her head. "He's okay. Why would you ask?"

"Don't most mothers worry about their sons?"

"I've no idea, but yes, in my case it comes with the territory. Did you never want children?"

"No."

"Still a child yourself?"

"You may be right," I reply.

While the kettle boils, I make a cheese sandwich. Obliquely I observe the sharp outline of her shoulder-blades raising the thin material of her jacket. She looks so fragile.. We have only known each other a few months yet I sense during that time, physically she's lost ground. I put the tea in front of her. "You look well," I lie.

She shuts the book. "As do you, Shona. I see you've been hard at work."

The shirt I'm wearing is marked with paint and charcoal. Our eyes meet. Hers seem to dance. With little encouragement, I could lean forward and hug her. "Yes, I'm painting. It's done me good."

"I'm glad." She clasps her hands around the mug, intent on the milky surface. "I have a favour to ask."

"Ask away."

"I believe you told me you had a partner," she says.

I shake my head. "I meant years ago, we *used* to be ... we were very close. Now I look after his house and garden and in return I live here at a reasonable rent."

"And is that an ideal situation?" She takes a sip of tea although it is still steaming.

"Is anyone's situation ideal?" My voice is sharper than intended.

"Surely somewhere in the world, people are enjoying ideal situations?"

"If they are, then good luck to them." There is now, definitely, something antagonistic at work between us.

"You said his name was Richard?"

"I did."

"And is he a student at the college?"

"Yes. Why do you ask?"

"I think I met him in the library. He was talking on his phone to someone called Shona which surely must be you. Do you have a photograph? Just so I know I'm not going ga-ga!" She pulls a horrible mad face.

I'm taken by surprise. All pleasure at seeing her has disappeared. I push back my chair. "Wait here."

She pushes back *her* chair. "Can I keep you company? I love looking around other people's homes."

The cheek of the woman! "Richard doesn't allow strangers into his part of the house."

She looks amused. "Whatever you say, dear."

In the front room, I close the door firmly and stand very still trying to control my annoyance. Surely you would have mentioned meeting Mrs Gifford? My internal narrative races from showing her a photograph, to *you* with the newly re-instated Raoul being invited to the Miller Building for dinner. *Stop Shona. Stop now!*

I turn to the bookshelves. Once, the two of us filled an entire photograph album: pictured smiling, being silly, our arms about each other. We swam together in warm foreign seas, shared restaurant meals, cars on a fairground ride, you threw parties with me at your side – our close friendship, our question mark to those who knew you, whatever our relationship truly was – was once immortalised in vibrant Kodak colour.

The album never travelled with you in the move from London to Hawksbridge. Just one photograph remains from that era. I believe it only survives because at some point you used it to mark your place in a book of illustrations by your favourite artist: H.R. Giger's. A book bought by *me* as a gift for *you* when we'd first met, a hundred pounds; a huge amount of money for a woman literally living on the bread line. Giger's work had never appealed to me, it was too precise, too cold, but one day out of curiosity, I'd suddenly had an urge to see the alien monster that had inspired the building blocks of your successful career. As I'd flipped through the pages, a photograph fluttered to the floor. There were the two of us, hand in hand in front of the Eiffel Tower. My face slightly blurred as if I'd just begun to turn away but you, tanned and confident stared back at whoever was taking the picture. Unbelievably in retrospect, on the back, I'd written, *To dearest Richard, love always, Shona.*

And Giger's illustrations? My reluctant but honest opinion was that I preferred your take on an alien being. You made me many things, but your illustrations allowed me some humanity.

On returning to the kitchen I discover Mrs Gifford asleep, her head dipped forward, nose resting on the table top. The hat lies on the floor next to her chair. I retrieve it, patting her shoulder at the same time. She jerks awake, gaze darting round the room as if she has no idea where she is.

"Mrs Gifford? It's me, Shona."

"Shona?" She looks up. For a second, there's not a flicker of recognition in her eyes.

I place the photograph in front of her.

Myopically she holds the picture close to her face. "Yes, that's him. What a good-looking young man he was. Still is. But older of course."

"And that's me with him," I prompt.

"So I see."

I'm irritated with her, irritated with myself. It's as if that afternoon we'd spent together in winter has been a figment of my imagination. Surely, we'd talked. We'd dropped our guards. Oh god, been on the same page. The process to connect with Mrs Gifford was like coaxing a feral cat. One moment they might rest their head in the palm of your hand, the next they'd lash out before retreating into their own dark corner.

"Would you like to see my garden?" I ask, desperately.

"I can see it from here. Very pleasant."

I stand by the open door, willing her to follow me outside. "There are roses further down towards the shed. Old roses with a wonderful scent. I'm trying to create a herb garden, just somewhere calm and sweet-smelling where I can sit and sketch." I'm gabbling, displaying my need for approval. I close the door, turn back to her. "Sorry. I see so few people, then when I have someone captive . . ." I flash a wry grin. "I bombard them with too much information."

Her expression softens. "Believe it or not Shona, I was once exactly the same: that desperate urge to over-share. Having a child knocked that on the head."

"Because you had to put Sonny's needs first?"

"Of course." She shrugs. "Not that a child is capable of sustaining the total interest of a parent but what choice did I have?"

"You never met anyone to share your life with or even friends?"

"For some it's not that straightforward, is it?"

Like two tired runners we sit facing each other and finally start to talk. Mrs Gifford tells me about an area she calls Bungalow City and how she hopes one day to live there. "All I ask is a year or two, to fulfil a dream."

I tell her that I've started painting seriously again.

"And what do you mean by seriously?" she asks.

"I'm absorbed completely: if not physically painting or drawing, I'm thinking about painting and drawing." My smile is spontaneous as is hers.

"And what else?"

"I'm trying to work out the past, the part I played, the people from those years – all dead now. Do you think much about your past?"

"Rarely. I worry about the future." She pulls her hat on any old how.

I lead the way into the hall. "Thanks for calling in," I say, opening the front door. I suddenly realise I'm on my own, there's no sign of Mrs Gifford. And then she appears, only just emerging from the kitchen.

She waves her cloth shopping bag at me. "I forgot it. I'd lose my head if it wasn't screwed on tightly." Passing me, she squeezes my hand. "And thank *you* for the tea."

I watch as she walks away down Canberra Road, swinging her bag as if it is light as a feather. It fills with air, like a beige balloon.

In the kitchen I rinse the mugs. It is two pm, several hours before you get back. Should I ask you about meeting her in the library? But, perhaps to you she *was* just some random elderly woman to take pity on. Thinking of you reminds me of the photograph. It isn't on the table where she left it. Surely, she wouldn't take it with her? But of course, she has.

*

Totally at peace now, I'm in the garden leisurely examining each plant, making plans in my head for the following seasons. Your garden isn't huge, it's very much a town garden, but from the weed-ridden concrete space it was when I first came here, it's now a lush and green sanctuary. I get secateurs from the shed and begin dead-heading the early roses. They are so beautiful, so heavily scented that I find myself regretting not offering some to Mrs Gifford. My thoughts keep returning to her. 'What a mad old bat she is," I mutter, not really meaning this at all.

"Who's a mad old bat?"

I hadn't heard you come in but suddenly you're standing in front of me. I'm desperate to find out about your meeting with Mrs Gifford, but I find myself hesitating. I know you too well: any curiosity on my part will result in your obsession of with-holding information kicking in. Better – for now – that I keep the knowledge to myself.

"Nobody you know." I squint up at you: "You're early."

"So stuffy in the college. Somehow the central heating came on. Everyone else, including the tutor, went to the pub, I came home."

You look full of health and vigour, a Costa coffee in one hand.

"You're doing a grand job out here," you say.

"Thank you but the garden manages pretty well with very little help from me."

"Still, it's a lot for you to cope with."

"I enjoy it."

"Even so." Having first dusted the seat of the bench, you sit down, placing your coffee next to you.

I'm struck by how handsome you look, how your clothes appear new, nothing I recognise from doing your laundry each week. You take off your light-weight jacket and lay it carefully across your thighs.

"So, where were you last night?"

"I stayed over at a friend's flat."

"Raoul?"

"Clever you." You turn your head towards me.

I can't see your eyes. You're wearing sunglasses. I wait but no further disclosure is forthcoming. It occurs to me that physically your shape is altering. You've gained muscle. This is particularly noticeable on your arms, shoulders and neck.

"You've joined a gym," I exclaim.

"Clever you," you say again. "Not before time. These last few years, I've let my body deteriorate. There's a gym at college and a pool. Do you think I'm having a mid-life crisis, Shona?"

There is something boyish about you at this moment that makes my heart soften.

"Maybe, but a good one. Maybe we both are."

"How do you mean?"

"I'm painting again. That means so much to me."

Abruptly, you get to your feet. "Not the same thing, babe. I'd call your mid-life crisis more of a mood swing." Picking up your coffee, you start to walk back to the house but then stop. From the herb bed you break off a stem of mint and sniff it. Frowning, you retrace your steps. "That was rude. Apologies. I'm pleased for you, Shona. Actually, you're looking great too. Never better."

"Thank you," I answer coolly.

"I mean it. I came back early because we need to discuss something. Can I get you a cold drink, maybe a glass of wine?"

I shake my head.

You pick up your coffee so that I can sit down next to you.

"Phew," you say. "Here goes." You stretch your legs out across the grass.

"So, what was it that you wanted to discuss?"

Before answering you finish the coffee, place the cup under the bench. "No biggie here, Shona. Well actually my plans for the house are fairly big."

My happiness is dissolving. "What plans?"

"You were disappointed when you first arrived – don't you remember?"

"Vaguely. Whatever, I'm happy here now. I consider myself fortunate to live in such a comfortable house for such a reasonable rent."

"Shona, don't gush. No gratitude. We're family. Take that for granted. Okay?"

Oh, how I dislike you when you talk to me as if you're on some business stage in America making a motivational speech! "Okay," I mutter.

"Imagine this, Shona: the entire ground floor opened up: kitchen becomes kitchen-diner not the cramped square it is now."

I'm puzzled. "But the space is limited. Where will the diner element go?"

You wave in the direction of the vegetable bed at the back of the house. "A two-storey extension. Several houses in the road have had this done. My planning permission came through at the weekend. There'll be a third bedroom. You'll have your own *ensuite* bathroom. No more need to share."

"Great," I say dully. "How far will the extension come out to?"

"About where we're sitting now."

"I'll lose the garden."

"It's not *your* garden to lose. You won't have to worry about it anymore."

"But what will be left?" I'm appalled, bereft.

You don't see this at all, you're too full of your own good-humoured excitement. "Well, I'm afraid these shrubs will have to come up right down to the end fence. I want a sizeable terrace and some more structured planting. Shona, I love what you've achieved out here but," you slap your forehead theatrically. "I want to create something, a garden suited to *my* taste. I'm feeling more energised than I've felt in years." You take off your sunglasses and squint at me. "Look, I know much of your life has been one hellish train wreck. But it's been years now. I've tried to help." You wave a hand in the direction of the house. "There's always been a place for you wherever I've lived. I want to keep things that way but I also want something that's personal to me."

"I don't think I've ever asked you for anything," I counter.

"But you've accepted all I've offered." Your expression hardens. "So, what do you think?"

Carefully I reply, "I appreciate your point of view but it seems a crime to destroy the entire garden."

"Eventually you'll have a garden totally your own."

"Hypothetically." I've gone too far.

"Just once in your miserable life, can't you be supportive? It will look amazing. Instead of being out here morning, noon and night, you can paint your fucking socks off."

We both sit in silence staring at the wooden fence panel opposite that is splintering and coming away from its supporting struts. His house. His garden. His rules.

"Richard, I'm here because I use the excuse of my illness, or maybe I'm lazy and obviously if I didn't live here, I'd be in a tiny flat somewhere above a shop – at best. But why do *you* let me live here? What's in it for you?"

I feel the tension leave his body. His shoulders slump.

Finally, he says in a normal, unexcited Richard voice, "As I've told you before, you're my family. All I have. As far as I know, I'm all you have."

"There's Raoul now."

"And maybe one day, if we keep getting along and that's a big 'if' he may join us." I let silence develop, wait for him to speak. When he does, he sounds dispirited. "And of course, you must know by now, that I like being seen as 'straight'. To all intents and purposes, you are my partner." His grin is painful. "At college I've even referred to you as 'my fiancé'! Single men approaching forty are still considered weird and that's not something I want for myself."

I believe you. I've known you long enough to understand how you try to create confusion over your sexuality, an 'is he? Isn't he?' Some lack of confidence, vulnerability. Not so very different from the way I use the word 'partner' when mentioning you while trying to validate myself.

"I'm sorry. Tell me again your plans for the garden. I promise I'll respond with enthusiasm. Really Richard. Not joking. Mean it."

"I'm sure you do." From your jacket pocket you take out your phone. Before I can turn away you've held the screen up to my face and taken a photograph. My hand shoots up defensively.

You study the screen. Hold it up to me. "Image of a lying bitch," you say.

And you're right. You've caught me at the exact moment as I switch my expression from resentful to conciliatory. My mouth is smiling, my eyes are full of hate.

The phone goes back in your pocket. You dribble the dregs of your coffee on the ground, squeeze the cup till it buckles. Your aim for one perfect red rose is perfect. The petals scatter. "That's what I think of your fucking garden."

Neither of us move. We both hold our breath. All of five minutes pass. With an angry movement of your body, you get to your feet and start walking back to the house.

20

MARTIN

Bulging backpack on his shoulders, Martin steps over the chain link fence cordoning off the entrance to the footbridge. He takes the steps two at a time. Below him the dual carriageway is almost deserted at this time of night. Out in the sharp fresh air, heading away from the tower block, he finds the strangely repellent fixation he has with the Giffords beginning to lessen; he feels more alert than he's felt in several days. And yet two months ago, moving in with them had seemed the perfect answer to the alternatives of either sleeping rough or going home. The last option was unthinkable.

He's left his watch for Sonny. It is the only present he'd ever been given. Not really a present. Dad – *call me Kenneth* – making space on a cluttered table as he emptied a cloth bag of gleaming men's watches. 'You can have one,' he'd said. 'Go on, take it. Your friends will think you're loaded.'

'They're not real then?'

'Not real? They tell the time.'

'I don't need a watch.'

‘Well you’re going to take one and wear it, whether you like it or not, you ungrateful little sod.’

That was the only way to get anything out of Kenneth. Let him force it on you. Not anymore, dad.

Reaching the top step, the broken footbridge stretches out in front of him. He feels the adrenalin kick in. Etched like a dark stain, the central section of the bridge is missing where the concrete blocks gave way a year earlier. Hanging on to the railing, feet constantly testing the jagged eight-centimetre-wide strip of remaining concrete, he edges forward. He daren’t look down. Instead he keeps his eyes fixed on the distant lights of the town. Finally, he steps back onto what at least feels like solid ground. With a silent ‘whoop!’ he leaps down the steps, over the wire fence, collapsing onto the gravel and grass. The night is cool but he’s sweating.

He looks back towards the Miller Building. As always it is in darkness. The Giffords are paranoid about being discovered. Their fear around so many things is getting to him. But Sonny, he can’t bear Sonny any longer. Martin doesn’t have the words to properly describe him, Sonny inspires a sense of horror, something he’s never experienced before. He’s wormed his way into Martin’s head. He won’t keep a distance. Sonny isn’t like a human being, he is a pale determined thing.

In Martin’s backpack are his few possessions, some clothes, food and a bottle of whisky he’d found in the larder. He can hear the glugging sound of the liquid as it sloshes around. His intention is to get as far away as possible and then just drink.

From his jacket Martin takes out cigarettes and a cheap plastic lighter. He sits on the footbridge steps and lights the cigarette. Ahead of him, in Hawksbridge, several points of lights go out. It must be around midnight or maybe even later but there are at least two clubs that stay open till four am. He stares up at the star-filled sky, the three-quarter moon half-concealed by one small solitary cloud. This far outside town, there's virtually no light pollution. There isn't a scrap of wind. Around him, the tall grass stands stock still.

Slowly he gets to his feet, stretches his arms above his head. The glowing tip of his cigarette drops a shower of tiny sparks. Martin stiffens. Something – probably a fox or a rat – is moving in the semi-darkness to his left. Like a Mexican wave, the grass ripples.

Then a flash of movement and fifteen metres away, a human shadow breaks cover. Martin feels a rush of air. An inch from his face, a stone whistles past. It ricochets off one of the railings.

"What the fuck!" he shouts.

The shadow is running parallel with the road, towards the empty tenements. Martin lets him go. He doesn't want a fight, but then as he turns away, a smaller stone cuts into his hand, makes him drop the cigarette as if it was a red-hot ember. The figure stands still, facing him, too far away for Martin to be able to make out any features but he's certain now that it's a man. Not too tall, slightly built.

They stay like that for a few seconds, sizing each other up, a safe distance between them before the moon emerges from the cloud, shines like a spotlight down on both of them. The assailant's hair shines like silver.

"Sonny, is that you?" Martin calls out. Fascinated, he watches as the figure raises his head to look up at the moon. It howls, a weird inhuman sound. At Martin's feet the cigarette butt has lit the dry grass. He's only aware of it when a flame shoots up and licks his fingertips.

21

SHONA

2014

My easel and paints are set up on the main beach. It has been another hot week, temperature in the high twenties and today the sun is fierce. I've paused to lather sunscreen on my face, neck and arms. This summer I've allowed my skin to tan a little. My scars appear less pronounced and I no longer feel a need to conceal them. Let people think what they like. Hands still oily from the lotion, I gather up my hair, twist it into a knot before securing it high on my head with two slim paintbrushes. The paintbrushes are an affectation I adopted during my first hospital stay. Initially inadvertently, then several members of staff commented on how attractive the style looked. 'Oriental' one said admiringly.

I'm working on a small painting. I'd roughed in the blue sky and calm turquoise sea, then added a small boat some distance out from the shore. Now there is a woman in the boat. She uses just one oar and as she rows towards me; the expression on her face is one I remember well: murderous. As a child that look annihilated me, brought me shaking to my hands and knees. I paint on. I am in control. Dorothy will never be allowed to reach the water's edge.

"Well done, Shona." Unobserved, Mrs Gifford has made her way along the wooden groyne and now sits on a plastic carrier bag, her thin legs swinging. Today she wears a simple cotton dress and green plastic sandals. The pallor of her skin compared to mine is somehow shocking. Its texture makes me think of white crepe paper.

I look into her face and am reassured by those clever bright-blue eyes. The young woman of my imagination shines through. "Thank you, Mrs Gifford. It's not finished yet."

"Will it ever be finished?"

"I hope so."

If someone interrupts me when I'm working, I'm annoyed knowing that once they've gone, I'll find it impossible to return to the place I'd reached in my mind. But today I'm delighted to see her. All my firm intentions of being a little distant when we next met have flown and to be honest, twice uninvited I've gone back to the Miller Building in the hope of finding her in. Each time the front door was locked. The actual building seemed asleep. On the second occasion I checked out the route along the side of the block. I pushed a way through a barrier of rampant shrubbery into what appeared to have once been a semi-underground carpark; the marked-out bays were only just visible through the dirt. There were some stacks of old tyres and wooden pallets. The interior door Mrs Gifford had said would lead to the staircase was also locked. It was a horrible place, head-room height constricted. I was aware of the weight of the floors above me. Every shadow posed a threat. I've watched too many crime documentaries for my imagination not to provide images of violence. I didn't hang around.

Now to Mrs Gifford, I say, "It's been ages. I thought I might see you in town one day."

"I've had a cold. It hung on but then Sonny caught it. Oh, he's such a baby when under the weather. He's been very morose."

She said this so glibly, I was almost certain the excuse was a white lie. But I went along with it. "You're both better now though? You look well."

"Actually Shona, there are days when every bone in my body aches, but considering my age, I'm pretty resilient."

Now, that had the ring of truth. I drop my brush into the water jar and climb up onto the groyne to sit next to her. She leans against me, her shoulder lightly touching mine. I wish that someone else was with us to take a photograph. The sun on the sea works its magic and we slip into agreeable silence. Eventually she recounts a story, how as a child she spent several summer holidays in Hawksbridge with her parents. I hadn't imagined her having parents. To me, Mrs Gifford represents my idealised matriarch. Never the child.

"It was very different in those days," she says. "Hardly anyone chose to visit the town. There wasn't much here. No shops or amusements. No college. Each afternoon I'd be left to play on the shingle while they went back to the guest house for an afternoon nap. Or that's what they called it."

"Were they in love?" I ask.

She pauses to think before answering. "I think they were. She was always touching his hair and face."

"What did you do, left alone on the beach?"

"I made miniature stage sets from seashells, bits of rock and seaweed."

"Were you allowed to go in the water?"

"Never wanted to. I only went in as far as the shallows, searching for shells."

"And what about when you were grown up? Did you love Mr Gifford?"

Mrs Gifford looks momentarily bewildered. "There was no Mr Gifford. I'm *Miss* Gifford but when Sonny was born it suited me to call myself a widow: plenty of sympathy for a wife whose husband died in active service." She hugs her knees. "No sympathy at all in those days for unmarried mothers."

So often, people fail to bring their stories to life. They pick and choose the bits they particularly like, that they believe will capture the interest of any audience. Often their choice is faulty. Not so Mrs Gifford. I clearly see that child, alone but not lonely, the parents walking away towards the shabby guest house. Maybe his arm lies heavily across the woman's shoulders. And I see Mrs Gifford, that feisty yet fake widow, beguiling sympathy from every stranger she met.

"Shona," she says. "I have an apology to make. Months ago, I stole the photo of you and Richard."

"I know." My voice is gentle. At this moment there is something dear and childlike about Mrs Gifford. "But why?"

"On a whim, I think." She touches her forehead. "And I intended to show my son. In the end I didn't. There was Martin. We all seemed happy enough. But now Martin's gone. Not even a thank you."

"Perhaps when autumn comes, he'll be back."

"I doubt it." Nimbly Mrs Gifford slips down onto the pebbles. She pauses in front of my easel. "That woman looks a lot like you," she says.

"I hope not."

"Very striking." Her nose almost touches the canvas. "Well, keep at it," she says.

"And the photograph?" I call after her.

She doesn't hear me or maybe chooses not to. With affection, I watch her toiling up the beach towards the promenade. Her legs look breakable. She has left her carrier bag behind. I fold it up, make it small enough to fit flatly in the back pocket of my jeans and return to my painting. I sniff the canvas as she did, then I begin again. With the intention of blotting out Dorothy's face I mix a pale flesh tone but I can't bring myself to use it. It seems too brutal.

I've done enough for the day but I'm not ready to pack up. Seated on the groyne I have a good view of the beach. For a while I puzzle over what exactly it is that draws me to Mrs Gifford. I come up with very little, the type of reasons that Richard would treat with derision. I would sleep well if she were nearby, I could imagine myself in some dull hotel in say, Eastbourne and looking forward to the low-key holiday in her company. I'm starting to be amused by my own foolishness. *Enough whimsy Shona!*

From my bag I take out a sketch book and flick through the pages. I stop when I reach a few lines of charcoal depicting Sheila Kirkpatrick lying in a deck chair, taken from memory, from my last summer with them. It is as if a cloud has moved across the sun.

22

SHONA

1994

Shona Blake was pretty. No doubt about that. No longer fostered, adopted now, almost fifteen and tall and slim with an attractive low voice. Obviously intelligent although school reports expressed concern over her inability to make friends or join in.

'She is not proving to be "a team player".'

Sheila was scornful on her behalf. "I don't want Shona to be a team player," she told the head teacher at a parents' evening. "She's an individual. Unique. We're so proud of her."

You might imagine that having been rescued from a toxic environment and sadistic mother Shona might be grateful. Not a bit of it. That 'toxic environment' was all she'd ever known of 'home'. In a perverse way, she was comfortable with cruelty, neglect and dislike. She understood it. Knew where she was and what to expect. Affection, kindness, adults assuming the best she found confusing and confusion so easily turned to anger.

When Sheila said, "Darling, we understand your frustration," instead of appreciating her empathy Shona became – well the word she might use would be 'incandescent'. She lit up with fury.

Brian Kirkpatrick – torn between his love for his wife and duty to a child he'd taken responsibility for was easier to get on with. She could tune him out. Forget for hours at a time that he was part of the cosy family equation.

When first Shona came to live with the Kirkpatrick's she was silent and watchful. They had been warned she would be. They had also been warned that she could develop quite violent mood swings, see-saw between bouts of trying to please and trying to hurt. The Kirkpatrick's imagined they were prepared for even the worst eventualities. There was the disappearance or destruction of anything Brian or Sheila professed to be fond of: a favourite ornament, the diamond missing from a broach Brian gave Sheila on their wedding day. Burn marks appeared on clothes, curtains, towels, bedding. Worst of all was the incident with the neighbour's daughter Lynda Wilson. The little girl had survived, but her mother called the police. Nothing could be proved. It was Shona's word against Lynda's, but the affair made the local newspaper. In the end, the Kirkpatrick's were forced to move rather than risk the frequent unpleasant scenes with Mrs Wilson and her daughter. Yes, in those early years, Shona made their lives hell.

Further psychiatric help was regularly discussed but Sheila was adamant that all her now adopted daughter needed was love. Their love would wear down her resistance. But no, it was Brian and Sheila who were worn down. By then Shona had entered her teens. She'd grown smarter and recognised that these two people were approaching breaking point. She set herself the task – although it was really more of a game – of winning their confidence. For hours at a time, she made herself a pleasure to be with. Ever the optimist, it was invariably Sheila who dropped her guard first. Patiently Shona worked on Brian. She was her funniest dearest self for Brian. His reluctant chuckle over some remark she'd made was a reward. Hah!

Duped again, sucker! And then, like a whirlwind, she'd shrug off her pleasing disguise and turn on them both.

Eventually repetition becomes repetitious. It all became too easy. Approaching her fifteenth birthday, she decided to extend the game, make it more challenging for the three of them. For a year she would be the daughter they'd hoped for. Convince them completely and then watch out!

Thoughts ordered and emotions under control, on her birthday morning she kissed their cheeks. Her accompanying hug was awkward but firm. She'd had to force herself to relax and accept the hug they gave back. She thanked them for her presents, tried on the clothes they'd bought and insisted that every gift was perfect.

"What would you like to do today?" Sheila asked. "Anything – the sky's the limit, isn't it, Brian?"

Ah, they both looked so hopeful. Often when Shona was with them, she felt that she was the adult, they the child. Although the sky was overcast, she suggested they spend the day in London Zoo in Regent's Park.

"Excellent idea," Brian and Sheila agreed, even though it was a long drive and parking would be difficult. They'd taken Shona there before. It was a place where she generally behaved. In the past they'd comforted themselves with the knowledge that their troubled daughter at least appeared to have an affinity with wild animals.

She was quiet in the car, but they didn't remark on this. They were determined not to let any wrong word or action spoil the day. On reaching the zoo, she concentrated on the animals, the power of the big cats, the compelling fascination of the reptile house. Brian and Sheila watched her while pretending not to. They had a pleasant lunch in the cafeteria before going into the shop.

"Choose anything," Brian said.

A year earlier, a month ago, the week before, Shona would have picked something ridiculously expensive – one of the huge stuffed animals – just for the pleasure of seeing their expressions alter.

Instead, she chose a small sketchbook with a blue cloth cover and some colour pencils.

They exchanged relieved glances. "What about a paintbox as well?" Sheila asked.

She shook her head. "Just these." Once outside the shop, she said, "Would you mind if I wander around on my own?"

This request alarmed them. They were thinking, she's going to disappear, hide somewhere, cause trouble.

"Don't worry," she said. "I'll meet you near the exit in an hour."

Sheila was about to remonstrate but Brian touched her elbow. "Great. We'll find a bench and enjoy the sun. These shoes are killing me!"

She was only a few minutes late but approaching them, she read the relief in their faces, which they immediately attempted to hide. On her part she felt an unexpected wave of affection for the two of them.

And then Sheila asked brightly, "Drawn anything nice, darling?" Which made Shona want to kill her.

Uneventful days followed. The emerging adult in Shona was fully aware of the fragile positive atmosphere now present in the house. Sheila slipping her hand under Brian's arm, squeezing his arm against her breast. Brian looking down at her with tenderness.

As expected, Sheila was the first to start trusting her. Having endured more than five years of misery, she was eager to embrace this altered daughter. The weight of anxiety lifting from her shoulders was visible. With Brian, disbelief fought harder against dawning hope.

As months passed by, Shona almost gave up the game. The experiment took its toll on her as well. The projected year of living differently created unforeseen side effects. She was rarely angry with them anymore. Few days seem to hold those choking moments of suffocation. As her behaviour continued to improve, she'd expected both of them to overwhelm her with their pent-up affection and expectations, but they proved surprisingly astute choosing to take several steps back. Finally, they understood that space and minimum familial communication were the elements needed for their daughter to function. Sometimes she experienced regret for what might have been, but she never allowed herself to lose sight of her ultimate intention.

There was a pivotal day so perfect even she was forced to take pleasure in it. Lying sprawled on the lawn, leaning back on her elbows, bare legs stretched out, for the first time ever she found herself aware of daisies in the grass: white petals, yellow centres. She had no memory of ever noticing them before. She remembers thinking, 'It's like closing down for the holidays,' because that is exactly what it felt like, as if her body and mind were insisting that she take the day, maybe take forever off. Let this be enough.

They sat nearby in deckchairs, sharing their Sunday newspaper with its many supplements. Brian's section of newspaper, held up in front of his face, had begun to quiver. His hand was shaking. She imagined he'd found a funny article and was quietly chuckling over it. Then with his free hand he took a handkerchief from his trouser pocket and wiped his eyes. He was crying. He laid the paper on his knees. Their eyes met. "So glad, Shona," was all he said.

"Me too," was her answer.

He sniffed. Blew his nose. Put the handkerchief back in his pocket. "So, ladies, who's ready for a lager and lime?"

"That would be lovely," Sheila exclaimed. "Shona?"

"Yes. It would."

If only Brian hadn't shown how much he cared. His tears, their unconditional love became in a second – unbearable. For the Shona she was then, it was a simple matter of self-preservation. Those two with their relentless affection would suffocate the life out of her. She visualised a steel door. With all her strength she closed it, turned the key in the padlock. Shona had made her choice.

23

SHONA

2006

From the moment it was established that I had an agent, my relationship with Richard began to deteriorate. In the past I'd accepted his opinion over my own but his criticism of the portrait of Dorothy affected me. Whether it was good, bad or indifferent, I was convinced the painting marked an improvement in my work. Perhaps he was jealous of my modest success, perhaps he just hated any loss of control, but without even knowing Beatrice Salmon, he developed a deep-seated hatred for her. His 'salmon smelling fishy' remark became a constant quip.

One morning as he gathered together his laptop and some papers he'd need later in the day, he announced, "Can we have words, Shona? I won't be in till around ten tonight and I'd like to get a few things straightened out before I leave today." Coat over the back of a chair, brief case and portfolio leant against the skirting board near the front door, he perched on the edge of the dining table. "You've been here a few years now. I love your company. We get on well, don't we?" Boyish grin.

I nod.

"But just a few guidelines to keep us both on track; ground rules really." The same rules that later became the 'usual rules apply' mantra. "All evidence of your work to be tidied away each evening before I come home. Please, no phone calls to be made or received during the evening. No shop talk with *La Salmone.* Confine your communications to within business hours."

"But you're on the phone constantly."

"Shona, I bring in the money. You don't. I take on well-paid but second-rate commissions so you can paint to your heart's content. Look, that apart, surely it's not unreasonable to want calm and quiet in my own home."

"But I don't make a noise."

"But you do make a mess and that woman telephones constantly." He'd glanced at his watch. "Got to go. Don't forget to take my jacket to the dry-cleaners – I need it back for the weekend."

I did as I was told and asked Beatrice to ring during the day.

"I'm happy to do that, but any particular reason?"

"Richard feels it affects our relationship."

"I'm sure you told me once that there was no relationship."

I stammered and stuttered. She said, "I see" a few times and then became silent. Finally, I said, "Is that all okay?"

"I suppose it has to be."

Our phone call made me feel sick inside, ruined my day, the week and longer still because after that Beatrice withdrew. Someone I'd never spoken to before rang from the agency. She introduced herself as Joan Vigo, Bea's new personal assistant. She would contact me every week or so at a time agreed by email, to check up on my progress. I missed Bea's calls, the affection in her voice, the sense that there was someone else in my life apart from Richard. I told him that I was lonely. He organised small dinner parties. People arrived for drinks at the weekend. They had no idea that Richard and I didn't share a bed. In public he'd re-arrange my hair, touch my face, arm around my waist, mock me in that way I've noticed men in long-term relationships often do, with their partners.

A friend of Richard's observed that I made him think of a 'Stepford Wife'.

At the time I'd smiled, imagining this to be a compliment.

"What or who is a Stepford Wife?" I asked Richard later.

He'd smiled. "You," he said. "You are what I tell you to be."

I allowed that statement to go unchallenged. It should have hurt more, should have made me furious but Shona, the child, the angry teenager with murderous thoughts was gone. Evenings when Richard was home, we watched TV together. In those days there was just the one enormous sofa, a corner each and space in between to fold our legs. Neither of us drank much during those evenings. Richard was obsessive about us both staying in shape. He was really thin but impressively so. This was before it became so universal for men to bulk up, when he saw himself as David Bowie's Thin White Duke.

As weeks passed, I achieved a measure of contentment during those evenings we spent together. It felt like some sort of family set-up that I could handle. He preferred me to be quiet and I was okay with that: to look attractive, match both him and the furnishings – again happy to oblige. I convinced myself that I too benefited from a calm, well-ordered life even if the calm and order depended on my doing as I was instructed. Better not to rock the boat. That apartment, the sofa we shared represented our boat.

By then, Richard was seeing Raoul but not often. The relationship hadn't yet become serious. The studio was busy with important design projects and they came before anything. I was Richard's sounding board. It made me feel useful because by then I'd stopped painting.

But suddenly, I found myself jolted back into real life. Joan Vigo rang with the news that an exhibition was planned, the venue arranged, a choice of dates available. Beatrice felt it would be good to see some of my new paintings. An image was needed for the marketing. In a bright false voice, I told her that I was making excellent progress. A week later she rang again and again I lied. I said nothing to Richard and yet ironically, it was Richard who brought matters to a head.

Each evening, I gauged his mood by his greeting. A peck on the cheek meant he'd had a stressful day, no conversation required; a peck on the forehead indicated that he was looking forward to me pouring him a glass of wine. Hugs were the best. Even now there are moments when I miss Richard's hugs.

One particular evening his terse greeting was, "White please, Shona."

"Not red?"

His gaze was level, his mouth a thin line. "I asked for white."

By the time I brought his drink, he'd opened his laptop and was staring at the screen. With a sinking heart, I saw the home page of the Beatrice Salmon Agency.

He read out, "*Now You See Me* – I wonder who came up with that vacuous title? An exhibition of new work from critically acclaimed artist Shona Blake is planned for this autumn. Watch this space. Interesting. What work would that be?"

I poured his wine. He took a sip. His tongue flicked round his lips savouring the taste. "I'm waiting," he said.

I started crying. They weren't real tears. They came when summoned. I excelled myself. He'd never witnessed a display of emotion from me before. I ramped up the noise, bawled like a lost child.

His anger and ice disappeared. He put his arms around me, pulled me close, stroked my hair. "It doesn't matter, sweetheart. It doesn't matter."

"But it does. I can't paint anymore. It's like I have to fit it in – but I can't. If I don't totally commit, nothing comes." I added a few more sentences. The shoulder of his shirt was soaked with my tears.

The change in him was immediate. He sat me down on the sofa, piled cushions around me in a caring, exaggerated manner, "Darling, you must paint. For the moment the exhibition comes first."

"But they want an image by Monday for the publicity."

"We'll both have a drink. Then show me some of your sketches. I'll choose an image – no Shona, let me choose – this is something I get paid big sums of money to get right."

He was as good as his word. The image he chose was from one of my darker paintings; a block-like edifice, not unlike the Miller Building, silhouetted against a fiery sky. He spent an evening playing around with it on his laptop. "What do you think, Shona?"

He'd enlarged the building, added one square of yellow light, placed the silhouette of a woman in the square.

"That's you," he said.

It was stunning. Unforgettable.

Those months preparing for the exhibition were probably the happiest that we shared. We were united. But even now, so long afterwards, I wonder: was his concern genuine or was he just content to be back in control of both me and what went on in my professional life?

The exhibition is held at the Labyrinth Gallery in Soho: a relatively small space that I was able to fill with three large paintings, ten smaller oils and the one of Dorothy. Clutching an untouched glass of champagne in my hand, I'm posing in front of life-size poster for the exhibition.

"Move a little to the left, Shona darling," the photographer says. "We want the backdrop in as well. It's a terrific piece of artwork. Your friend Richard knows his stuff."

Yes, Design and Art Direction by Richard Christopher Maplin is also credited in fairly large type along the lower margin of the poster.

On the other side of the room Richard has his back to me. He's holding court within a group of friends. The room is crowded. I'm relieved because outside, the rain is pouring down. I'm not sure what I expected from the evening, maybe that more people would be interested in the art on the walls. Instead, there is a party atmosphere but I'm not included. Leaving the photographer, I make my way through the crowd in search of Beatrice. We have spoken briefly on the phone during the run-up to the exhibition but her tone has been reserved. I spot her by the drinks table. She wears a black trouser suit with satin trim on the reverse of the jacket. As always, she looks incredibly elegant – out of my league. I take a step towards her before realising that she is in deep conversation with someone I know to also be an artist. Is she disappointed with the reaction to my work and now signing up someone better, more accomplished, a man? Earlier Richard explained that the interest in male artists was far greater than in female artists. "You'll be in your fifties before anyone will take you seriously. Fact of life, babe."

Fearing being seen to 'hover' I move away from Beatrice. I've no idea what to do with myself. I go into the powder room. In the mirror my skin looks flushed, my eyes horribly bright. I drink cold water straight from the tap. Dab my mouth and chin dry with a paper towel. The door starts to open.

"Shona, I'm so proud of you."

I spin round.

It's Beatrice. Her eyes are warm and friendly, she's smiling as she holds out her hand. On the palm lies a small sheet of waxed paper. On it are lines of red dots. "Come with me," she says and takes my elbow. "Help me stick these on. Everyone loves your work. But that portrait – is incredible."

We walk back into the gallery. I'm hyper-aware of her hand on my arm.

As I approach the long wall of canvases, I realise how the painting of my mother dominates the display. On the wall next to the frame there is already a sold sticker.

"Oh," I say, feeling both pleased and bereft. "Someone's bought it."

With a flourish of her hand, Beatrice bows.

"You bought it?"

"I did."

"Where will you hang it?"

"Come and see."

The following afternoon, carrying a bottle of champagne, I made my way across London to Beatrice's flat. For the next two years we were lovers.

24

SONNY

He leaves the building through the empty underground carpark. Rays of early evening sun penetrate the shrub barrier concealing the entrance. He's wearing a base-ball cap, jeans and a sweatshirt belonging to Martin and discovered in the laundry basket a week after he'd left. The clothes feel constricting. Sonny has rarely worn anything that adheres to his skin. He particularly dislikes the cardboard feel of the denim jeans.

Pushing his way through branches and leaves, he emerges on the tarmac drive running around the side wall. He hasn't stepped outside since, well he'd rather not think about when, rather not think about what had prompted him to howl like an animal in pain. He stands in shadow, adjusting his breathing. Less than half a mile away he makes out the outline of the derelict tenements. Sonny psyches himself up for the sprint across the stretch of open ground, heading to the footbridge. The bridge holds no fear for him. Like his mother, he is nimble footed with perfect balance. Sonny starts to run. Faster and faster. He is fifty years old but he can still run.

*

Half-an-hour later and he's slowed to walking pace as he approaches the outskirts of Hawksbridge. Dusk is falling. He slides his hands into the pockets of his jeans, adjusts the baseball cap to what he believes to be a fashionable angle, with a curl of his thick silvered hair brushing one eyebrow. Across the road a man walks his dog. It has been years since Sonny last saw a dog apart from in pictures. A woman and two children unload shopping from the boot of a car. He has to fight the urge to speak to them, just to see if he can. If he is understood. He wonders how they see him and hopes they assume that he is young. His skin is pale but almost devoid of lines. He shakes away the intrusive fear that the light from the streetlamps will shrivel its smooth surface.

Sonny reaches a parade of shops: a hairdresser, a bank, an estate agent. Only the mini-market is open. He peers in curiously, narrowing his eyes against the glare of shiny tins, packaging, vividly coloured heaps of fruit and vegetables.

"Can I help you?" someone calls out.

Sonny shakes his head and keeps walking.

The destination he's making for is the town square his mother so often speaks of. His imagination has created a wondrous place not only central to the town, but the centre of an exciting universe. He stops to lean against a wall. Breathing deeply, he fights a rising sense of panic.

"You okay, mate?" A man lays a hand on his shoulder.

"I'm fine," he says. "Getting my breath back. Been running."

The hand slides away. "Take care." Footsteps fade, heading in the other direction.

Sonny sets off again. He can still feel the pleasant sensation of the hand on his shoulder. What had the man looked like? The voice hadn't been young but not old either. Kind, reliable, adult.

Nothing prepares him for what happens next. One minute he is turning into a narrow dark street of shuttered shops and the next he steps out into the town centre. His mouth falls open, eyes wide – he stumbles and has to clutch the back of a bench to stop himself from falling. He's standing on the perimeter of an enormous paved expanse filled with people, all on the move. Surely there must be hundreds of them? Unthreatening in their quantity, these alien figures appear benign. He sees tall trees and a fountain, kiosks with striped canopies. From his mother's cooking, he recognises the smell of garlic, bacon, fried potatoes. All smells that have hung about their apartment and the corridors of the Miller Building for days: stale and unpleasant when confined, entrancing in the fresh evening air. His mouth becomes one wide, joyful smile.

Unsteadily he feels his way to the front of the bench and sits down. Used to a world of cushions and comfort the wooden slats beneath him feel strange, quite painful. For a moment he closes his eyes, resting them before returning to the wonder of it all. He listens to the sound of the sparkling water. He picks up the whirr of cycle wheels, voices, laughter, snatches of music and singing coming from at least two different directions. He opens his eyes. Twenty yards away is the college's main entrance. To Sonny, the college is extraordinary: higher, wider, glossy and glassier than the Miller Building. Students are still spilling in and out through the college doors. Hungrily, he observes their clothes, their hair styles. He's a little disappointed. What had he expected? People dressed as if they'd stepped out of the magazines his mother brings home.

A group of young women walk past. One of them glances towards him. She starts to smile. He freezes. Her friend tugs her arm.

"Creepy," she says loud enough for him to hear.

His bubble of enchantment bursts. It is as easily done as that. In the distance he hears the sound of a clock tower beginning to chime the hour. In front of him, the chrysanthemum spray of water from the fountain stutters and stops and the crowds begin to scatter. A breeze picks up. Suddenly all his fears around leaving the confines of the Miller Building overwhelm him. Sonny has been outside before but always keeping the building in his sightline. Now this solid safety net is so very far away. He's gasping for breath. His heart thunders. He is going to die.

Someone squats down next to him. "Put your head between your knees."

"I can't."

"You can." The man places one hand on Sonny's neck and eases his head forwards. "Let me help you. Breathe in and out, deeply and slowly."

"Raoul, we're going to be late," another voice says.

"Five minutes won't hurt."

"You're a soft touch."

The man with his hand on Sonny's neck laughs. It is a warm sound. Sonny's panic attack begins to ease. "So frightened," he whimpers.

"Don't worry. We're here." The man removes his hand. Sonny continues to breathe as instructed. He feels himself growing calmer. After a few moments he straightens up. "Thank you."

"Can you walk?"

"Not yet."

"For Christ's sake, Raoul, he'll be fine. Look, I'll wait for you in the wine bar."

"At least we could put him in a cab."

For the first time Sonny looks directly at them. His first

thought is that the two men are somehow a pair. He is seeing what his mother saw from the library steps. Both are younger than him, yet he recognises that they are adults, years older in life, in experience than him. They have powerful bodies. Raoul, the kind one, wears a navy tracksuit, the disgruntled friend, already beginning to walk away wears charcoal grey, a scarlet towel slung around his neck.

"Cabs don't go to the Miller Building." Sonny says.

"You live in the Miller Building?" The disgruntled friend has stopped and turned towards him.

Sonny nods.

"Are you Sonny?"

"Yes. Sonny Gifford." He hates his voice. It sounds child-like and unformed.

"Come on Richard, we have to help him."

Richard is no longer annoyed, he's smiling. "Of course, we'll help you." Richard holds out his hand for Sonny to grasp. "Good to meet you, mate. Look, we'll drop you home." He grins at Raoul. "The wine bar can wait."

The three of them begin to walk. The pavement once they leave the square is narrow. Sonny walks with Richard, Raoul behind them. When they reach the car, Sonny climbs into the back. Again, as he settles against the leather upholstery, he experiences that feeling of wonder. The car interior smells ... extraordinary, new, clean. Raoul drives. Sonny is seated behind Richard. As they head out of Hawksbridge Sonny touches Richard's shoulder, just lightly, to show gratitude. Richard's hand brushes his fingertips.

25

SHONA

2014

It's chaos indoors and outside since the renovations began. I spend most fine days setting up my easel on the beach. If it rains, I sit in a shelter and just draw.

Hawksbridge main beach stretches for a couple of miles. It's a mix of pebble and sand. There are camping and dog walking areas, safe waters to swim, sail or fish. And then book-ending this sociable stretch, to the right there's the lonely expanse leading in the direction of the Miller Building. Here the currents are uncertain; the visually pleasing reddish-coloured sand can suck your legs under up to the knees with no reassuring lifeguard seated on a high platform to save you. If you know the town well you will have heard about the other book end, turning left instead of right at the promenade and walking till you can clearly see a line of dark cliffs jutting out into the water. It's a good long walk with no access for vehicles. Here, the sand is cream-coloured and fine. Some foundation of rock beneath it supports the grains – you can walk or run with confidence.

In the past, I've always chosen to succumb to the pull of the Giffords and their glowering home. However, this morning – because even at seven am the temperature was in the low seventies – I decided to turn left on reaching the seafront. Already the promenade was filling up with tourists and the idea of somewhere less populated appealed to me. For once I travelled light, taking no paints or sketch book, only a towel, water bottle and sandwiches. In the back pocket of my jeans was a slim paperback. I'm no great reader and can rarely concentrate once a novel goes over a hundred-and-fifty pages!

Arriving at the beach I found about a dozen people, most of them in my own mid-thirties age group. No families. A few couples, the rest on their own. The tide was in, the sea an almost Mediterranean turquoise. Two women stood up to their waists in the water, just talking to each other. I berated myself for not at least bringing my camera.

I chose a space close to the rocks where there was some shade and spread out my towel. Under jeans and a long-sleeved t-shirt, I'd worn a two-piece costume. Blue-and-white striped, bought when I'd first lost the weight added in hospital. Up till now I'd never found the confidence to wear it. I sat on the towel, facing the water, hands hanging loosely between my knees, sun on my forehead. Oh, how I lapped up the heat. From jaw down to neck, to shoulders and spine, my body loosened. I kicked off my sandals enjoying the warm sand under the soles of my feet. *Ready Shona, have courage.* I began to struggle out of the t-shirt. The long sleeves were tight and I wasn't paying proper attention; I seemed to have a mouthful of cotton. As finally I emerged and threw it down next to me, I realised that someone had placed their towel quite close to mine: a man only about four yards away. He was in the process of erecting his beach umbrella, packing the base with large stones so it didn't get taken by the breeze. All his attention was focused on his preparation for a day on the beach. His clothes were already in a neat pile on his rucksack. Putting on my sunglasses I observed him. He was in good shape, muscular and tanned, wearing navy swimming trunks. I wasn't the only one watching him. The two women had waded out of the sea. As they walked past him, they glanced across then looked at each other. 'Fit' one of them mouthed. It was Raoul, looking much the same only . . . improved. I doubted that he'd recognise me. I was vastly different from the Shona he'd known ten years ago.

Across the space between us, I could sense his good humour, that he was happy with his day. He lay down, then sat up again, rummaging in his rucksack for a small tube. He squeezed a glob of white cream onto his nose and lips. "Ah," he said – pure enjoyment – and lay back down again.

I slipped out of my jeans, made a pillow of them, rubbed on factor fifty suntan lotion. I was thorough. My scars are vulnerable to too much sun, but a little is beneficial. Satisfied, I too lay down. The sound of the waves was soothing as were the conversations drifting towards me: indistinct but convivial. I felt that perfect sense of pure enjoyment. I didn't want to sleep: it was enough for me to listen and observe. From behind my sunglasses I scanned my fellow sun worshippers, bodies spread-eagled under the mid-afternoon glare. The thought occurred to me that on occasion my work lacked colour. Possibly due to too many hours spent indoors, all attention focused on the small square of canvas. Too focused. Precision taking over from creativity. Against my will I grew drowsy, but then a figure seemed to float across my line of vision: stick-thin, torn jeans, ragged shirt and dark hair flying. At each prone body or group, he stopped. People shook their heads or ignored him. He was asking for money.

He arrived at Raoul, hunkering down next to his towel. I don't know what he said, but Raoul laughed. The figure scooped up sand and dribbled it across Raoul's chest. Raoul batted his hand away but then sat up, reaching under the edge of his towel for his wallet. I think it was a tenner he handed over.

I was next in line, the last on the beach. I hid behind my sunglasses.

"Can you spare some change?" He blocked my sun.

I recognised the voice. I'd recognised the figure. I took off my sunglasses. Our eyes met. "Sorry," he said. "As you were."

Before I could reply, Martin was running awkwardly across the sand, picking up speed once he reached the footpath. The image stayed with me; it's in my sketch book now – man as light as air – fleeing.

26

From my bedroom window I'm looking down at the destroyed garden.

The weather is stormy and there is no solace to be had anywhere, not even up here. I can hear the muffled sound of a radio behind that of hammering and loud voices. When you told me, quite casually, that you planned some changes in the house, I had no idea you meant the entire house. Downstairs every floor has been ripped up. The kitchen is in the process of being extended out into what was the garden, the back door filled in and ugly bi-fold doors to be fitted. The beech shelving in the front room lies in a skip. A carpenter is in the process of building units in the alcoves each side of what will soon be a log-burning stove. Which means a woodshed – and not any old woodshed – taking up yet more space outside.

"Will there be any garden left?" I'd been close to tears at the destruction of my years of work: plants trampled underfoot; shrubs dug up: left to die on a heap of rubble intended for yet another skip at the end of the project.

"Not as we know it," you replied. "I'm sorry Shona, but I want something more streamlined."

"What does that even mean? You've destroyed a lovely space."

"But it was *your* lovely space. I want my garden to be—"

"Contemporary?" I couldn't keep the sneer from my voice.

"Why not?"

"You use that word all the time, what you mean is—"

"It's my fucking garden, my fucking house."

Each time you get in from college, there are more paint swatches, mixer pots and interior design magazines arriving with you. I dread hearing your footsteps on the stairs. You march straight in, as if it's any room in the house and not my bedroom.

"What do you think, Shona? For the hallway. Maybe one of these contemporary dark colours? I'm so over basic white."

"It's up to you."

"But you have an eye for colour. Choose one."

"But I told you the last time you asked; the hall is already dark, white works best."

"Same old, same old."

"Then don't ask."

This constant demand and then rejection of my opinion is driving me mad. "Shona, can you spare a minute?" is a phrase I dread. I hear it several times a day, sometimes animated, sometimes querulous. If you're determined to disrupt my work, you're succeeding.

There are days when I hate you. When you found that Wikipedia page, your eyes shining, reading out, "In the noughties, award-winning media designer Richard Christopher Maplin ..." banging your fist against your chest, " ... combined illustration and technology to create incredible works of art. Babe, listen to this: Maplin was a game-changer in the use of 3D digital techniques."

I attempted to tune out, continuing to mix paint while making a total mess of what I was doing.

"I wonder who put this together. Must be a fan of my work. Are you listening?"

"Richard, I'm trying to concentrate."

"You're not the only one. I just thought for one fucking moment, you might be interested in someone other than yourself."

I could have, should have replied, 'Yes but you've shared something about yourself at least a dozen times today,' but you would come back with, "So now you're counting?" I'd say, "But Richard, you have respect, money, made a name for yourself – I'm just starting over," and you'll snarl, "Whose fault is that?" The builders will fall silent and look at each other. You've made it clear to them that you're in charge, the man who pays the bills, makes the decisions, so they'll agree with you that I'm an ungrateful harridan and they've no idea why you put up with me.

"Just don't call me 'babe'," I say through gritted teeth.

"I didn't mean to." You turned back to the page. "Obviously I no longer class you as a babe."

The magic time: four o'clock when the builders pack up for the day and the house falls silent. As I hear their vans pull away, if you're at college, I go downstairs and walk through the rooms that are vastly changed even though there's still work to be done. Your constant conversation removed, chaos quietened, I am in awe. The newly plastered walls feel silky: they're a pleasing coral pink. If this house were mine, I think I'd leave them like that. There's a smell of fresh wood and paint.

I step into what will soon become the new extension. Reluctantly, I can see your vision. At the moment plastic sheeting covers the bi-fold door space. It pulsates in the wind, creating a groaning sound I imagine a swaying galleon on a stormy sea might make. I press my face to the plastic. Yes, a streamlined garden will suit you and your renovations very well.

There is no kitchen for the moment, just one chair and the table pushed against the wall with the kettle and a microwave. It looks disgusting. The builders drop their tea bags, their sandwich crumbs, anywhere. They never clear up after themselves. Sometimes I'm tempted to leave everything just as they've left it so that in the morning, they'll come in to filthy mugs with congealed tea and coffee dregs at the bottom.

I'd tried to explain to you how I felt. "I'm not their servant."

You looked at me as if with infinite patience. "It's not much to ask, is it? With the house the way it is, there's no cleaning required at the moment. Can't you just make it easy for once?"

"I feel they're watching me all the time."

"In your head." You actually tapped the side of your head to indicate my madness. "They're just blokes who earn a living doing work that people like you and me can't or won't do for ourselves. They come highly recommended."

"I'm not getting any painting done."

"You're at the beach every day."

"Not when it's raining. Not when the temperature drops. I come home and sit in my bedroom till the builders have packed up."

"I know." You started laughing. "The foreman said he hardly hears a sound coming from your room. His theory is that you're having a kip.

"You've been discussing me?"

"Lighten up. It was just a joke." You grinned. "But maybe you are kipping. Just joking!"

If I could hold a mirror up to your face, you'd see what I see; someone being hateful.

Then your expression softened. "Look, I'm sorry. I know it impacts on you far more than me. But once it's done, you'll have your own bathroom and a new kitchen."

"Fair enough." It's true, I will benefit. Having a bathroom to myself will be wonderful. "I'm over-reacting. Forgive me? It's just that the time I have to work is so precious."

You placed a hand on my shoulder, expression concerned. "Of course, your time is precious. Who knows that more than me?" Your fingers tightened. "But that's no reason for you to behave like an absolute bitch."

Shocked, I twisted out of your grip.

Like a schoolboy relishing his freedom, you grabbed your jacket. "Won't be back till tomorrow afternoon," you shouted as you flung open the front door, "And no, you can't watch my TV."

But there you're wrong. You've left five small bruises on my shoulder. Two of them fall each side of old scar tissue. I tell myself, none of this is any big deal, I've sustained far worse. The front room is the only room downstairs still vaguely habitable. I *will* watch your television and drink red wine and if I spill it, well I can't imagine those Italian sofas will survive this renovation anyway.

Outside it's almost dark. I can hardly make out what's left of the garden. *Goodbye*, I mutter as I open a bottle of your best red wine. *Fuck you, Richard Christopher Maplin.*

27

I pour a second glass. The wine has a bitter taste. I don't even like it but when have I allowed not liking something to stop me? I'm still in what remains of the kitchen, sitting at the cluttered table, my thoughts in the past.

I said that my affair with Beatrice lasted two years but if I placed the days that we actually spent together end to end, I might find our affair only covered the shortest month of February. As to the nights, they'd add up to no more than a couple of Bank Holiday weekends. Yet those days and nights made the years seem wonderful, filled me with hope and optimism.

Bea was in her late thirties, not much older than I am now. She was married. There were two children in their early teens: a boy and a girl plus a husband called Harry. I was the lover she hid in plain sight although I think Harry might have known and accepted it. I can't imagine I'd have seemed any threat. The Salmons were in a very different league from Shona Blake, stroke Kirkpatrick. I thought of them as a 'glossy magazine family', two generations of money and entitlement behind both. There was a holiday home on the Dorset coast, two red setters called Ping and Pong, a French au-pair and a separate gardener for both houses. I'm not sure where I came in this order of importance or if the family even credited my existence as any more than my being just another of Beatrice's coterie of artists. And even Beatrice, although she insisted that she loved me – I'd provided her with few clues as to who I was. Yes, she knew I'd been adopted, during my teens suffered a breakdown and spent a long time in various hospitals. I did share a little about life with Dorothy. In the beginning she was curious about my scarred body, but I had a talent for rebuffing curiosity with a few light dismissive phrases. Her understanding of my responses reminded me of the Kirkpatrick's – that Shona opening up was just a matter of winning my trust.

"You'll tell me when you're ready, Shona. We have plenty of time."

I would never have shared the full story.

The moments I felt most secure and relaxed in her company were when I stayed at her *pied-à-terre* in Islington. The Salmons lived on the other side of London and little in the north of the capital interested them enough to make the journey across. Beatrice's apartment was spacious, the bedroom opening through French windows onto a lovely garden. The apartment itself wasn't grand at all: two bedrooms, one living room, all with unpolished floorboards, a few bright mats, pictures on the walls that didn't scream to be taken notice of. I remember how cool and shady the interior was. Painted in a pale grey-green, I felt calm, almost serene in a way I never felt at home in Richard's company. And Beatrice – once the front door shut out the world – she was different, slipping out of the elegant trouser suits she adopted to suit her public persona into loose shirts, cotton trousers, one gold chain around her neck, no shoes. Her dark hair, shaken out of its tight French pleat, hung in loose waves around her mobile face. She gave me what I believed to be love and I responded as best I could and my response seemed to delight her. I felt petted, desired . . . liked. Liked might seem inadequate but it meant something to me. Her laughter, her touch, her heat, her distance: she was everything I'd never known I needed. Our every encounter seemed important and highly charged.

And so, to our last day together.

Mid-summer 2008. The terrace doors to Bea's bedroom are thrown wide open. From her bed I can see stone tubs of vividly coloured flowers, but it is the variations of green and bronze foliage that always seduce me. That afternoon, it is as if she's planned the clear summer sky as a backdrop. It is wonderfully hot. We sprawl naked on the bed. Her body is compact, brown and smooth, legs not quite as long as mine. How I love her shoulders. They are so strong and muscular! A swimmer's shoulders, she'd told me.

Next to the bed is a vase of cosmos flowers, picked from her garden before I'd arrived. With one of the flower heads she lightly traces a heart shape on my back. She kisses the line of raised flesh below my collar bone, moving lazily down to kiss the burn mark on my hip.

"Shona darling, I wish I could change your past. Each of these scars tells such a sad story."

Drowsily, without thinking, I murmur, "They're my reward for pain inflicted."

Abruptly she moves away from me.

I open my eyes. "Is something wrong?"

"What a stupid thing to say." She rolls back to her own side of the bed, her face flushed and angry. "Is that why you stay with Richard? Why you accept his controlling behaviour, his destruction of your confidence?"

I've never seen Bea angry before and have no idea how to respond. No words come to mind, no actions. "I – I – I," is all I can stammer out.

She swings her legs off the bed and starts to pull on her clothes. Her voice calmer she says, "Darling, you're like a cat, content to sit in the sun and be admired, knowing you have a home and an owner to go back to. You'll never leave Richard. Already you're probably thinking about the train you have to catch and what lie you'll spin."

I grip her wrist, kiss it hard. "I love you."

"Then leave him. Come here to me. No strings. Surely almost anything would be preferable to staying in such a toxic relationship. The two of you as a couple are a fabrication. You don't love him, do you?"

"No, of course not. I never have."

"Well then, why stay? We could pack up your stuff during a day when he's at the studio. You'd never need to see him again. He won't know where you are." She laughs, claps her hands, good humour apparently restored. "Grab a week's worth of knickers, a few basics and whatever you're working on – I can fill in any gaps."

Looking back, I clearly see that moving from one dependency to another would have eventually meant death to our relationship. How many years of therapy have I gone through? Enough to know that to get fully well, one day I'll need to stand on my own two feet.

"So, what do you think?" Fully dressed, Bea stands in the doorway.

"What will your husband think?"

"He'll be glad that someone's in the flat while I'm away. Henry hates this place standing empty. Come on Shona, how much longer can you remain in that weird, Victorian relationship where he has the upper hand? It's so unhealthy."

I double the pillows behind my head. My face and breasts are bathed in fractured sunlight. The cosmos blossom lies next to me. I pick it up, tuck it behind my ear. "I will move out. I promise. It's a wonderful offer. Let me think about it." And I do want to think about it. I like the idea of living with Bea, but I'm unused to new ideas. Richard and I have been . . . unchanged for so long.

"If you don't leave now, you'll never leave him. You're too comfortable. Budge up," she says.

I move across the bed, draw her towards me. She takes hold of a hank of my hair, pulls my face into hers. "I'm willing to wait but not forever."

From the other end of the apartment, her work phone begins to ring. The sound breaks the moment. I sense her body tensing: for Beatrice, agency business always comes first.

"I want to share a life with you." She lets my hair slide through her fingers.

Before I can answer, she is already stepping out into the shadow of the hall.

I fall asleep. When I wake, I look at my watch. Only about ten minutes have passed but with a prickle of unease, I realise I do need to be back at the apartment, to shower, become the Shona Richard expects me to be as I recount a fictional day.

I sit up, "Bea," I call out.

She doesn't answer. I dress. Check myself in the mirror. The cosmos flower hangs at a comical angle over one eyebrow. I ease it out of my hair, carefully wrap it in a tissue and place the blossom in the side pocket of my bag. As I enter the hall, I can hear her voice, slightly strained, coming from the room she uses as a home-office. "Of course. Leave it with me. No, I'll make my own enquiries."

The door is open. Bea sits at her desk, her back to me. She is holding her phone but in front of her a laptop is open.

"Something sounds serious," I say lightly.

With an abrupt movement she shuts the lid of the laptop. In the half-light her face looks colourless, her full lips drawn into a thin line.

"Is there a problem?"

She shakes her head. "Some difficult news. Nothing I can't deal with." She begins to rub the palms of her hands together. "Look Shona, I'm sorry to hurry you out but—"

"Don't worry. I'm late anyway. I'll think about your offer."

"Yes, do that." Her eyes slide away from meeting mine.

"Are you free next weekend or maybe an afternoon in the week?"

"I'm not sure. Let me check my diary and get back to you." Her tone of voice is distant, as if she's speaking politely to a total stranger.

Silently she leads the way to her front door, opening it and stepping back. I lean forward to kiss her mouth but she turns her head so that my lips brush her cheek. "I have a deadline."

I feel a small flicker of anger. It's as if I'm being dismissed.

"Fair enough," I shrug my shoulders and then, "Are we okay?"

"Of course we are."

But we're not. The following day, Bea terminates my contract. Richard is furious, insisting that he will find me a solicitor, we will sue her.

"The cow," he snarls. "I never liked her. I hope you're angry. Really fucking angry."

I'm too stunned to respond, to even think coherently. She's blocked her personal phone and email. While Richard is at work, I ring the agency; I'm told that Mrs Salmon isn't available to speak to me. I ring multiple times, always the same reply.

"Your name's been removed from her website," Richard informs me.

I write just one letter. Three days later it's returned in a brown envelope. On the back, Bea's written, 'Please don't try to contact me again.'

By then Richard's affair with Raoul has become all-consuming. Increasingly I'm left alone. I find it difficult to concentrate on even the simplest drawing. I retreat from the outside world spending hours staring down at the street from my bedroom window. In much the same way Richard later takes care of me in Hawksbridge, when at home, he cossets me as if I am a sick child. Dimly, I'm aware that he likes this vulnerable yet withdrawn version of Shona, sitting as still as a statue, hands folded in her lap, nothing to say, nothing new to impart. Sometimes he takes photographs – random – in passing. I can see him now, walking through a room, glancing across to where I am sitting and holding up his phone. He never shows me the images. I don't ask. I don't care.

Another fine summer morning. Whether by accident or intent, Richard sets off for the studio leaving the door to the apartment wide open. Still in my nightdress, my feet slipped into thin-soled red-satin slippers, I made my way down the three flights of stairs. The communal hallway was in shadow; the sun hadn't reached that far down in the street. I recall the front door; it was solid wood with a coloured glass panel: red, green and blue. I stood with my face against the cool glass peering out at the distorted image of a sunny street. A woman from one of the other apartments asked me to move. "I'm late already," she said. And then she looked at me properly. "Are you okay?"

"It's hot upstairs," I said.

"We all envy you and your boyfriend. I'd love a roof terrace."

Later that same day – with no memory of how I got there – I found myself standing in front of the house where I'd lived with Dorothy. I waited patiently until someone came out: an elderly man pulling a brown canvas shopping trolley. Seeing me in crumpled nightdress and flimsy slippers, he hesitated.

"Does Dorothy Blake still live here?" I asked.

He shrugged. "Died," he said. "Couple of weeks ago. Funny old bird."

"She was my mother. I was eight years old when I moved away."

"Do you want to see the flat? I've got the keys. It's empty at the moment."

I followed him up the one flight of stairs. He unlocked the door and stood back to let me enter.

"I'll wait outside," he said. "Call me when you're ready to leave and I'll lock up."

I didn't stay long, just peeped into the rooms. Dorothy had always kept everything clean and tidy. "The clients expect it," she'd frequently said. And it was clean, very little dust on the windowsills, the drainer shone. I stood where my fold-up bed had been. I imagined myself living there, taking my mother's place. What would I become?

I went out onto the landing and sat on the stairs, pulling my knees in tight to my chest.

Eventually the man came to find me. "All done?" he asked.

I didn't answer. I was outside myself, watching my body

rocking from side to side. I could hear a thin keening noise. On and on it went.

I carried no money, no identification. He left his trolley in the hallway and shepherded me out into sunlight. I got into the back of his car and he drove me to a hospital where I was later sectioned. That was so kind of him.

I empty my wine glass into the sink, upend the still half-full bottle and watch the wine, like blood, trickle away leaving behind a reddish stain.

28

SONNY

His mother won't be back for several hours. He'd watched her from the living room window, head bent forward against the wind, her shopping trolley bumping over the uneven tarmac. Through binoculars, he'd tracked her progress all the way to the seafront, till he could no longer differentiate trolley from person. Only then he'd let the curtain fall.

The previous evening they'd argued. After a day of rain, he'd said from frustration more than anything, "This place is a prison. You've made me your prisoner."

Mildly, without looking up from her library book, she'd said, "I didn't intend to."

"And that makes it all right, does it. Do you even care?" He'd unwound from his coiled cat position in front of the dying fire.

Placing her index finger against her page, she'd looked up. "Of course I care. But darling, aren't we too far along this road for blame to be an issue?"

"But you're my mother," he'd shouted.

"For my sins." Her mouth had twitched with a supressed smile. "Let's not argue."

He'd stood in front of her not knowing what to do or say. At that moment he hated her but had she held out her hand, told him she loved him, that he was wonderful, he'd have crumbled, been happy to let her soothe away his resentment.

"I'm going to bed," he said, knowing how much she hated to be left on her own in the evenings.

"Take some biscuits with you. I could make tea."

"I'm sick of tea and biscuits."

He'd marched towards the door.

She called out. "Night-night darling. Sleep tight."

He'd ignored her.

"I said night-night, darling."

"I heard you the first time."

"Then why don't you answer like you always do?"

"Because I'm sick of these rituals. Sick of repeating the same childish words just to keep you happy."

As he'd stepped out into the corridor, he heard her: "Darling boy, did you know that your hair is thinning? From over here I can see your lovely pink scalp."

Horrified, he'd stalled, his hand automatically reaching for the back of his head.

"I made it up." Her voice was shrill with false jollity. "I promise you, I made it up. Just say 'night-night' like you always do. To please your old mum?"

At her bedroom door Sonny hesitates. Till recently this room had been a haven, a place of good memories. As a teenager he'd spent Sunday afternoons curled up on her bed as she read out pieces from the *Sunday Express*. (Those were the days when newspapers were still delivered to the Miller Building.) There'd been a woman journalist, Veronica Papworth, who wrote about fashion and a 'dizzy god-daughter'. They'd both looked forward to her column. He'd never been sure whether he liked the god-daughter – maybe he was jealous of her – but he'd enjoyed the way the writer wrote about someone she obviously adored. Those cosy Sunday afternoons are long gone.

As ever, the room is seductively comfortable, the temperature so pleasant he's tempted to just sit. Here the windows are left bare. The view is of fields rather than sea or the tenements. His own room is always untidy but his mother's room remains quietly neat – that's how he thinks of it. The colours pastel: shades of pale mint and cream. From their scavenging forays, she chose well – an antique blanket box, a Persian carpet in watery blues, an ornate headboard, a dressing table with a three-way mirror she'd painted white and a stool to match. On the side table next to the bed, the jigsaw she'd started, is spread out on a tray. All the puzzle edges are in place and much of the vivid blue sky. The box lid depicting a highly coloured illustration of the Taj Mahal is propped up against the lamp. There are tigers, an elephant and people wearing jewel-coloured clothes. He removes three pieces from the finished areas and pockets them. He then forces three different pieces into their places.

Job done he sits on the stool in front of the mirror, hands in lap, eyes lowered. He's anxious about what he will see when he raises his head. There is very little on the dressing table: a pretty box of Woods of Windsor True Rose dusting powder and a Wedgewood dish in which she keeps both hair pins and a blue hair net. The dish was something she'd found and liked in one of the empty rooms. *Three, two, one,* he murmurs before raising his head. His breathing quickens and then slows. *Not bad at all.* He is delighted with his boyish reflection. There are few lines, his forehead is almost smooth. He looks rested. He laughs. Why shouldn't he look rested? Resting has paid off in maintaining the illusion of youth. *No illusion. I do look young.*

And then as he twists his head, this way and that, all concentration focused on his jawline, the very fine lines – almost non-existent – fanning out from his eyes, nothing too disastrous – he catches sight of something, a tiny circle of skin visible in both of the side mirrors. He repositions them, tips his head so that he can better see the crown. His mother was right. He is losing his hair. Fearfully he touches his scalp. He can feel skin! Now his reflection is repugnant.

As he turns violently away from the triple images, he notices a card or rectangle of paper tucked under the Woods of Windsor box. He slides it out. It's a colour photograph. He recognises one of the men who had brought him home from Hawksbridge: Richard. In the photo he looks younger. A young woman is with him. In the background is the Eiffel Tower. Sonny turns the photograph over: *To darling Richard, love always Shona.* Shona – his mother's friend. Since that night, when they'd dropped him off near the underground entrance, he hadn't seen the men again, never felt brave enough to make the journey into Hawksbridge. For the first time since Martin's desertion, he feels a return of his determination to make a change. It has been weeks since his last visit to the seventh floor. Weeks wasted. The photograph has served as a distraction. He replaces it under the box.

From a neat pile of spare bedding at the bottom of her wardrobe, he removes two pillows. If she notices their absence he'll say – oh he'll think of something when the time comes. He turns to the blanket box and takes out a sheet and two pillowcases. About to close the lid, Sonny notices a purple plastic folder. Out of curiosity he slides it out. Through the plastic he can see a brightly coloured logo. He tips the contents onto her bed. All correspondence from local estate agents. Methodically he works his way through pages of details about bungalows sited on the far side of Hawksbridge. Some sheets are starred. On one, dated only mid-July, next to the price his mother has written, 'Maybe they'll take an offer?' In the corner of the page, she has drawn a felt-tipped heart. But why? The single-storey building is ugly, box-shaped with a pointed roof. He skims through the details. It has a gravel drive and car-parking space. There is a landscaped garden, desirable kitchen and two spacious bedrooms. Bewildered, he wonders if one of those bedrooms was earmarked for him or perhaps her new friend, Shona. He finds several letters stapled together dated from two years earlier – she has registered with a solicitor. She has made a will. He searches the file, searches the blanket box but finds no will. What other secrets does his mother's dear little head hold? Only minutes before, he'd felt desperate to cut the ties between them, to forge forward on his own – but to discover her in the process of severing them – that is so very painful.

By the time she arrives home in late afternoon, he's changed out of his kimono into cotton trousers and a vest. He may be losing his hair but he's proud of his body. Like his face, he's taken good care of it. He welcomes her cheerfully, makes her cup of tea, as always using the required cup and saucer. When he complains of a headache, he accepts her concern gratefully. Yes, he will have a bowl of tomato soup, and yes to a slice of cake, but if it's okay with her, he'll take them to his room. Perhaps sleep for an hour or two or make a start on one of his library books. At nine that evening he brings back his soup bowl and plate.

The tray with the jigsaw is on her footstool. "Not so grumpy?" Smiling, she looks up.

"I'm fine, Ma."

"I've almost finished the sky. Just a corner and that one white cloud left."

"I might go for a run," he says.

"Darling, I thought you had a headache."

The 'darling' sticks in his throat. He can't stop himself from wincing.

"What is it? You don't seem well."

"I'm fine. Get on with your jigsaw." Sonny pauses in front of the tray. "I think you'll find some of your pieces are in the wrong place."

Returning to his bedroom Sonny gathers up the pillows and bedding. He checks the corridor before moving silently towards the staircase. His heart hammers as he approaches the apartment door on the seventh floor. He's never felt it before, but there's something eerie about a door that has stayed locked for a considerable time. A sense that something else may have taken over the emptiness on the other side. As soon as he steps inside, his mood starts to change. The tightness in his whole body since his mother's comment about losing his hair melts away. He drops the pillows onto the bed and then throws open the doors to the balcony. Night has fallen but the sky isn't in absolute darkness. It's raining. He doesn't care, enjoying the soft rain on his face and arms. Sonny salutes the heavens, raising his clasped hands high above his head. The stretch feels so good.

Now think. What do you need? The two rooms are enormous. There's no way he can duplicate any of the comfort he enjoys three floors below. Leaving the balcony doors open he sits on the bed. Wishes that he'd brought pencil and paper. But a list – what if she found it? No, he won't put anything in writing. He's reminded of all the estate agent details, the formal letters from a solicitor. With the heel of his hands he bangs his forehead. *Think of Martin. Imagine someone like Martin.* In the past Martin thoughts had always helped. They did now.

'Sonny, just stroke my back.' Martin, naked but for boxer shorts, lying face down on one of the single beds, his body in the red light from the lamp turning his skin to rose. Sonny given permission, stroking first Martin's neck, moving down to his shoulders, finally – an hour passing, sliding his hand under the waistband of Martin's shorts, over the perfect curve of his buttocks. Sonny unable to breathe.

Sonny goes into the small kitchen. He opens a kitchen cupboard, drawing out a rusty metal toolbox. He pushes back the lid. There are several compartments holding a jumble of tape, picture wire, chains, a screwdriver, hammer and hundreds of nails and screws of different sizes. This box originally belonged to another tenant, left behind when he and his family moved away. Sonny sits on the floor, stirs the detritus with his index finger till underneath he locates a small cardboard box. He opens it. There is Martin's watch; wide faced, metal strap. And there is the folded piece of paper that Martin left with it. *To my mate, Sonny x.* Beneath the watch and paper are other keepsakes: a two-pound coin, an earring, three strands of hair, each a different colour, a set of keys, a torn leather glove.

29

SHONA

2014

In Hawksbridge library last year, I'd checked my birth mother online. Dorothy Hazel Blake was in a small way notorious, linked to the deaths by asphyxiation of two men but not enough evidence found to prosecute her. And then almost a decade after my adoption, she was jailed on a charge of manslaughter but released only six years into her sentence. On her death, a short obituary appeared in several less well-known newspapers. Although I knew she was dead it helped me to see details of her death in print. I now have copies of Dorothy's birth and death certificate. She was forty-one when I was born. By then she might have believed herself infertile, which would coincide with her belief in her own invulnerability. Dorothy would have faith that her iron will would protect her from all inconvenience.

If as a child, I'd remained in her care I've no doubt *I'd* be dead by now.

"Don't breathe," she'd whisper.

Sometimes I'd struggle awake to find her hand over my

mouth and nose. She always smelt of cigarettes. I don't know why but I find the smell comforting. I think of my mother's legacy, her gift to me, a belief that all can be solved by pain. Those cigarette burns weren't inflicted on me every day, not even frequently: they were saved for when Dorothy felt … driven to the limit, when she could take no more. I've only worked this out as an adult. Her actions were a transference. I link my shadow self's actions against Brian and Sheila Kirkpatrick as a natural progression from mother to daughter. I was still a child in many ways and so I had no concept of boundaries. I went further than marking the innocent with the glowing tip of a cigarette.

1995

As Shona's sixteenth birthday approached, she experienced increasing anxiety. The task she'd set herself was challenging. At night her dreams were haunted but during daylight hours she was able to blot out all thought of repercussions. Had Shona been a few years older she might have reached the conclusion that the game had gone far enough. But maybe the extra years still wouldn't be sufficient to stop the destructive chatter of devils inside her head.

In those final few weeks, she became a spy: the shadow listening in to conversations between Brian and Sheila that might include her while appearing totally preoccupied. For instance, as she pretended to be engrossed in one of Sheila's favourite novels, Colleen McCullough's The Thorn Birds, *she was actually tuning in to Brian's murmured aside to Sheila as they watch the Nine O'Clock News: "Eleven months, two weeks and counting. Surely that means something?"*

"I'll draw breath." Sheila reached for his hand. Their clasped hands lay between them on the sofa.

Were they smug? She believed so. Deserving to be blotted out, Shona? Oh yes.

She'd reached the point of fight back or allow herself to be forever altered.

This wasn't the house where Lynda Wilson almost died. The family now lived in a London suburb. Each weekday Brian and Sheila caught the Piccadilly Line into the West End. He was an accountant for a large store; she managed a coffee bar just off Carnaby Street. Shona's birthday fell on the following day, which was a Saturday. This was Friday and she had two study periods at home to revise for end-of-term exams. Her textbooks were spread out on the dining room table.

"Don't work too hard," Sheila said. Her hand rested lightly on the crown of Shona's head.

"Don't worry. I won't."

"Sheila." There was a cautionary note in Brian's voice. "We'll be late."

Sheila came no closer. "I would have hugged you." Her eyes were warm with affection.

"I know, but best not to," Shona had replied.

She let an hour pass. Several times she read the same poem, 'Wild Swans' by Edna St Vincent Millay, which she had torn out of a book in the school library.

> *House without air, I leave you and lock your door.*
> *Wild swans, come over the town, come over*
> *The town again, trailing your legs and crying!*

And then she left the 'house without air' and went into the garden. In the night it had rained. The air smelt fresh. No wild swans flying over but a good enough day.

Brian no longer had a garage to work in but there was a

brick-built workshop. As before, he used the space for his DIY projects: a bird table, a pergola, painting a cupboard door. There was a sink with a cold water tap and shelving along three walls. The previous weekend he'd begun to put together a flat-pack garden bench. Now it was almost complete. Lengths of wood to form the back struts lay across two trestles. Even when Brian had all day to complete a job, he was easily distracted: Sheila calling from the kitchen with offers of coffee and yes, Shona as well, with her own practical problems: a malfunctioning hairdryer or the latch on her bedroom window that refused to stop sticking.

She pulled on a pair of Sheila's gardening gloves before crouching down to peer into the gloom beneath his work bench. In a cardboard box against the wall Brian stored empty bottles and jam jars for recycling. She chose two wine bottles that still had their screw caps. In a cupboard under the sink she found his stock of white spirit, three clear plastic containers, one only half-full. Carefully, she filled the bottles from the two full containers, topping the containers up with water before replacing them. The bottles she carried indoors. Sheila had left some laundry in the washing machine to do when she came home from work. She peeled off the gloves and tossed them in. Switched the machine on. The wine bottles were placed in her school bag which she hid upstairs in her wardrobe. Through Shona's head ran a phrase, 'no real or lasting damage'.

In the evening Sheila and Brian invariably drank wine. They were social rather than heavy drinkers. The sparkling crystal glass, the deep red colour of the wine, the 'cheers' as they raised their glasses enhanced the enjoyment of the meal. After dinner, they sometimes poured a second glass but Sheila rarely finished hers. Together on the sofa, they watched two hours of television, then up to bed.

"Good night, Shona." They'd pause outside her bedroom door.

"Good night," she'd call back.

"Don't read for too long. School in the morning."

"I won't."

She was used to the sounds they made moving around their room, the shower from the ensuite, cupboards opening and closing, the low murmur of their voices. During the week they rarely had sex. For fifteen minutes they read their books and then she'd hear his book snapping shut, hers dropping to the floor. A kiss, a loving smile, Shona imagined them turning away from each other to switch off their matching bedside lamps. Quiet settling over the house.

They both slept well. Shona poorly. They were aware of this. On the edge of sleep themselves, they'd become used to the careful sound of their daughter making her way back downstairs to curl up in the armchair with her sketchbook and herbal tea. If either came close to waking, they'd feel reassured. Ah, it is only Shona.

Part 2

30

MRS GIFFORD

Standing on tiptoes in her tiny spotless kitchen, stretching up to a high shelf for her best wine glasses, the tiredness dogging Mrs Gifford since mid-summer is gone. From the living room drifts the sound of male voices arguing good naturedly.

Richard's is by far the loudest and he has the most to say, however she recognises that his friend Raoul's quiet responses contain an authority that the other's pronouncements lack. Only her son's voice is missing.

The two men had arrived unannounced, coming in through the underground carpark. Their rap on the door had been a shock.

"Hide yourself, Sonny."

"Who is it?"

"I have no idea."

He'd gone into the kitchen and on into the pantry.

Fearfully, she'd opened the door.

"Sonny's mum? Didn't you and I meet in the library? *Quelle* coincidence. Can we come in?" Richard took her hand in both of his. Behind him in the gloom of the corridor, another man waited.

She'd stepped aside, letting them bound past her. Suddenly the room was crowded with tanned, well-built bodies. Both men exuded health, their faces lightly sheened with sweat. They wore shorts, t-shirts, dazzlingly white socks and trainers. She picked up the scent of fresh air and some sort of cologne.

"I'm Richard, and this is my friend Raoul, a tutor at the college. We've been knocking a ball about on the college tennis court but it got too hot and so we thought we'd call in and check up on Sonny."

"I don't understand. How is it you know my son?"

"We gave him a lift home from the town centre one evening – oh, it must have been six weeks ago. We've left it far too long, but here we are." His gaze swept the room. "What a fantastic place you've got."

"It will be a travesty if they pull this building down," Richard says as she carries the tray of wine and glasses into the room. "Any plans yet as to where you'll both live?"

Sonny looks at her. Quietly he answers, "My mother makes the big decisions. If I had my way I'd never leave here. It's my home. The entire building: the ground the Miller Building stands on, the view from every window – I've spent a lifetime in these rooms."

She's astounded. Never before has Sonny put his feelings so completely into words.

"I get you," Raoul says. "Living here since you were a child, obviously there's a strong attachment. Where could the council house you that would come close to what you have already?"

"Sonny, the fold-up table, please," she says.

Languidly he unfolds it. She sets down the tray.

"But what are you both going to do?" Richard persists. He directs this question to Sonny. "From the article in last week's local paper, work begins in January. That's only a matter of months away."

Sonny shrugs.

"But the council meeting to decide one way or another is this week. It's going to happen. No use burying your head in the sand."

"Richard, stop hectoring the poor guy."

"Just being realistic."

"A glass of wine?" Mrs Gifford holds up the bottle, "It's a good one. Pouilly Fuissé."

Raoul takes the bottle from her. "You're right, it is a good one. Let me pour."

"I didn't mean to 'hector'." Richard places his hand on Sonny's shoulder. "Tell me, what was it like when you first came here? Is it okay to open the curtains?"

Mother and son exchange looks. Mrs Gifford nods. "Of course."

At the window Sonny points out the distant terraces. "There used to be a corner shop years ago. It seemed to sell everything. But in those days this area was busy. Families, artists, musicians."

"And you'd wave to me from this very window." She hands her son a glass of wine.

"What was that comic called I bought you every week?"

"I don't remember." He frowns at her.

"So, did you never go outside?" Richard asks.

"Rarely. I had everything I needed here. All of us kids played on the stairs, in the corridors–"

"Oh, they had a whale of a time: hide and seek, ball games,"

"I meant as an adult," Richard cuts across her. "That

night we brought you home, to be honest we thought you were having some kind of panic attack."

"It passed. I've had panic attacks before."

"Have you? You've never said." She looks at Richard. "My son is agoraphobic."

"I am not! Will you stop butting in?"

The room falls silent. Abruptly Sonny moves away from the window, away from Richard. Her voice shrill, she calls out, "Crisps? Olives anyone?"

Raoul gently takes her arm. "Don't worry, Mrs Gifford. We're going soon – we'll leave the two of you in peace."

With relief she sees that her son and Richard have returned to their place at the window. They're talking quietly.

"I worry," she says.

"Of course, you do."

"Thank you for coming. My son needs male company but gets none."

"We'll drop by again."

"I wonder . . ."

"Yes?" Raoul prompts.

"Well, it's months away but I'm having a small gathering on Christmas Eve. Could you both come? Just look in for an hour perhaps?"

He hesitates. "We'll try."

"There'll only be me, Sonny and Shona. Do you know her? Richard's other friend?"

Once they've gone, the living room seems particularly peaceful. She's cleared away the glasses and the bottles, Sonny lies stretched out on the chaise longue, head and shoulders supported by cushions. His eyes are closed but she knows he's wide awake.

She says, "I met Richard in the library some months ago."

"You never told me."

"I didn't think it would come to anything. *You* never mentioned you'd met them either."

His eyes open. "Actually, I didn't want to share my memory with you."

"You sound angry."

"Why shouldn't I be? *They* have a life, together or apart. People find you quaint. Endearing." His voice is full of venom. "They don't know what to make of *me*."

"Sonny, can we stop this now? Another drink? There's walnut cake, perfect with red wine."

"No and no! I'm like a fly caught in your horrible sticky web. That's how Martin felt about you. Why he left. It was all your fault." Sonny face is contorted, tears spill from his eyes. "You couldn't bear to see me happy. Just for a change someone liked me better." He slaps his chest.

"That simply isn't true."

He sits up, leans forward. "So, it's my fault he left? Have I got this right? You were the mother Martin never had but I never even stood in as a brother? He couldn't fucking stand the sight of me?"

"Please, let's not argue."

His head swivels first to one side, then to the other. He reminds her of the nodding dog she's sometimes noticed in the back of car windows.

"I hate you," he says.

"Only in the moment. It will pass. Deep down, I know you love your old mum."

"And you know that for a fact, do you?"

Mrs Gifford is weary. She goes into her bedroom and shuts the door. After a few minutes, she hears Sonny out in the corridor and then his footsteps on the staircase, heading upwards to the seventh floor. He thinks she doesn't know how much time he spends up there, but of course she does. He is her son; she needs that knowledge to reassure herself of his safety. In the quiet she thinks about Richard and Raoul. She'd liked them both. Very much. The interest they'd shown, their sensitivity towards her son. When Richard kissed her on the cheek as they were leaving, she'd felt something far more emotive than just flattered. When was the last time a man had kissed her?

"Your skin smells of rose petals," he'd said.

Only at the end came a jarring note. As she stood in the doorway watching them walk towards the lift, she distinctly heard the friend say, "Richard, you're so full of shit."

31

SHONA

2014

I am painting systematically with none of the manic intensity of that younger self. For now, all I'm searching for is consistency: that quality Mrs Gifford – as a young talented dancer – told me she'd lacked. I'm convinced that one day this work will form an exhibition, somewhere, sometime in the future. When this happens, I'll provide my own title: *Turning inland*. At the end of August, it had struck me that a number of paintings were now finished: nine canvases. Lined up and turned to face the walls of my bedroom. Once each picture is complete, I don't look at it again. It's always at the back of my mind how your self-congratulation brought you and any progress to a standstill.

I don't discuss my work with you but nor am I secretive about it. Most mornings I spread out on the island in the new kitchen area. We now have all this space but so far neither of us have produced a cooked meal. We depend on the microwave and ready meals as we did before. However, work-wise, I have to admit that the extension is a success. You have the dining table with a view of your precious minimalist garden. There is enough space between island and table to avoid conflict. You, too, are absorbed. Frequently, I arrive downstairs to find you're already there with your cup of black coffee, magazines and books stacked next to an open laptop. My mean side whispers that there's something self-conscious about your entire set up, as if this is how you imagine creative people are when they work from home. You're too vain to smoke, yet will a Gitanes cigarette *à la* David Bowie be added to the display?

But this morning you're late. I've already laid out some visual reference collected yesterday from the beach: sea-shells, pebbles, a piece of wood scarred and whitened by the waves. Mrs Gifford's story about her childhood holiday when her parents left her alone to play near the sea has made me consider the lack of memories from my own early years. Living with Dorothy, space was limited to two rooms and a stairwell. There was school. I was always clean and tidily dressed. I was polite, never wanting to draw attention to myself. I don't recall daydreams except around periods of suppressed anger. Mrs Gifford's story comes like a gift. If I'm unable to picture myself in her anecdote, I can be the observer of that woman as a child.

You incline your head as you hurry past. "Morning," you say.

"How's your course going?"

"Not bad, although I sometimes feel my age. I'm the oldest by at least a decade." You set your laptop and a thick leather file down on the dining table. "Orange juice? Coffee? Carbonated water?"

I shake my head. With a palette knife I begin to mix colours on a saucer. Although I'm aware of your movements as you switch on the coffee machine and begin opening cupboards and jars, I don't feel any of the resentment I used to feel, as if you were intruding on my space. The room is huge now. Any noise you make is in the background and almost reassuring.

Finally, you settle down in your chair, eyes fixed on the screen as you spoon muesli into your mouth. I test out a shade of greeny-blue on a board. Just a hint of red required. You carry your empty bowl to the sink and then I'm aware that you're standing directly behind me. Suddenly both my neck and shoulders feel vulnerable. Your hand shoots out and picks up my sketch book.

"Put that down, please." I keep my tone even. Ignoring you, I reach for a tube of vermilion and squeeze out a pin-head of liquid.

"Hmm Shona, quite the aspiring Rembrandt. You'd be the star pupil in the adult ed. art class at the college."

"I expect I would."

I can feel your breath against my neck. I refuse to acknowledge you.

Taking my sketch book with you, you saunter back to your table and sit down. For a while you continue to flick through the pages. Your face is expressionless but I know that non-expression of old and my heart sinks. I keep on with what I'm doing although now I'm only pretending to be busy with the colours. I can't leave the room. There is no garden left outside to lose myself in. My only option would be to sit in my bedroom. But then, Richard you would have won whatever game you've set up for me this morning. Finally, I ask, "Richard, what's wrong?"

"Why should anything be wrong? You're imagining things, Shona."

"No, but I may be mistaken, that's all." Still not looking at him, I try to smile. "Not imagining anything."

The sketch book hits the saucer and green paint splatters on the white marble work surface. "And what do you intend to do with these daubs you're working on? I can guarantee *La Salmone* won't be interested. The fine art world's moved on since you played a tiny part in it."

"And what would you know about fine art?"

You flinch as if I've slapped you. Your reaction makes me feel good but is also a little frightening.

Abruptly you switch off the laptop and push it away. "This won't do," you say.

"As in?"

You run your hand across your face. When you look at me again, I can see that you're struggling. "As in, I've never been a sharing kind of guy. The truth is I can't bear watching you steaming ahead with your ideas and energy. When it comes to being creative, nothing gets in your way, does it? Not a nervous breakdown, lack of friends, love, dislike – you just keep going, while I'm standing on the side-lines as yet another minor 'masterpiece' comes off the production line."

You're on your feet but you've not finished with me yet.

"And I'm deeply sorry," (said with heavy sarcasm) "but I happen to care what happens in here. Yes, I'm responsible for the saucer spilling, I apologise for taking your sketch book and chucking it at you, but Shona, you make a mess! Now you're painting again, you've gone back to being that careless, self-absorbed woman that did my head in when we lived together in London. It may seem *bourgeois* to you that I care so much about my property but that's how I am. I paid for it."

You yank open a kitchen drawer, take out the breadboard. "This breadboard was a thing of beauty. Extremely expensive. New a week ago. It's made from olive wood. Did you know that?"

I shake my head. A few days earlier I'd cut out some small pieces of card on it, my scalpel had slipped, made a tiny nick in the wood.

You place the board in front of me. "You've taken off the top layer."

"I tried to sand it down."

"It looks like shit." Flipping open the kitchen bin you drop the breadboard into it. "You're going to trash the place within a year."

"I'll be more careful."

Your voice is gentle, fake sorrowful, "The thing is, when you're on your own personal roller coaster nothing else matters. You're not capable of being careful."

"I cared about the garden and you destroyed it."

Big sigh. "The garden's gone. In the past. I reiterate, it was always my garden. Okay. Come on, I want to show you something."

"What exactly?" I don't move.

"The loft room."

"What loft room?"

You hold out your hand. "Trust me. Please, I'm trying to help us both."

I don't take your hand but I follow you into the hall as you take the house keys from your jacket pocket. Choosing one, you hold it up, then mount the stairs two at a time.

On the landing you unlock and push open a narrow door that for all the years I've lived here, I've believed to be nothing more than a cupboard. A rather eerie flight of un-carpeted stairs ascends into darkness.

"After you, Shona."

"No, I'd rather you led the way."

"I'm not Blue Beard, you stupid cow." Your tone is almost affectionate.

There are twelve narrow steps in all with a turn on the sixth where the staircase suddenly becomes bathed in light. You lead me into a spacious room. The door swings shut behind me. I turn. After all this time I still have a problem with closed doors. You read my face, grab a chair, wedge the door open.

"Don't worry, I'll find you something better," you say. "So, what do you think of your new studio?" You are boyish Richard wanting my approval.

"It's a lovely room." The walls and pitched ceiling are painted white. There are two large dormer windows, invisible from the pavement or back garden. The only furniture is a simple table and that one chair. In the far corner is a butler's sink with draining board. "When did this happen?"

"Before your time. The decorators gave it a fresh coat of paint in the summer while you were on the beach painting."

"But why don't you use it? It's a perfect place to work."

"When I first moved in, I did imagine myself up here producing amazing illustrations that would, I don't know, re-instate my reputation. Drawing board over there, plan chest under the eaves. Some Bowie and Talking Heads prints on the wall. It looked great. I took photos at the time. Came to nothing. Embarrassing really. Finally, I went back to my laptop and the buzz of a busy studio and like-minded people kick-starting ideas. I never mentioned it because as you know, failure isn't something I like to brag about." Crossing the room, you lean on the edge of the table. "However, recently seeing you almost like the old Shona again – or should I say the young Shona?" He grins. The grin doesn't reach his eyes. "I thought you might prefer to have your own space up here. You could make as much mess as you like. Fine by me . . . up to a point. Do you think that would work?"

For once, your voice holds such sweetness as if all the crap between us has been cut away. I feel myself softening. To hide my own emotion, I walk over to the sink and run the tap. Cold, clear water gushes out. I let it run for a moment. "Yes, I think it would work. Thank you."

You remove the key from your key ring and place it on the table.

"Thank you," I say again. "It's very generous of you."

Immediately your expression changes. "You're doing me a big favour. I get my new kitchen back. Yay!" You punch the air.

What a strange creature you are. To you, everything's about scoring points where I'm concerned. You take the stairs noisily. There's a thud as you reach the landing as if you've leapt the final two steps.

Key in pocket, I sit on the chair in the doorway and consider our exchange. I always fall for the same thing: the lure of your being just – nice, pleasant, friendly. And then comes the slap back. I've worked at getting well, while you work against that ever happening. Moments like these I think you serve no good purpose. Moments like these I don't exactly wish you dead, just a painless blotting out would be sufficient.

32

Months had passed since my one and only successful visit to the Miller Building. During the hot summer I'd arrive on the beach by nine am and set myself a three-hour maximum to work. Then I'd pack up but before going home and working in the loft room, I'd call in at my usual café, sit outside with a coffee and sandwich. I never saw you and Raoul together there again, but at least once a week Mrs Gifford appeared, always as if by accident, just passing by. She wore the same absorbed expression as on that first encounter and I would half-rise to my feet and hail her. Gratifyingly her expression would soften. She'd accept the chair I'd pulled out. I'd order a pot of Earl Grey tea for her. In the café they now knew that a cup and saucer were required for my elderly friend.

We talked non-stop. There were times when her mood changed from good natured to hostile but I believed I was beginning to better understand her. Although on the surface Mrs Gifford seemed happily settled in those three rooms she and Sonny shared, her life was perilous. Unlike me with my complaints and resentments but an almost determined inability to make any changes, every day she had to be brave. The walk she made to the town and back, her battered trolley, her spirit: the more I knew of her, the more open-mouthed admiration I felt. To me, she was heroic.

I told her a little about my childhood with Dorothy. Because they'd both been single mothers, Mrs Gifford seemed to have some sympathy for her, suggesting that without a child, my mother's life might have turned out very differently. When she reiterated that, "Not everyone's cut out for motherhood," I knew she was speaking about herself as well.

I never mentioned the Kirkpatrick's. Generally, we tried to keep our conversations light, giving each other personal compliments. I believe Mrs Gifford would have preferred her compliments to come from a man, but any was better than none at all. She admired my hair. I was effusive about her grace and pleasantly musical voice. "I would recognise your voice anywhere," I said.

"It's an old woman's voice."

"Nonsense." Actually, it was an old woman's voice, croaky, tremulous – which made it so wonderfully distinctive.

I thought a lot about these encounters. I knew I was allowing affection for her to develop. Sometimes it worried me. Was I still looking for a fairy-tale ending? Good mother replacing bad mother? A couple of times Mrs Gifford had patted my hand. Once she turned my hand over on the café table and traced my heart line which ended between my middle and index finger. "You value your independence, Shona. Your actions speak louder than your words." And then she'd folded my hand between hers. "Strong hands. Not pretty but reliable."

It was her touch that affected me. Her fingertips were quite leathery, and somehow silvered. I could almost convince myself that traces of silver were left behind on my skin. I had to force myself to turn away from thoughts of her tracing out my scars. With her, I was hyper-aware, imagining the scars under her touch, quietening, becoming less sensitive, less linked to my emotions.

But as we moved into a wet autumn, I saw less of her. I didn't enjoy sitting in the café on my own staring out at a grim grey sea, pretending to sketch or read a book but really all my attention focused on the café door.

A fortnight had passed with no sign of Mrs Gifford. I imagined various explanations: it had been too wet for her to make the walk into town, Sonny was taking up all her spare time, she might even be ill. I decided to go to the Miller Building uninvited. We were friends now. Surely, she would be pleased to see me.

Following three days of good weather when it seemed that summer had returned, I set off mid-morning. There was a warm breeze but the beach was almost empty, just a few people with their dogs. I snapped photographs of driftwood, pebbles, clouds and waves. I grew so engrossed that the shelter signifying my turning inland came as a surprise. It was empty and I sat for a while contemplating the sea. But then my eyelids grew heavy. In a few seconds I'd be asleep and so I set off again. I found myself wondering why I'd found the Miller Building intimidating. That day it seemed to sprawl as if too exhausted by the unexpected sunshine to plan any wickedness.

I liked the scrunching sound my sandaled feet made on the yellowing grass, the heat on my neck and shoulders. I felt remarkably strong, rejuvenated as if I'd sloughed off Richard and Canberra Road like a hateful overcoat. I stopped, slowly turning three-hundred and sixty degrees. There was a heat haze developing: over the sea, the distant terraces. From a distance the footbridge resembled the skeleton of a dinosaur. Then came the Miller Building, behind it the rooves of Hawksbridge. I felt at peace. Quite happily I could settle down on a fallen tree branch, take out my sketch book and just draw. *Keep going, Shona.*

The change in my mood was gradual; from contentment to unease, a heightened awareness that something was wrong. I could no longer hear the repetitive whisper of the waves only a hundred yards behind me. I stopped, took off my sunglasses and listened. The only sound was a distinct aggressive buzzing coming from an area to my left. Nothing to see apart from a line of tall waving grass. Just to do something to alter the strange dynamic, I picked up a stone and hurled it in the direction of the sound. A black frenzied cloud of flies rose into the air. Horrified, yet fascinated, I waited. It took a couple of minutes before the cloud dropped and the noise lessened.

Treading carefully, I crossed the grass. I expected to find the rotting carcass of a dead animal, some discarded meat from an abattoir: even so, I was curious. The flies hovered above a long roll of filthy carpet. Taking off my cotton jacket, I used it to flap my way closer. The smell as I approached made me choke.

As I peeled back one corner of the roll, the insects went mad, flying into one another, into my face. This was no dead animal. A body lay face down. I thought I was going to be sick, but nothing came, just dry retching. I pulled the neck of my sweatshirt up over my mouth and nose. I was looking down at a youngish man, his eyes closed. He wore jeans and a checked shirt, the sleeves rolled up to just above the elbows. Had I not found him wrapped in a carpet, I could have believed he'd died of heart failure while contentedly stretched out asleep in the sun. I saw no blood, no sign of violence. The clothes, his unkempt hair reminded me of Martin, Mrs Gifford's lodger: same age, same hair colour, similar style of clothing. Whoever this was, he'd lain here for some days; the face no longer looked quite human and the smell – oh god, the smell! Actually, there was some blood, but not much. One ear lobe was split, as if an earring had been torn off. But he was thin. Horribly thin.

I'd had enough. Dropping the carpet back over the man, I took a step backwards and then another step and another. I glanced towards the Miller Building. I would swear there was a movement as someone drew back into the Giffords' living room. At that moment I had no desire to see anyone. I turned, walked away, back towards the sea.

On reaching the outskirts of Hawksbridge, I found an unvandalised phone box. Finally, I got through to the police switchboard. "There's a dead body," I said.

"Just a moment. Your name is?"

I thought of Mrs Gifford and her son, that in a matter of months they would be homeless. If the police came, the obvious place to search would be the Miller Building. The entire area would be overwhelmed.

I replaced the receiver. As I walked away the phone began to ring. I concentrated on the picture in my mind of what I'd just seen. I kept coming back to Martin. I'd seen plenty of Martins in the town. Aimless. Rushing towards nothing much. They were a type.

33

I wake struggling for breath. From your bedroom I can hear your voice. "Raoul, you fucking worthless cunt."

I look at the clock. It's just after one am. My heart must have been pounding because I'm aware the beat is slowing. Swinging my legs out of bed I stand listening at my partially open door. For a few minutes there is silence and then I hear you say, your tone defensive rather than angry, "But I've bought the tickets, the hotel's paid for," and then, "You know it's not about the money. *Please* don't let me down." Silence again. "You bastard, you fucking bastard." Almost a whisper, you're talking to yourself. Quietly I climb back into bed. Counting your footsteps as you go downstairs, I fall asleep.

In the morning, there's no sign of you. No text, no message left on the kitchen table. Your keys don't hang from the hook in the hall.

Initially the peace and utter stillness that falls over the house is wonderful. That first day as I wait for you to either ring or turn up, I keep hoping that you won't. The atmosphere doesn't feel anything like when your 'usual rules apply' hangs in the air. This feels like freedom. The second day I spend working on a new painting in the loft room. I treat the house as if it's mine, stopping for breaks, making coffees in the kitchen, putting on a jacket and despite the rain, going out to inspect your garden. For all my initial resentment I wouldn't alter a thing. I can easily imagine myself lounging on your new patio furniture, now covered for the approaching winter with black tarpaulin. I allow myself to daydream that you're dead or dying, a car accident or a confrontation with Raoul that became violent. I imagine you leaving a will, everything left to your long-term friend, the artist Shona Blake.

Nothing will ever be that simple and on the third morning I wake feeling anxious. Suddenly the house seems too quiet, almost eerily empty. If anything has happened to you surely I'd have heard by now. I remember the first time Raoul dumped you, how devastated you'd been, so unlike your usual self. In my head I re-run the words I'd overheard, the desperate note to your voice in '*please* don't let me down'. This third day is a reminder that on some tortuous level I care what happens to you because again on some level, I believe you care about what happens to me.

Most of the time, we observe a certain code of behaviour with each other; you and I connect within the house but never outside, anything that needs to be said is said face to face. I have a ten-year old basic mobile, a burner: it can phone and send texts. No internet access. In my Contacts I have only two numbers: yours and more recently you've given me Raoul's. "Just in case the roof falls in and you can't get through to me," you'd said. "Only emergencies Shona." I'm reluctant to ring you. I can predict your response, 'For Christ's sake, can't I go away for a few days without you chasing after me?' However eventually I do ring. You don't pick up, nor does your phone switch to 'answer'. I text, 'Are you okay?'

The day drags. There's no reply to my text and I can't quite bring myself to call Raoul. I'm unable to settle. Just after four in the afternoon, I pull on a coat and head off to Hawksbridge town centre. I stride along streets that are wet with sea mist my hands deep in my pockets. At the college reception desk, I ask for Richard Maplin.

The receptionist checks her screen. Brightly she says, "Richard rang in sick a couple of days ago. If you have proof of being a partner or close relative, I could give you his contact number."

"Not necessary."

She looks surprised. I've been abrupt. "Sorry," I say. "I'm a little worried about him, although I'm sure nothing's wrong. There's a tutor here he knows, Raoul?" I realise that after so many years I have no idea what Raoul's surname is, but she's smiling.

"I can help you there. He's on a week-long course in . . . Paris. Lucky man! He has classes here on Monday so he should be back by then."

"Thank you." I'm about to turn away when a thought occurs to me. "Do you know when he left?"

"He signed out from the college yesterday morning."

As I approach the house, the hall light has been switched on. I unlock the front door and step into the comfort of warmth. "Richard?" I call out.

"In the kitchen."

You're perched on one of the new chrome and leather bar stools that flank one side of the kitchen island. You look tired. There's an open bottle of red wine and a glass, two-thirds full. Also, olives in a bowl specifically crafted for olives. Gosh, haven't we become sophisticated? You're facing the doorway, ready with a greeting when I appear.

"And where have you been on this chilly afternoon?"

"Just in town." I pat my shoulder bag. "A few sketches of Christmas shoppers."

"Might I see them?"

I shake my head. "They're going in the bin."

"Fair enough. Wine?"

"Yes."

While you take another wine glass from the shelf, I hang up my coat in the hall. In the past I'd have draped it over a chair but now the chairs are some distance away in the dim gloom of the dining area. My hands tingle painfully as warmth starts to creep back into my fingers. For the first time I try out one of the stools. There is a metal bar for me to rest my feet and I'm surprised to find that really, they're okay.

You place my drink in front of me. Sit down again. Folds your arms and lean forwards as if about to impart a juicy piece of information. "So, what's with you, Shona?"

"Nothing. I did wonder though—?"

"Yes?"

"You usually let me know if you intend to be away overnight." My mouth twists. "The usual rules apply thing."

"I'm sorry. Of course, I should have called. Life got in the way."

"Did you get my text?"

"Not till this morning." You twirl your wine glass. You seem embarrassed. "You must have heard me shouting the other night. Sorry about that. Raoul and I, we were going to spend a few days in London. At the last minute he cancelled. Said he had to attend some course in Paris. He was lying. Don't know why he bothers. His lies are always pathetic." He pauses, thinking. "Probably his approximation of honesty."

"So, what did you do?"

"Went to London. Stayed at the hotel. Hooked up with someone I vaguely know."

"Would I know him? Her?"

"Him. Just passing trade. Horrible couple of days."

I want to offer sympathy but already you're moving on, talking about the courses you intend to take in the new year, about your disappointment with Hawksbridge College. I sip my wine. You gulp yours. I see again the bewildered boy in the man. It is good to remember. So often we treat each other as adversaries. I quell the impulse to reach out to you; my head nodding and bland expression are adequate.

It grows late. Neither of us have eaten. This enormous room is full of shadows. You switch off the overhead lighting, leaving one candle burning on the dining table, another in front of us. Your face is rosy from the alcohol, expression sad. There is a moment just before you get up and place your glass in the dishwasher when I think you're about to cry. You close your eyes as if they're sore, but when you open them again, I see the barrier is back.

"Can I leave you to clear up?" you ask.

"Of course."

"After you've put out the candles, once the wicks have cooled down, stand them in the sink?"

"Will do."

"No but really, Shona. Are you paying attention? I don't want you burning down the house, do I?"

"I'm not a fool, Richard."

"One can't be too careful."

"One? What are you talking about?"

You don't answer. You stretch and yawn. "See you in the morning, Shona."

34

SONNY

The bedroom on the top floor of the Miller Building has been transformed. Wax candles standing proudly in the necks of wine bottles are arranged along one wall. There's a brightly coloured rug brought up from his own room. His mother's contribution, had she known it, was the orchid that Shona gave her. He'd thought its disappearance would be noticed but so far nothing has been said. In pride of place above the bed he'd hung a print, Michelangelo's *The Creation of Adam*: God and Adam, their fingers touching, generating life.

The hardest item to manhandle up had been his full-length antique mirror. The gold plasterwork frame was incredibly heavy. For three hours while his mother slept, he'd heaved it by degrees, along the corridor and then into the lift. By the time he reached his destination, Sonny was exhausted but triumphant. Mirror leant against the wall, he'd lain on the bed laughing, his legs dangling over the side. Yet another step achieved towards a goal. The mirror is in place now. The bed has been moved a couple of feet away from the wall. There remains a vast expanse of floor between it and the mirror. He imagines he and one other dancing, play-fighting, fucking, synchronising with their reflected selves.

These weeks he's felt happier. More like the Sonny of old, the 'little show off'. Her crack about his thinning hair he's managed to stifle. Face on, there is no difference.

Physically he tells himself the passing of time has had little effect. When the Miller Building was still home for at least thirty adults and a dozen children he could remember their immediate neighbour telling him, 'Sonny, you never alter and yet you must be all of . . . '

Sonny had rested one slender finger against the neighbour's lips and said, "Hush. I choose to ignore time. Nights and days, that's all time is for me. I don't count out weeks, months or years."

"But don't you ever feel the impulse to go out into the daylight?" the man persisted. "See what's going on."

"Absolutely not," he'd said firmly. The night was a different matter. A time when younger Sonny welcomed the dark, the unnatural quiet and the importance of the smallest sound. In those years his nocturnal excursions went undisclosed. Not exactly kept secret, just not set out for public scrutiny.

He has his own dialogue memorised, hasn't varied the content in years, hasn't found the opportunity to use it in even more years. It would never have worked with Martin or someone Martin's age. But Richard?

Standing in front of the mirror, Sonny strikes a pose, one hand on hip, head half turned, thumb supporting his jawline, index finger pressed against the cheekbone, tightening the skin. "Why, nowadays Richard, I hardly recognise the seasons. Time passes in the smell of my mother's clothes. I see the rain drying on her face, feel the cold or heat emanating towards me the moment she comes in from out. It's as if my face is sinking into a cloud of lightly perfumed steam. Very intimate. Very incestuous." Pause as he pats his pale cheek, "Ah, so this is winter, this is summer. Here a change, another season passing away." And then he smiles to imply that he doesn't take himself seriously. "My mother says I should have been in the theatre. I'm a bloody little show-off!"

35

MRS GIFFORD

"My favourite winter weather," Mrs Gifford mutters as she journeys with her shopping trolley towards the shoreline. The sky is coldly blue, the sun hovers low on the horizon. There's been no rain for over a fortnight which means the ground underfoot is packed and solid. She has prepared several lists: things to do, things to buy, non-perishable party food, drink, sub-divided into alcoholic and non-alcoholic.

It's been weeks now since Richard and his friend visited. Each time she's walked into Hawksbridge, she's hoped to see one or the other. In the final years of the twentieth century (she and Sonny still think of these as the Miller Building's glory years) there was never a shortage of people to talk to. They spilled out into corridors: drinking, eating, talking laughing, singing and later who knew what went on, on the turns and twists of the badly lit staircase? Most weeks she meets Shona but that holds none of the excitement Mrs Gifford feels in the company of men. Approaching eighty, more physically vulnerable now, she finds herself painfully missing male company. She blames the rift developing between herself and her son.

The path reverts to sand and takes her uphill for several yards. After so many years her spirit still lifts in anticipation as she comes within full sight of the sea. Despite the cold, she stops, surveying the scene with approval. Oh, but she loves this particular part of the beach. To her right, the coastline curves away to become cliffs; to her left lies the promenade, cafés, the faded grandeur of the two Victorian hotels. Panning inland, the university dominates the horizon – such a bright beacon in the shabby town.

In spite of not wanting her anxiety around Sonny to spoil her improved mood, Mrs Gifford looks back over the path she's walked. The sun's rays have reached the top story of the Miller Building. At this time of year, they will travel no lower. A lemon-coloured circle is reflected in five of the six rectangles of glass. She frowns. The balcony door must be open. What should be glass is just a dull black rectangle. Suddenly as if the page of a book has been turned the sun reasserts itself. Sonny has closed the door.

A sharp breeze comes off the sea. Mrs Gifford tightens her scarf of black fake fur, pulls up the collar of her winter coat.

The square is packed: a Christmas Market set up, each stall pitched under green or scarlet awnings. A group of foreign students – all talking animatedly, push in front of her. Stepping back to let them pass, she finds herself almost crushed by the weight of shoppers eager to reach the stalls. Rather than lose her bearings she uses the trolley to forge forward. Finally, like a cough, she is expelled out onto the tree-lined perimeter. There is a bench with one small space available and Mrs Gifford lowers herself gratefully into it. Snuggling into the warmth coming from the bodies on either side, she observes the fast-moving, youthful pageant. *Young people these days look so tall and healthy as if they've been fed a diet of honey and ambrosia*. 'Ambrosia' is a word she once knew the meaning of. Not anymore. Even so she remains convinced that it is the word she wants.

Removed from the crush, she searches the young faces for someone who will remind her of her son. Knowing there are misfits everywhere, she sees not one person who matches up. Maybe like Sonny, by the time they reach their middle years, someone or some organisation has absorbed them, removed them from the public eye. The thought horrifies her. She muses on how he might have fared if she'd forced him out of their safe cocoon into an environment like this. If that morning when he'd arrived home from the new school, she'd taken him firmly by the hand and marched him back. Would it have been the equivalent of placing a Spartan baby on a hillside in winter, to thrive or die?

"This won't do," she tells herself. It is hard to turn her back on the college and the hope she might spot someone she knows, but it must be done. Stiffly, Mrs Gifford gets to her feet. Before she's taken two steps, someone slides into her vacated space on the bench. The Co-Op calls, but oh, she'd leave the ruddy shopping for another day were someone, anyone to offer her an hour's conversation over a hot drink. Reaching the supermarket hope fades.

"Just essentials," she tells herself.

Mrs Gifford is sitting in the seafront café watching the rain pour down the window. Her mind is completely blank.

"So, there you are," Shona says. "Don't we usually get the table away from the door? The usual?"

"Yes please." Mrs Gifford looks round for her trolley. With relief sees it leant against the wall.

"Been shopping?"

"Can't be arsed."

Shona blinks. "Are you okay?"

"Not sure. Tea will help."

Shona orders a pot of tea for two and a chocolate brownie which they always share.

By the time the brownie is eaten, Mrs Gifford is herself again and glad to be out of the wet. "I missed the downpour. It wasn't forecast."

"How will you get home?"

"Lord knows." She says this so comically, they both burst out laughing. "And, how are you? You look well."

"I believe I am well. I like your fur scarf."

"Cat." They laugh again. Mrs Gifford's laugh ends oddly. "You know he doesn't love me anymore."

"Who doesn't? Surely not your son. He thinks the world of you."

"He says I've made him a prisoner. I've taken away his freedom. Shona, I never meant to. I've tried to make our lives happy ones." She slumps back in her seat. "Don't have children. They only cause you grief."

"It will pass. Perhaps next year if the council re-house you?"

"He won't leave. He's made up his mind." Mrs Gifford wipes her face on her coat sleeve, leaving behind a smear of pink face powder. "Don't mind me. Better now," she says.

"Another cup?"

She shakes her head. "I'll never make it home before I need to pee."

"I can't imagine you ever squatting behind a shrub."

"I've squatted more times than I care to remember. That walk takes its toll."

The rain is lashing the café window. Mrs Gifford reaches for her trolley.

"Don't go yet. You'll be soaked," Shona says.

"I've walked in worse weather than this, my dear." She frowns. A dim memory is trying to break through. She is in the Miller Building; the curtains are slightly parted so that she can peer out of the window. There is Shona, some distance away looking up. In the background there lies a roll of pale-coloured carpet. She remembers stepping backwards, letting the curtain drop, horrified. In the distance, in her head are the words, 'Here lies.'

Shona is saying, "I could get us a cab back to my house for an hour or two. See if the rain stops."

"But *you* don't have a house. Richard owns it."

"But *I* live there. He won't mind."

Mrs Gifford seems quite serene, relaxed in her chair, as she pulls on a pair of cotton gloves. "It's time you learnt to mind your own business."

"I'm trying to help."

"That's way beyond your capabilities. Don't get up. Get yourself more cake."

She sees Shona's startled face but at that moment she couldn't care less.

Eventually after what seems as if she's travelled through one endless nightmare, she's home. Having bumped the trolley up three flights of stairs, she finds their apartment in darkness, no welcoming fire, no Sonny filling up the kettle. She feels bereft and too weary to do anything but remain upright standing in the centre of the room, using her trolley for support. She is soaked through. Far above she hears an unfamiliar sound, as if something heavy is being pulled across the floor of one of the upper apartments. Then it stops. Silence. Kicking off her wet shoes she pads into the kitchen, fills the kettle. On a shelf is her battery radio. She tunes it into the afternoon play. With much clattering she takes out crockery for their dinner later. The noise she makes drowns out the sounds resuming above.

36

SHONA

2014

The square in front of the college is already decked out for Christmas even though it's still November. From my vantage point in a window cubicle at Hawksbridge Reference Library I look down on strings of red, green and white fairy lights looped between the leafless trees while next to the fountain in the centre, Santa's Grotto is being noisily erected. On my way into town via the promenade this morning, I watched council workers as they prepared to suspend unwieldy golden angels from each lamppost. I remember how dismissive I used to be of Christmas and the festive season generally, how overwhelming I found the stacks of food, sweets and toys in every store. You and I in our capacious stylish overcoats, the buttons undone so that the material swirled around our long legs as we marched through the supermarket aisles, proclaiming everything naff. So tawdry. *We* would never be a part of this commercial pantomime. (Do you remember, we felt exactly the same way about actual pantomimes?)

I've changed my mind since then. Maybe you have too. Over the last couple of months, you've definitely mellowed, no doubt Raoul's influence. The other day you observed that I'd 'calmed down'. I think you meant it as a compliment. Richard, you've been so pre-occupied with the novelty of being a college student once again – a student in a relationship with one of the more desirable tutors – you haven't realised that for 'calmed down', read 'withdrawn'.

I return to my computer screen, securing my plait in a business-like fashion with a couple of long pins on the top of my head. It's been a couple of months since I found the young man's body; so far there's been no mention of it in the local paper but I always feel the need to check. Today is no different. There are missing persons and victims of stabbings, but no unidentified bodies discovered.

I start as someone touches my shoulder. It's the librarian. "You have half-an-hour left on this computer," she says.

"Thank you for the reminder. That's all the time I need."

Quickly I turn to the page of artists' agents. Some of the names are still familiar from when I was not only an artist but part of the artistic community. Beatrice Salmon's contact information has changed. She's moved her agency from north London to central. Common sense tells me she won't acknowledge any communication coming from Shona Blake. She's no longer married although she's kept the name Salmon. I knew that already. You mentioned it several months ago. I remember how foolishly I'd relished the news as if it would mean that Beatrice was now free to search me out again. My face turning towards you had been an open book.

"I don't think so, Shona," you drawled. "It's been years. You're not the fresh faced, new kid on the block artist anymore."

I'd hated you but I smiled, my upper lip sticking to my teeth, my mouth was that dry. "I just hope she's happy," I said.

"Of course, you do." You had that horrible knowing look in your eyes.

Whatever Beatrice thinks of me, I *will* contact her. I check out several other agents – there are at least three that might be interested in my work.

It's getting dark outside. The library lights have been switched on. The heating in here is inadequate and I shiver. I glance up at the clock. Damn, I've run over my allotted time slot but I can't resist the urge to type in 'Brian and Sheila Kirkpatrick'. Nineteen years ago, aged sixteen, I had recently been transferred from a burns unit to a psychiatric ward and waking to find a police man and woman seated each side of my bed. I hit 'search'. I'm almost a hundred percent that nothing will come up. That worst part of my history has long been erased. A Wikipedia link appears: *Brian & Sheila Kirkpatrick – the good Samaritans. Accident, suicide or murder?* Horrified, I start to read further: *The only survivor was the couple's adopted daughter Shona Kirkpatrick.* At least the author of this hadn't known my true surname.

Someone tugs hard at my hair. My head jerks up as my plait, taking on a life of its own, uncoils against my neck.

"Hi Shona." Martin is grinning down at me.

I haven't seen him since well before I discovered the young man's body. Somehow, over time, I'd begun to convince myself that had I looked more carefully, I would have realised that it was Martin. I'm not sure whether or not I'm relieved to see him.

"You're okay?" I ask. He looks healthier, less like a scarecrow than when I'd seen him on the beach during the summer. And his clothes look clean. A leather jacket is slung over one shoulder.

"Why shouldn't I be?"

"I've not seen you about."

"Did you miss me?" He grins.

I switch off the computer and begin to gather up my papers. Without looking at him, I say, "I was worried that something might have happened to you."

"Dead in a ditch?"

"Possibly." In my sketch book are a series of drawings of the dead man, each one progressively becoming more like Martin. I'm upset: the cold analytical side of my nature battling against the truth that Martin's alive and on some level, I'm really pleased to see him.

The same librarian interrupts us, pointing at the clock above the exit. "We have someone waiting for this cubicle. It really isn't fair. You've run over time before."

"I'm just going."

"Well, if you could hurry." The woman holds up her hands as if my extra fifteen minutes represent a serious threat to the running of the department.

Seeing the Wikipedia page has un-nerved me. Hurrying makes me clumsy. The paperwork takes on a life of its own, slipping from my hands and floating away at hip height. My files slide out from under my arms, but I'm incapable of action. Instead like an idiot, I just stand there, hands hanging limply.

"Oh, for goodness sake," she exclaims. "Whatever is the matter with you?"

"It's okay, Shona." Martin says. "Let me help. Did you have a bag?"

"It's under the desk," I mumble.

"There you go." Martin slides the files into my bag, loops the strap over my shoulder. He attempts to take my arm but I shrug him off.

The librarian looks as if she'd like to say more but together Martin and I make for the door. He patters down the staircase ahead of me. On the ground floor he waits while I catch up. "I'd have told the cow to fuck off but I assume you're in the library quite a bit. Wouldn't want you banned." He is grinning again.

I try to respond but still feel shaky at just seeing him so very much alive.

His eyes are questioning.

I shake my head. We step out onto the pavement.

I'm desperate to get home but I force out, "Can I buy you a coffee? Maybe something to eat?"

"I wouldn't say no."

"What would you say?" Finally, my face cracks into a smile.

"I'd say, why not?"

It is obvious he knows the centre of town far better than I do. Martin leads the way to a small café in a side street. From some distance I pick up the heavy smell of frying food and realise how hungry I am. Facing him across the chipped Formica table-top, a mug of strong tea in my hand, I start to relax. The café is hot and crowded, windows running with condensation. I order bacon baps: one for me, two for him and coffees. At first, we have little to say to each other. I'd like to ask him where he's been all summer, but I don't. It seems too personal. As he spoons sugar into his mug, I notice a white line around his wrist where his watch had been.

"What happened to your watch?"

"Left it for Sonny when I did a bunk from the Giffords'. I still see her sometimes if our paths cross here in town. I let her buy me tea and whatever." He laughs. "She always slips me a packet of fags. She's great. He's weird. Or do you think that's an act? So, everyone tolerates him?"

I shake my head. "I've never met Sonny. What's he like?"

Martin rests his chin on the heels of his hands. "He's a child in a man's body. Perfectly harmless, but annoying. He wants attention all the time. In the end I couldn't bear to be in the same room with him. I'd choose her to be my mother any day of the week. He doesn't know how lucky he is."

"I feel like that about her too. But perhaps having such a loving mother hasn't been good for the son. Asphyxiating."

He looks surprised. "I wouldn't go that far. She's seductive: not sexually – but she drew me in. Mrs G was the reason I stayed as long as I did. More a good granny I suppose."

The bacon baps arrive. He has ketchup, I have brown sauce. I was expecting the worst, but the roll and crispy bacon are delicious.

Wiping my mouth on a paper napkin I say, "I had no idea bacon tasted like this."

"Haven't you ever eaten bacon before?"

"First time."

"You've led a sheltered life, Shona." He has his head on one side as he looks at me.

"Yes."

"Don't want to talk about it?"

Lightly, I tap the side of my head with my hand. "Just can't."

"No problem." His voice is kind. His eyes look kind. I 'm used to neither. "Finished?"

"Yeah. Thanks Shona."

I pay the bill. Outside the café I'm at a loss to know how to bring the encounter to a close.

Martin solves the problem for me. "I'm going now," he says.

"Yes."

"Don't follow me."

"Why would I?"

"You wouldn't. I'm more likely to follow you."

"Please don't." I walk away. I don't look back and then as I turn into the next street, realise that I have no idea where I am. Eventually I spot the sea in the distance between two houses. *Turn right, Shona.*

I'm back thinking about the Wikipedia page. I need to read it in full. So many years later, what interest could there be in it? Reaching the house, I stop this train of thought. *Let it go, Shona.*

37

It's rare for me to go out during the evening but last night I went to an exhibition in what the Hawksbridge local paper calls the 'Artists' Quarter'. I've been to very few exhibitions in my life apart from ones where *my* work was also featured. But it was in my head that if an agent wasn't forthcoming, I could exhibit my work locally to test the water. Richard, you may well be correct in your belief that the art world has moved on in the decade I'd been out of it but perhaps now is the time for me to find out.

The exhibition wasn't in a gallery, only a large room above a restaurant. The space was packed. Initially daunted I worked my way around the perimeter concentrating on the artwork, trying not to let myself be affected by the noisy, confident crowd. I found myself wishing that you were with me. In the old days we would have enjoyed quietly demolishing each artist's painting because the work *was* bad. As I was about to slip away a young woman with a clip board approached me. "Have you seen anything you liked?"

"Several pieces," I lied.

"Can I put you down on our mailing list?"

I nodded. "Shona Blake," I said.

She looked startled. "I know your work. There was a

picture in a Liverpool Art Gallery a year or so ago: a woman seated in an armchair, a glass falling from her hand. It was mesmerising."

"Was it for sale?"

"By the time I arrived, it had already sold. Fifteen thousand pounds."

So – Bea had sold the painting of Dorothy. It had held no sentimental value to her. "That's a lot of money," I said. "Three times the amount I received for painting it. Not that I'm bitter." I tried to smile.

"Would you ever consider putting perhaps a sketch into one of our exhibitions? We stage them two or three times a year. Something not out of the financial range of our clients?"

"Yes, I would." She handed me the clipboard and I wrote down my name and email address.

"Could you tell me which of the paintings you really liked this evening? The artists would be thrilled to know."

I held up my hand. "I'm so sorry but I'm running late. I'll try and visit again before the exhibition closes."

Walking home in the sharp night air, I didn't feel so bad. Beatrice Salmon was part of my past but in many ways it had been a positive interlude. I reasoned that relationships collapse. One person gets hurt. Nothing out of the ordinary. And if she had sold the painting for fifteen thousand pounds then my work was still worth money. That thought heartened me.

Letting myself into the house, I heard voices.

"Shona, join us," you called out.

You and Raoul were lounging at the dining table over a mess of food and drink. You haven't smoked in years but an overflowing ashtray was next to your plate. Even though it was a chilly night the bi-fold doors stood open. The only light in the room came from the lamps outside on the terrace.

You got to your feet, crossing the room towards me. "Shona, you don't have to join us but we'd be very grateful if you did, wouldn't we Raoul? I had no idea Raoul was staying to dinner otherwise I would have texted you." You reached for my hand. "May I?"

I nod. Let you lead me to the table. Raoul pulled out a chair for me. Like some invalid I allowed myself to be lowered onto it.

"Wine or tea, Shona?" Raoul's voice was as elegant as his face and body.

"Tea please."

"I think I'll join you. More wine Richard?"

Richard hesitated but then reached for the wine bottle. "No way am I drinking tea at my first ever dinner party since the renovations."

Over the years I've built up my own idea of Raoul. That first sighting in the London wine bar, outside the café, on the beach, I'd observed him with an artist's eye. It is easy to understand why you remained besotted because Raoul is a beautiful creature. Whatever you claim, Raoul had been in the house before. Moving with grace between cupboards and drawers he knew exactly where everything was kept. I glanced across at you. Your eyes were fixed on your lover. Reluctantly they moved to me and you smiled and shrugged expressively as if saying, *what can I do, I love the man.*

It occurred to me that Raoul possessed a quality of remoteness that you once saw in me. You will never properly know us, know what we are capable of or what we will do next. However, I am captive, Raoul remains free. I think I say that with no bitterness.

Raoul placed one of our rarely used bone-china mugs in front of me. "You don't take sugar, do you?"

I shook my head.

"I thought not." He beamed down at me as if delighted. "Shona, you make me think of a Saluki. I had one once but she was unhappy. It was when I was a waiter, out all hours. She was thin and sleek and gentle."

"What happened to her?"

"Nothing awful. She went to a friend who had a house surrounded by fields outside London. She missed me at first. Salukis are very loyal but eventually she enjoyed a happy life. Far more freedom than anything I could offer."

"So, Shona, how do you like being compared to a Saluki? I'd be rather pleased."

"Richard, you are an Alsatian. Also very loyal. Very loving." Raoul placed his hand on your shoulder before kissing the crown of your head.

They talked on as if I wasn't there. I didn't mind. I tuned out. Their voices became a pleasant background noise to my own thoughts. I felt tired but not quite ready to confine myself to the quiet of my bedroom. In fact – like a Saluki – I could happily have crawled under the table and slept. This is one of the few things I miss about being in hospital, having noise around me during the night, unbearable at first but gradually it became necessary – a comforting awareness that I wasn't alone.

"I find them fascinating," Richard's words were slurred. "Trust me Raoul, when I'm there on Christmas Eve, I'll mention the idea."

Like a dog aware of the scent of food, I was suddenly wide awake.

"Don't get involved."

"I'm interested in the project not the people. The

mother's ga-ga and the son's possibly a psychopath." As if you'd said something very amusing, you started to laugh.

"Where will you be on Christmas Eve?" I asked.

You slapped your forehead. "Oh fuck, get me out of this, Raoul."

"You're on your own, mate, but Shona might like to know."

"What might I like to know?"

Only one cigarette dropped out of the packet as you upend it onto the table. "It's a long story," you said. "Some time ago-,"

"Weeks, months?"

"Couple of months?" You looked at Raoul. He had nothing to add.

"We met your pal Mrs Gifford's son in town. Long story short, he was in a bit of a state and we dropped him home."

"Is that it?"

"A while later we checked up on him. He's weird." To Raoul, Richard said, "He's weird, isn't he? There's a problem somewhere."

"I'm not sure."

"Long story short-,"

"You're repeating yourself."

"Well Shona, I am sorry. Didn't know I was being interrogated."

"Oh, I think you did."

"Okay. Due to my interest in the architecture and history of the Miller Building, we called in. You were intrigued, weren't you Raoul?"

"Not really. The building is incredibly ugly. Arts and Crafts meets Modernism – I don't think so."

"Yeah, yeah, yeah, you're the tutor."

"I'm more than that." Raoul pushed his mug of tea away and reached for the wine bottle.

"Don't you start as well." Richard turned back to me. "We didn't get a chance to look around the interior but your friend Mrs G. asked us to some party they're having on Christmas Eve. She told Raoul that you'd be going but I've put off mentioning it, well, because I didn't want a row. I imagined you might think I was encroaching on your friendship with the old lady. I definitely don't want to make friends with either of them. I'm all about a forgotten building that was amazing in its day, the Giffords represent MY way in. End of story."

"I wish you'd told me at the time." But really, I didn't wish for that. It would have been no easier to hear or bear. I'd tried not to think of Mrs Gifford's hostility towards me on the last occasion we met, but now I'm wondering, had she made up her mind to choose Richard and Raoul over me? Why wouldn't she?

"I'm sorry but I can never be sure how you'll respond," you said.

Oh, how I hated you. I sipped what's left of the tea before turning to Raoul, "So, did you enjoy Paris?"

He looked surprised. "That was a few weeks ago now, but yes I did."

"Richard missed you."

"Did you miss me, Richard?"

"Of course."

"Don't worry Raoul. He amused himself while you were away."

Raoul pulled a face. "I thought you were miserable – read books and went to bed early?"

"Shona's trying to make trouble."

"Of course, I'm not. I assumed Raoul knew."

"Knew what?" Raoul was staring directly into Richard's face.

"That I went to London, stayed at the hotel and slept with someone else. Satisfied Shona?"

"It's nothing to do with me."

"Then why open your ugly mouth?" Hand raised he lunged across the table towards me.

My head jerked back to avoid a blow.

Instead with the back of his hand he sent my tea mug flying, brown liquid splattering across the pristine white wall.

38

SHONA

1995

Shona drops a chamomile tea bag into a mug. It is late at night, already her sixteenth birthday and moonlight floods the kitchen. She's changed into pyjamas and fluffy slipper-socks. She places her school bag on a kitchen stool before switching on the kettle. All perfectly normal in the unlikely event that Brian or Sheila will come down to check on her. With care she removes the wine bottles from her schoolbag and decants some of the white spirit into Sheila's plastic plant spray. From the sink, she retrieves Brian's heavy glass ashtray. Every evening he leaves it there, full of ash and cigarette butts till the morning. 'For safety's sake. Call me neurotic' so often she's heard him say.

The kettle boils. She makes her tea and carries mug, spray and ashtray into the living room, quietly closing the door. Brian's ashtray is returned to its daytime place on the occasional table next to his side of the sofa. Without pausing she switches on a side lamp and begin systematically to spray the sofa, two armchairs, the curtains at the bay window and the patio door frame.

There is no turning back.

From the log basket next to the open fire she retrieves the packet of firelighters. On the coffee table, she spreads out Brian's discarded Evening Standard newspaper. There is a photograph of John Major who has resigned as leader of the Conservative Party. He has a bland, unthreatening face. It is now twelve minutes past one. Brian's alarm is set for seven. She has plenty of time. She tears the newspaper pages into strips: John Major divides raggedly down the middle. Some of the strips are wound around firelighters; others are left on the coffee table. At strategic intervals firelighters are positioned: under rugs, between the venetian blinds, tucked down between the sofa and armchair cushions. The remaining waxy crumbs are scattered on the floor as if feeding pigeons in a park. From the second bottle of white spirit, a trail is dribbled, beginning at the patio doors and out into the hall. The smell is now overpowering. She needs to work faster. The dregs of the bottle are emptied over the lower stairs.

All that remains is to light the fire. She'd assumed there were matches. Would have sworn on oath that there was always a box of Swan Vesta matches on the mantelpiece. That Swan Vesta box proves a figment of her imagination. To light the logs in the fireplace, Brian uses his cigarette lighter, which will be upstairs in his jacket pocket. For the first time she feels something close to fear. Any moment now, like two innocent tussle-headed children, Brian and Sheila will emerge from their bedroom to investigate the smell infiltrating their dreams. They will see Shona's handiwork and every last shred of affection and hope that she's worked to build behind their eyes will change to horror.

Her demons rescue her. "The workshop, Shona. Hurry!"

Stepping out onto the patio, a peal of birdsong breaks the silence. She holds her breath, praying that the cry won't be taken up. Not a sound, not even the subdued murmur of traffic and she's in luck. On Brian's workbench she finds an old tin box, years ago a container for Oxo cubes. The scratched logo is still visible on the lid. He's kept it as a receptacle to store screws, nails and rawl plugs. Inside, is the box of imagined Swan Vesta: at least two dozen matches and a cheap plastic lighter. She flicks the lighter. A small blue flame appears. Hurrying back across the lawn, her heart is thundering loud enough to wake the living and the dead.

Picking up a strip of paper from the heap on the coffee table she lights it, lets it float down to the carpet. Happy Birthday, Shona! Not so happy: the tiny yellow flames vanish. She ignites the fire-lighters between the blinds, slides wads of newspaper into curtain hems. Lights them. Nothing but smoke. Starting to panic, Shona tosses random lit matches. They singe her fingertips. Suddenly, at her back, she's aware of heat. There is that indescribable sound of burning as the fire takes over. Fascinated she watches the flames, only a few inches high, start to consume the curtains.

The white spirit on the hall carpet catches – so fast she's forced to leap backwards as they begin to lick their way along the flammable zig-zag path. In her right foot she feels a stinging pain. The idiotic slipper sock is smouldering. Ripping both off, she tosses them onto the stairs. Oh, how the flames love them. Her eyes are streaming. She's beginning to choke. She's failed to factor in smoke inhalation. To her left comes a furious roar. Hand covering mouth and nose she stops for a moment to observe her handiwork before tossing the empty box of matches and lighter into the fire working its way up the stairs. Above her head, the lampshade is alight. Suddenly, the entire fitment explodes. Her shoulders and arms are pierced by shards of burning glass.

Footsteps are hurrying across the landing.

"Shona," a voice calls out. It is impossible to tell if it belongs to Sheila or Brian.

Throwing open the back door, she runs out of the house. A strange moaning sound is coming from her mouth. She looks up at her bedroom window. There is Brian backlit by dancing orange light. As he sees her there is a look of relief on his face that has nothing to do with happiness. She imagines him calling back over his shoulder, "Don't worry darling. Shona is safe. She got out in time."

He tries to open the window, but the catch he's tried so many times to fix for her still sticks.

At that point, Shona begins to unravel. "Smash the window, Dad," she shouts. She's never called him 'Dad' before. "Dad, smash the fucking window. Please."

He gives her such a rueful look, almost apologetic. Then he raises his hand, a wave goodbye before turning away and disappearing into the burning house. Her face is soaked with tears as she fights to hang on to some self-control. Surely, at any moment, he and she, Brian and Sheila, Mum and Dad, will somehow erupt laughing with relief from the house. They will be dressed in summer clothes and ready to take her . . . on a picnic, to a park, to the zoo. But Shona had done too good a job.

In agony from the burns on arms and shoulders, she staggers over the pebble driveway. To keep her balance, she presses the palm of one hand against the side wall, feeling the burning heat and a deep vibration. Out on the pavement, people have gathered, their night clothes covered by coats and dressing gowns. Someone throws a blanket over her shoulders. She screams with pain as the material touches her burnt skin.

They sit her on a neighbouring wall. She can still feel the heat of the flames on the side of her face.

"Poor mite," a woman says.

39

MARTIN

'Oh, but it's fucking cold.' Martin pulls the sleeves of his sweatshirt down over his hands.

With Christmas only weeks away a Salvation Army band has assembled in front of the central fountain, transforming 'Away in a manger' from a gentle lullaby into a rousing march. People, entertained, are dropping money into the scarlet buckets. Mrs Gifford has stopped to listen. Martin picks her out immediately. There is something in the upright way she holds her body that makes her eye-catching. In his sentimental alcoholic state, he sees her as the saintly spirit of Christmas past.

He's with a group of men gathered outside their preferred off-license: a shop that opens early, closes late seven days a week. It is on the other side of the square to the library. When it rains, the men decamp to shelter in the library's wide doorway. Providing they are courteous to the library users, they're rarely moved on. At night, once the building closes, some of them sleep there. Not Martin. The doorway is an 'elite abode' – that's what the regulars call it. "We've put in the time, mate," they tell him.

Martin is the youngest rough sleeper by at least twenty years. The men make a fuss of him; they look out for him when they're able. Once again, Martin seems to have landed on his feet. He is the object of some affection; there is camaraderie up to a point. Each man has his limit. Later on in the day they are all less friendly. As night falls it's everyone for themselves. He doesn't mind. There is something about the impermanence of this life that suits him. Only the extreme cold (the leather jacket he wore when he'd bumped into Shona is long gone) he finds hard to handle.

Over his can of lager, he continues to watch Mrs Gifford considering the possibility of asking her for money. He can't quite bring himself to do it. In the past, she's always been generous but she wants to talk and talk. He'd love her coat, even that tatty piece of fur around her neck.

As if sensing his interest, she turns to look straight at him. Frowning, she puts her head on one side.

'She can't place me,' he thinks.

The band starts to play 'God rest you merry gentlemen'. Her face breaks into a smile and she's back with the music.

"Do you know her?" One of the men asks.

"A little. Last winter I stayed with her and her son. They live in that big old building near the footbridge."

The man nods. "The Miller Building. I used to live there in the 1980s. I remember her. She was middle-aged but always looked amazing. Sometimes she came to the parties. After a couple of drinks, she'd start dancing. She could still do the splits and high kick. Kicked my hat right off my head one night. When her foot came up towards my face, I thought, Christ Almighty, I'm going to lose an eye. She was great – old now though. Aren't we all? Well not you. The son was a pain IN THE ARSE."

"In what way?"

"Always weird. Bit Bowie-esque, although he wouldn't have had a clue about Bowie. Lived in a dream world. Thought he was the dog's fucking breakfast. How was he when you stayed there?"

"The same. Looks young still. Creeped me out."

Someone shouts, "Wetherspoons?" Everyone starts to move off. Martin lets them go. He'll catch up later. Two men have stopped to speak to Mrs Gifford. They belong to the college. Martin's seen them several times in the square. During the summer on the beach one of them gave him money. The other, Richard, he knows a little better. Both wear leather gloves, expensive winter coats. He sees a flash of a scarlet lining. A friendly smile on his face, he starts to walk towards them. Too late. They've each taken one of Mrs Gifford's hands, tucking it under their arms. The three of them, Mrs Gifford, face radiant, feet barely touching the ground, walk right past him. He is invisible.

"Perhaps a sweet sherry, Irene?" Richard asks.

"That would be lovely."

Much later in Wetherspoons, sprawled on banquette seating in front of a table full of glasses and greasy plates, an idea occurs to him. It's prompted by the log fire blazing on the other side of the bar. He can feel the heat. It's making him pleasantly sleepy. He's reminded of that first night in the Miller Building when his expectations had been so low; Mrs Gifford, as if on a magical journey leading him out of the freezing cold into all-encompassing warmth, a fire in the grate, food, drink and a clean bed for the night. He made up his mind. He'd go soon. Maybe not wait till Christmas. She'd find him a coat, feed him, fill him up. He could manage Sonny. This time he'd know when to leave. Martin is almost asleep. "I'll go soon," he mutters.

40

SHONA

2014

As I enter the kitchen, you're making toast. The pleasant smell has drifted out into the hall. This is the first morning in the days that have passed since Raoul was here for dinner that you haven't left the house before I've come down.

"Want some?" you say, indicating the toaster.

"A couple of slices please."

I sit at the breakfast bar. I far prefer this part of the room to what I suppose could be called 'the dining area' although I may feel differently when spring comes and the doors can be left open. From the cupboard you take out a clean plate and a knife from the draining board. You drop two slices of bread into the toaster and push the tub of butter nearer to me. The toast pops up.

"There you go, Shona. Jam, marmalade, Marmite?"

I shake my head.

"Coffee? Tea?"

I smile up at you. "I'm good."

You raise your eyebrows but say nothing, picking up a

piece of your own toast and walking across the room to look out over the terrace. I spread the butter thinly regretting saying no to marmalade.

"So, how's the painting going?" you call back over your shoulder.

"Fine."

Earlier in the year, inspired by my first sighting of the Miller Building, I'd begun preliminary drawings of a black cube. In each succeeding painting the cube lightened in colour and density, from carbon finally moving into bright leaf green. Within the cubes, tiny images emerge: Mrs Gifford's plastic sandals, her wayward linen carrier bag. From the top floor balcony drifts a murmuration of tiny birds. The most recent painting is very different: the imagined child who became Mrs Gifford, squatting on pebbles, thin hand dipped into a rock pool, the building in the background, a malevolent presence that due to some quirk of emotion, watches over her.

"Ready to show me?"

"No point really. You never seem to like my work."

"I'm harsh but fair." You grin at me. "Waiting till Beatrice Salmon gives you the nod ... or the thumbs down?"

For a fraction of a second, I hesitate. It's as if you've read my mind or at least seen my list of possible agents. "Maybe."

"Only funnily enough, she rang me a few days ago." You take a bite of toast and turn towards me.

Something unpleasant is coming. I'd been a fool to think I'd got away with embarrassing you in front of Raoul. "Don't Richard," I say gently.

"Don't what?"

"I don't want to hear anything negative." I stand up. "I think I will have a coffee. No, I'll make my own." I switch on the electric kettle. My shoulders are so tense they ache.

"Please yourself." You take one of the bar stools. "To continue. You do want me to continue, don't you?"

"Go on."

"She called me on my mobile while I was at college. I was surprised she had my number, probably got it from one of my mates in London. She asked how you were."

"And?"

"I told her your mental health has greatly improved. I've got that right, haven't I?"

"Yes."

"Do you want to know what else she said?"

"Of course."

"Then could you at least do me the courtesy of sitting down when I'm attempting to have a conversation with you."

"I don't want to sit down."

Through gritted teeth you say, "Then just stand still! Honestly Shona, everything's such hard work where you're concerned." You take a vicious bite of your toast. More calmly you say, "She wondered if you'd started painting again. I said, yes, you seem to be working most days. I told her I'd turned my loft room into a studio for you-,"

"It was already a studio. You did that for yourself."

You sigh. "But then I made the space available for you to use undisturbed."

"Okay."

"She wanted to know what I thought of the work you were doing these days, whether it had suffered due to your erm . . . breakdown."

"How did she know I'd had a breakdown?"

"No idea. Anyway, I told her your work was still fucking brilliant. Although maybe I should have said, 'Actually *Beatrice* I'm not sure what her mental health is like, but I find Shona disturbingly secretive and so far, haven't seen a single painting. Which would be closer to the truth but not much help to you."

"In what way am I 'disturbingly secretive'?" I fold my arms across my chest and then unfold them. I will not adopt a defensive position.

"I don't think I'm imagining it. In the past you valued my opinion. You used to show me your stuff. That doesn't happen anymore."

"If you want to see what I'm doing in your loft room, I can hardly stop you."

"That isn't the same as asking me for feedback. I've earned shedloads of money from *my work*. Won major industry awards. I'm a known name."

I can't resist. "One Wikipedia page doesn't make you anything very much."

At that you rear back as if I've sucker-punched you. "You fucking miserable cow. I was trying to help."

"And I thanked you. I've thanked you constantly for everything you've done for me." I head for the doorway.

"You've not finished your toast."

"I've had enough."

"I thought you'd be pleased to hear your ex-agent had phoned and I'd given her positive feedback." Your tone has changed to plaintive.

I'm alert now. At long last I've learnt that any olive branch is followed by a renewed attack. "Actually, I am pleased. Amazed as well, that Beatrice Salmon would still be interested in me."

You too are on your feet. You've come around the table and stand between me and the door, your chin jutting pugnaciously. "You've been out of the game for so long, there's no way the quality of your work, even your perceptions, haven't been affected." Because you know you've overplayed your hand, you produce a sort of embarrassed snigger.

I straighten my back. "Are you still so jealous of me?"

"You must be joking! Why would I be jealous of you? You're a failure, a loser. A fucking wreck in every way it's possible to be a wreck. Perhaps I should ring Beatrice Salmon back and give her my honest opinion."

"Go ahead." My eyes look steadily into yours.

The expression on your face is chilling. You move towards me. I step back, my hip banging against the corner of the table. I have no idea what you intend to do. And then your shoulders slump. "It's not worth it, is it, Shona? You're immune to slaps, cigarette burns, insults. It's affection you can't deal with."

41

Laid out on my bed is my burner phone and a list of artists' agents. Right at the top are Beatrice Salmon's details. Common sense tells me she's the last person I should contact. I not only had a work relationship with the woman, there was a personal one as well and she ended both with no kindness, no explanation. But she has kept in touch with Richard, checked up on me, even sold a piece of my work in the last year, that surely means something. I pick up my phone, my heart thundering, make the call.

After the third ring, a remembered female voice answers, "The Beatrice Salmon Agency. Joan Vigo speaking."

I disconnect. So, Joan Vigo is still with the agency. I remember her chilly phone calls to check up on the progress of my work years earlier. She would have been with Bea when I was cut adrift. She'd be aware of whatever sin Bea had found me guilty of.

An hour later I phone again. This time I have my response ready. "I'd like to speak to Beatrice, please."

"And you are?" There is a no-nonsense tone to her voice as if she's used to fielding calls from aspirational artists.

"Shona Blake."

"Ye-es?" she prompts.

"You probably don't remember but Beatrice represented my work several years ago. I wondered if, actually I have some new paintings."

She is still on the line, I can hear her quiet breaths before briskly she says, "Ms Salmon isn't in the office at the moment. I'll let her know you called."

"I've been ill for quite some time, but I'm fully recovered." *Oh god, shoot me now. Why ever did I say that?*

"And your email address is?"

"It's still the same one."

"We no longer have it on file."

I stammer out the address. "Or you can text me on this number."

She rings off. Over the following week, I visit the library to check my email account on a daily basis, phone three more times in the hope that Beatrice will answer. Always Joan Vigo, her tone of voice never alters as she keeps our exchanges to a minimum. *Ms Salmon is in the north of England for a few days, at a conference, out with a client.* My imagination takes flight: Beatrice and Joan have become a power couple, Beatrice finding the artists and buyers, Joan fielding calls and organising their power-couple's social events. She sounds far more suited to Beatrice than I ever was.

This first foray into the world outside Hawksbridge unnerves me. I fail to contact the other names on my list. I grow smaller as the world becomes bigger. I'm ill-equipped, have made little progress in how to be a successful human being in the twenty-first century.

And then, on what I swear to myself will be my very last call before I make a start on the other agents, Joan Vigo appears to soften. "Look Shona," she says. (This is the first time she's used my name.) "Take photographs, email the images."

"I don't have a camera."

I've irritated her, she snaps, "Then borrow one. Surely your mobile takes pictures?"

"Yes, of course it does," I lie. "Good idea. I should have thought—"

The line is dead. I don't care. I feel like a determined spy or burglar, as if I've found space for my fingertips to ease open an outside window leading in to Beatrice.

Richard has a digital Pentax camera that he's never used. It's in a cupboard in his front room, along with at least a dozen other defunct devices. He'll never know it's missing. I carry it up to the loft room. Learning how the camera works occupies most of the afternoon but at last I'm satisfied with the images. The process makes me feel quite emotional. As if the paintings are by someone else, and what that artist has to say resonates. Task completed, I sit quietly, hands folded in my lap. It is late afternoon but already dark. The house is silent apart from the faint hum of the central heating. There is no one to say, "Well done, Shona," so I say it to myself, over and over as a soothing mantra.

Downstairs I hear Richard's key in the front door lock. His footsteps in the hall, his shout of, "Shona, it's bloody pitch dark down here!"

He sounds exasperated, but not angry.

The next morning, I book an hour at the library. The email to Beatrice Salmon is written, the images attached, I hit 'Send'.

42

Over the days following my email to Beatrice, hope has slowly faded. I've ceased daydreaming that Joan Vigo welcomed my ex-agent and lover back from some European ART festival with the news that quite startling work had arrived from the artist Shona Blake. I tell myself that given our history, Beatrice would be unwilling to appear too eager. She will wait till the weekend, till the Monday following the weekend or the weekend after that. Or I won't hear from her ever again, not even a terse, 'Sorry, this isn't for us.'

Richard is out most evenings with Christmas parties, Christmas drinks. He and Raoul attended a carol service and Richard came in full of it.

"I sang my heart out, Shona. Amazingly once I got going my voice was pretty good!"

I wanted to yell, *So what? Who cares? Big fucking deal!* But hey, where was my festive spirit?

For the time being I've lost all interest in painting. It takes all my time to get out of bed each morning. I force myself into Hawksbridge, check my emails at the library, I've met Mrs Gifford just once to help her with shopping. Like Richard, she seems happy, looking forward to her festive *soirée*. I told her that I knew that Richard and Raoul had visited the Miller Building. This released a floodgate: how wonderful they both were, how kind, thoughtful, generous, handsome. I asked how Sonny felt about the two of them.

"Oh, he loved them both but he's taken a real shine to Richard." A frown passed across her face. "Nothing sexual, Shona."

Stiffly I answered, "I believe Richard and Raoul are a couple but there's always room for friendships." What a meaningless sentence that was, but it seemed as if everyone is having a good time except me. My happiness lies in the hands of a woman who has rejected me in the past. In the loft room, once again I've turned the paintings to face the wall.

It is freezing cold today. Sky an iron grey. Before leaving this morning, Richard turns the central heating down to eighteen degrees centigrade. To warm myself up, I walk to the seafront, have a coffee in the café. No sign of Mrs Gifford. I'm relieved. I've had enough of hearing about the wonder of Richard Christopher Maplin.

On to the town centre. My lowest point comes as I stand in Waterstones looking at their display of Christmas cards. Not all, but many of the images are beautiful, the sort of card you'd send to someone you loved or valued. And then it strikes me that there is no one in the whole wide world I love or value. Not a single soul. Not you, Richard, nor you, Mrs Gifford. Definitely not you, Beatrice Salmon. If Dorothy were still alive, I might have bought her one of these cards. She's done no worse to me than I've done to others. She too has been a victim. I don't remember ever shedding real tears before but today in the bookshop, I actually cry. I think of those six years I spent with Brian and Sheila and how they'd loved me. No strings attached. They'd found something in Shona that was loveable. At fifteen I'd rejected their love; twenty years later, I yearn for it. I think of Mrs Gifford's words a few days before, assuring me, "Nothing sexual, Shona." I've never met Sonny but it seems we might share common ground. Someone please, I'll take affection. Affection will serve me for now.

"Fucking hell, Shona, this won't do." I feel a sharp tug at my hair. I drop the handful of cards I'm holding.

It's Martin. I'm pleased to see him again. "Martin, I wish you'd leave my hair alone." I'm laughing and crying still.

"Yeah, yeah, yeah," he says, picking up the cards, looking round quickly before slipping them into his grubby canvas shoulder bag.

On a couple of occasions, since bumping into Martin in the library, I've spotted him in town but never to speak to. Each time I've felt that same sense of relief that he's alive. I can't quite get out of my head a link between him and the dead man I discovered. Once he passed quite close to me, gaze fixed on something at the other side of the square. I'd looked where he was looking. There was nobody, just a wide well-lit alleyway – nothing sinister. Both shoelaces of his trainers had been undone. I'd wondered if that were some fashion statement I knew nothing about. But the laces were filthy as if they'd trailed in mud for days. Martin doesn't seem to walk, he skates forward, all his weight on the ball and toes of his feet. He'd seemed totally caught up in a world of his own. No coat, just a sweatshirt and it was freezing. I'd considered looking in Richard's wardrobes for something rarely worn that he wouldn't miss. But I knew Martin would hate anything Richard had.

"Lunch? You buy," he says cheekily.

I follow him up the store escalator to the cafeteria.

Settled at a table, all he says with reference to my tears is, "It's not a good time of year for us."

Once I would have chosen not to be linked with someone like Martin. Not anymore. We eat sandwiches, then cake, drink Coke and talk till the staff begin closing up. I've never trusted anyone enough to allow myself to speak about my childhood but I tell him about Lynda Wilson and the noose, and how her shoes started to waggle and I knew she wasn't dead. That my adoptive parents, Sheila and Brian had known it wasn't a childish game yet still they continued to love me for another six years. That there is something about Mrs Gifford, her unconditional love for her son that reminds me of both of them.

"What happened at the end of the six years?"

I close up then. "Oh, by then they'd finally had enough of me. Don't blame them really."

Back out on the pavement I'm tempted to offer him *my* coat. Canberra Road is only fifteen minutes away whereas Martin might end up spending the night in a shop doorway. I hesitate and then it's too late. He pinches my nose. "See you," he says. I watch him zig-zag across the square, cutting around groups, startling shoppers with the intensity of his movements. A group of men are waiting for him. I hear one of them say, "Your bird?" Martin has his back to me so I can't hear his reply. But nobody laughs. Instead, he is welcomed, like a son.

43

SHONA

1995/6

While in hospital recovering from burns to my arms and shoulders, the same two policemen interviewed me many times. Invariably I answered their questions with one of my own: Why didn't Brian smash the window?

And they'd say, "Shona, what do you think? What's your take on his reaction?"

And I'd answer, "I don't know."

Not impossible for them to escape. The bedrooms were all on the first floor. The windows: plain glass, no double-glazing. He could have used the bedside table, or the lamp to break the pane. I'd imagined Brian helping Sheila onto the window ledge. "Don't worry. I've got you, darling." Holding her by the wrists he'd lower her down. What would the drop have been? Four metres? Five? Sheila's feet dangling with only a meagre distance to fall. They'd had time to think, to make a plan.

"Shona, were your parents regularly heavy drinkers?"

"Shona, we can imagine your mum or dad – a bit worse

for wear – leaving a smouldering cigarette, say on the coffee table? Were they having problems? Arguments? There was an orderliness to the path of the fire, as if the conflagration had been planned."

"Shona, neighbours said your house was in darkness by ten pm. The fire started two hours later – your thoughts?"

And I'd give them my lost and vulnerable look and ask, "But why didn't Brian smash the window?" There were times when I'd have loved to add, 'Your thoughts? Any ideas?'

My repetitious answers, my background, my fragility eventually had a powerful effect on the interrogators. Their objectivity became compromised. Both were parents. I sensed the change in the tone of their voices when they started seriously looking for answers rather than evidence.

It would have been so easy for the newspapers to take up the story. Just under two decades earlier the film *Carrie* had been a major success. Carrie White, a young woman whose telekinetic powers enabled her to set the school gym alight and burn to death the students who mocked and bullied her, was still referred to in cases of arson. Had it been a different time I might have made front page headlines: *Is Shona Kirkpatrick a Carrie-Copy-Killer?*

But the murderers Fred and Rose West were dominating the news; a fire in a suburban home and two deaths by comparison were insignificant. There was one mention in the *Daily Mail* but it didn't make the front pages and my name was withheld.

While in hospital I stopped talking. This was diagnosed as 'selective mutism' caused by the trauma I'd undergone. I looked pitiable, for a long time the burns I'd suffered were a cause for concern. When finally, much later, I was able to produce the words, "Could I have a glass of water?" the female nurse had been astonished. "Did you say something, Shona?" she'd asked.

"Could I have a glass of water?"

"Of course, you can." The nurse poured water from a jug into a paper cup and handed it to me; I'd wanted to reach out and touch her hand more than to drink the water. That was a milestone in my life: the first time I'd ever sought to touch or be touched.

I was transferred for assessment to yet another hospital where I was initially diagnosed with schizophrenia. While in the psychiatric ward, the nurses encouraged me to draw and paint. One afternoon, the art teacher took me aside. 'You have an aptitude," she said. "You could take this further in the future. Get some office skills but think about trying for college.' I'd looked up the word, aptitude: a natural ability to do something.

There followed a year of skin grafts and therapy. Once well enough, I walked in the hospital grounds, talked a little, thought a little, spent an hour most days with a psychiatrist. In all that time, I never admitted starting the fire. The hospital staff came to like me, although had the police ever thought to have asked their opinion I believe all would have agreed that 'yes – for whatever reason – we believe Shona may have started the fire'.

Just before my nineteenth birthday I was considered well enough to begin my journey back into the community. I'd been diagnosed as having a severe personality disorder resulting from the sadistic treatment received from my birth mother during the first years of my life. With a regimen of prescribed drugs, the condition could be controlled. All being well, as I moved further into adulthood, I would come to fully understand how to monitor my behaviour.

At this point due to insufficient evidence, the police

withdrew from their enquiries where I was concerned but the case was left open. My repeated question had eventually placed doubt in their minds. They had no satisfactory answer. Nor did I.

44

SONNY

Christmas Eve. Five o'clock. Night has already fallen. On the seventh floor of the Miller Building, Sonny is making his final arrangements. In a few days' time these rooms will become his home. It hasn't been easy but progress has been made. He'd been aware of his mother's constant scrutiny but now her focus has shifted.

The French windows are open. There's no electricity and the temperature in the room is near to freezing. A fat white candle flickers in a saucer, set on one of the two chairs. All around the room tapered candles have been squeezed into the necks of empty wine bottles. He's lit just a few to throw a pleasing light. From Martin's old room he's taken the nest of tables; from his own bedroom have come rugs. His mother's orchid – white ceramic pot, white buds, two glossy leaves – still thrives in the chilly air.

And then the bed, the beautiful bed where he'd lain with Martin just the once. If Martin could see it now, made up, pillows propped against the backboard. Over his mother's pastel-coloured bed linen, he's spread the army blanket. He sits on it now, in a half-Lotus position ensuring he doesn't lean back and crease the pillows. Within a few minutes, his head nods forwards and he sleeps, a better sleep than he's had in years. Sonny dreams of Martin but no, it's a different man that looks like Martin. He is walking towards Sonny and smiling in recognition. Sonny can hear his footsteps approaching across the scrubland. His eyes open. The sound is still audible.

He goes out onto the balcony. As a shadow steps onto the tarmac, Sonny recognises his mother's friend, Shona. From up here, he's watched her arrive and leave before.

45

SHONA

2014 Christmas Eve

As I turn inland, my torch beam flickers. A few seconds later it goes out. I shiver but not from the cold. It's easy to imagine that someone waits for me, lying on their belly in the high dry grass. I walk on. Over my shoulder I can still see some semblance of light in the sky; in front there's nothing but black, the Miller Building an even deeper black. After fifteen minutes I reach the area where I found the body so many months ago. There is no roll of carpet, no flattening of the grass. I shake my head to rid myself of fear, that the ghost of the young man might rise up behind me and lay his cold dead hand on my neck. I regret wearing a scarf. So easy for someone to take hold of both ends – pull them tight.

A few days ago, I received an email from Joan Vigo.

Hi Shona. We are interested in seeing more of your work. However, the agency is very busy at the moment. The only date we have available is Wednesday 31st of December, otherwise it would have to be towards the middle of January. Kind regards, Joan Vigo.

I read and re-read the email searching for some warmth

apart from the 'kind regards', each time taking exception to the use of 'we'. But although it's not the response I'd hoped for, it's positive. Bea wouldn't agree to see me if she doubted my ability. Even when we were together she was a businesswoman first and foremost.

I said nothing to Richard. He's wrapped up in his own world. All is not going smoothly due, I think, to Raoul and *his* inability to commit. This I've gathered from overheard phone calls, conversations which Richard makes no effort to conceal. Once or twice a week now, he's spending nights at Raoul's flat. To be honest since this house has been extended, I sometimes feel nervous there on my own. The darkness outside the bi-fold doors is impenetrable once night falls.

I increase my pace. The Miller Building is no more than fifty yards away. A pulsating glow is coming from the windows on the top storey. Fanciful but to me, tonight, the building resembles some ghostly ocean liner. I step out onto the tarmac. Up close my fears begin to fall away. In a matter of minutes Mrs Gifford will welcome me into her room. I know she will have enjoyed making it festive. I'd dreaded the journey, dreaded the entire evening, but now I'm here, I'm cheerful. Hungry too. I reach the front door. The knob turns easily in my hand and I step into the cavernous hallway. No lanterns this time; it's lit by the quivering flames of at least twenty scarlet tea-lights set in jam jars. There's a hint of warmth coming from an old-fashioned stove in one corner and I'm grudgingly accepting that the Miller Building suits Christmas. The decaying plasterwork glows a soft pink. The staircase bannisters have holly wound through them. Even in the lift an attempt has been made for it to seem festive. Another flickering jam jar. There is tinsel and a sign above the metal entrance wishing me a Merry

Christmas in scarlet gothic script. Without any qualms this time, I'm confident that the lift will support my weight. I enter the lift. This evening as the lift rises, instead of 'The Blue Danube', Bing Crosby is reminding me that *Santa Claus is coming to town.*

On the fourth floor, I step out into the corridor: more tea-lights, more jam jars. Has Mrs Gifford been collecting the jars all year? And here she is, scurrying towards me, her shadow, like the silhouette of a dancing puppet, keeping pace along one wall.

46

MARTIN

His energy levels have dipped over the summer. In the past he'd run everywhere, always trying to sustain the adrenalin rush. He's injured his ankle. Just a fall down some stone steps but Christ, it still hurts. Just getting up onto the bridge has been a problem. What resembles a tapestry of barbed wire has been fixed around both entry and exit, impossible to scale or push through. He's been forced to crawl like a spider along the side of the bridge, clinging on to the base of the handrail. Even then he'd caught his damaged leg on the wire. High above the ground he'd managed to lever himself up and roll over the rail. Not far now.

On the road below a solitary car approaches. Enviously he watches. In the passenger seat someone lights a cigarette. The car passes underneath the bridge. Martin turns to follow its direction. He frowns. The car has taken the slip road leading to the Miller Building: the wall of foliage concealing the entrance to the underground carpark is illuminated in the beam of headlights.

Martin begins the descent. He's reduced to hopping down the metal steps. Again, the barbed wire forces him to go over the handrail. He braces himself for the pain as he lands but it's not too bad, the ground is soft. In the shadow beneath the bridge he waits to see if the car emerges. Ten minutes elapse and then suddenly there's the roar of an engine. The car passes him at speed. No passenger this time. He glimpses the driver: male, face set and angry. Martin limps towards the shrubbery and silently slips through the opening into the underground carpark. A rectangle of light shows on the far wall. It's the door leading upwards to the hallway. He sees a man's silhouette. The door swings shut behind him. After a few minutes, Martin risks switching on his phone, panning the light around the walls before crossing the dirt floor. He opens the door. The air is warmer. One floor above he can hear the lift cranking upwards. And music. The Giffords are having a party! The lift stops. Someone gets out. A few seconds later he recognises Mrs Gifford's voice, too faint to make out any words. There is an unintelligible response and then the voices fade away. He steps out into the hall. The dancing tea-lights feel as if they're welcoming him back. The last month has been hard but suddenly his ankle doesn't feel quite as painful; it's no longer an impediment, a sign of weakness. Actually, he feels okay, ready to party, to hold a greasy leg of chicken in one hand, a lager can in the other.

But that's not the plan. First there are flights of stairs to climb. He can do that. And he does. More tea-lights. Far down the corridor, the Giffords' door is shut. He slips off his trainers, drops them into the only item he now owns: a plastic carrier bag containing a few filthy clothes. He's heading for his old room, the windowless store cupboard. He forces himself to silently run. The pain in his ankle instantly becomes excruciating. Face contorted in an effort not to cry out, he reaches the room. Key in lock, smoothly turning and he's inside, leaning with his back against the door. Martin doesn't believe in fate or any kind of god, but at this moment he could shout out a prayer from sheer gratitude that he's reached some sort of sanctuary. He has no idea how he'll access the food and drink next door, but he believes everything will be possible.

He feels his way towards the twin bed and almost falls forward. Again, he risks his mobile although the battery's going. Both beds are made up but have been moved together. Is this for one of the Giffords' guests? "Fuck it," he mutters. He *has* to lie down. He presses his face into the pillow. It smells wonderful. He remembers thinking that very same thing on the first night he'd slept here. He gets into bed. What is the worst that can happen? She'll never chuck him out on Christmas Eve in the middle of winter. He'll be cared for. *Don't fret, mate. Sonny will be thrilled you're back.*

Almost immediately, he's asleep.

47

SHONA

2014

"Welcome, welcome, welcome." Mrs Gifford hugs me. "Is it too early to say, 'Merry Christmas'?"

I am overwhelmed by the unfamiliar physical contact. I want to hug her back but remain stiff and awkward in her arms. "Not at all," I murmur.

She looks extraordinary. Normally her hair is pulled back into a smooth French pleat. Tonight, it hangs loose. I'm amazed to see that it's about the same length as mine, reaching more than halfway down her back. Into it she has woven green and red tinsel. In the flickering light her face looks young and smooth. I'm unnerved. I may not have intended to but in my head, Mrs Gifford has been catalogued as 'old woman with fascinating background'. I've thought of her as of the past, at most a mere few inches of life left to look forward to. There is more tinsel around her wrists. The dress she wears is black velvet, floor length, long medieval sleeves finishing at a point at the back of each hand. Her hands have always been her big give-away: they'd looked old, as if they'd experienced a hard life not always apparent in Mrs Gifford's face. I'm small-minded enough to envy her the dress. The fitted bodice and bias-cut skirt suit her slender figure. I regret my own choice of woollen trousers and fleece and shapeless overcoat. An ugly knitted scarf from a charity shop.

"You look lovely, Mrs Gifford. Wherever did your dress come from?"

"Ossie Clark," she says with some pride.

"And he – she – is?"

"Before your time, dear. 1970s. He designed wonderful clothes." Taking my hand, she pulls me forward into the room. "You're the first to arrive. What do you think, Shona? Does it look festive?"

"Everything is beautiful," I say and I mean it.

There's a smell of spices. I'm thinking fruit cake, mince pies, a festive punch – instantly I see all of that laid out on a table. Firelight dances on each facet of the crystal wine glasses and what I assume to be her best crockery; the crimson velvet curtains are a perfect backdrop. Oh, this is a beautiful room!

"My son has excelled himself. He's responsible for everything except the food."

"He's done a brilliant job," I tell her as I unbutton my coat.

She takes it from me. "I'll hang it up. And your rucksack?"

"I'll keep that if you don't mind; presents for you and Sonny."

Left alone, I study the room. Someone, surely not Sonny, has brought in branches of holly heavy with red berries. They decorate the top of each door frame and the wide mantelpiece. Silver and gold bells are pinned to the picture rails, coloured paper streamers criss-cross the ceiling. I'm ready to be charmed. Mrs Gifford's welcome has been so warm, even the thought of seeing Richard and Raoul has lost the power to hurt me.

I cross the room to the tall Christmas tree, its branches weighed down with glittering baubles. Close up I realise that the glossy pine leaves are plastic and many of the baubles broken. Some of the branches are held together with festive Sellotape. And then I notice the little naked dolls, Barbie and Ken – at least a dozen – painted gold or silver. A bigger female doll is tied with gold wire to the top of the tree. She too is naked and the colour of cinnamon. As she peers down at me, she looks like a tiny human being, making ready to attack. I shiver.

Mrs Gifford's touch on my shoulder startles me. "Nothing sinister here, Shona. We use what we can find, or rather, *I* can find. Does our tree look so very tawdry?"

I smile at her. "Ingenious," I say and we both laugh. Outside in the corridor, I hear footsteps. Mrs Gifford – mistress of ceremonies, exclaims, "And here is my boy!" Love for her son shines in her eyes.

A young man stands framed in the doorway. He's dressed simply in a white shirt and loose cotton trousers. He strikes a pose, balancing on one leg. His other foot is placed flat against his inner thigh. Although slight he has the spare muscular physique of a dancer. Theatrically, he raises his hands above his head as if in prayer.

"Namaste, Shona." His voice is high and light, hard to say whether boyish or girlish.

"Sonny, meet my dear friend Shona," Mrs Gifford says.

He almost skips towards me, takes my hand and places three light kisses across my knuckles. "Enchanted."

Close up, I see that the skin of his face is finely lined, as if covered by a pale cobweb. Whatever his age, he is maybe not a fairy-tale fawn but definitely something magical.

"Come closer to the fire Shona," Mrs Gifford urges. "You'll soon warm up. Mulled wine or cava? Or should we wait for Richard and . . . his friend?"

"Pour wine," Sonny says. "Who knows what time they'll get here."

"I'm sure they'll be punctual." Mrs Gifford looks at me. "Is Richard a good timekeeper?"

"I've no idea." My happiness is dissipating.

Sonny pulls up an enormous tapestry cushion and sinks into it. "Shona, join me."

I sit. The softness of the cushion means my body feels too close to Sonny's. I'm trying to hold myself together. Proximity is a problem I've never had the opportunities to find ways of overcoming.

Mrs Gifford hands me a pewter cup of mulled wine. I swallow it greedily. I'm hoping it will soothe me. Sonny too has a cup but he sets it aside to fold paper napkins into star shapes. Mrs Gifford remains standing. She looks impressive: wise and elegant, the epitome of grace. I catch her eye. She smiles. "It's always difficult at the start of an evening," she says. Her body stiffens. She turns towards the door.

Sonny also raises his head from his task and like a wild animal, sniffs the air. In one fluid movement he's on his feet. "They've arrived. I can hear the lift. Forgive me, Shona." And he's gone.

I scramble to my feet, carry my cup across to the table. Mrs Gifford, wiping her hands on a tea towel joins me.

"I'll give us a re-fill once everyone is settled," she says.

We wait. Finally, Mrs Gifford breaks the silence. "Shona, I may not always show it but I've appreciated your friendship this year." She pats my arm. "At my age, I'd given up hope of finding anyone I could talk to. I like your Richard very much, but men are impossible when it comes to conversation." But now she's distracted. "And here they are!" she cries out.

Richard, rubbing his hands as if for warmth although he's come by car, follows Sonny into the room. "Greetings, Mrs Gifford. I bring wine and pretzels." He turns to me. "Shona, you made it. Cab or did you walk?"

"I walked. Where's Raoul?"

"Prior engagement, I'm afraid." His good-natured social face disappears. For a second his expression is bleak. "I'll text him later and he'll pick me up. We can drop you off on our way back to his flat."

And so, the evening turned out well. My worry over walking home disappeared. Richard, although subdued, showed a kinder, funnier self. Mrs Gifford and her son immediately picked up that he was upset by Raoul's absence and they fussed over him. "More food, Richard? More wine? Come closer to the fire." By my third helping of mulled wine I felt no jealousy; I was pleased. For me it was a new experience, watching someone being comforted. I believe it was a novel experience for Richard too and timed just right for his dark mood. I'd moved from the cushion to the footstool. Richard took the cushion. Mrs Gifford, once she'd laid out the food on the table near the window, relaxed in her armchair, Sonny sat on the hearth rug, leaning back against her legs. They talked about the Miller Building when it teemed with life, how everyone had known everyone else; not necessarily liked everyone else, but the shared differences enriched their small universe. Mrs Gifford showed us another dress she'd worn twenty-five years ago.

"I won't model it," she said. "It still fits but having a face like a torn boot spoils the effect."

The dress was sleeveless, green satin, low neck, a kick-pleat at one side. We admired the dress, laughed and dismissed the 'torn boot' comment. At first Richard was quiet. I was amazed: Mrs Gifford had researched him online in the reference library. She coaxed him to talk by asking about his early successful career. He didn't brag, he spoke with regret and some finality, how a moment in time like that wouldn't happen again. I found it soothing listening to his voice, pitched low. I was dimly aware of Mrs Gifford getting up. Very gently she took my arm and somehow just eased me from the stool to a soft fur blanket on the floor.

"Just snooze, Shona," she said.

It was heaven. Perfection. To be warm. For worries to step back into the shadows. To feel utterly safe.

48

MRS GIFFORD

Shona's present lay open on her lap: a paisley shawl in shades of purple and inky blue. Seated in front of her dressing table mirror, she wrapped the shawl around her shoulders. She looked awful, like a bedraggled old witch.

Next door she heard Sonny moving about in the living room. Head on one side she listened intently. On Christmas morning would he for once make her a cup of tea? Would he rake out the grate and lay a fire? Today the cold outside had breached the walls and single-glazed windows. She recognised the squeak made by the pantry door hinges. He was looking for food, the greedy devil. There was plenty. Let him fend for himself today. Placing the shawl in the blanket box, she opened the curtains and then she remembered Shona, curled up on the fur throw, so deeply asleep that even the sound of Richard's drunken laughter had been unable to rouse her. Pulling on her dressing gown, she opened her door. The living room was empty. No Sonny, no Shona. Shona's bag and coat were gone. The fur had been folded neatly and laid across the back of the armchair. From outside in the corridor, she heard the lift gate open and then slam shut before the lift began its downward journey.

Crossing to the window she waited till Shona appeared, head bent as if struggling against a gale-force wind. What a relief. One less person to feel responsible for. The solitary log in the grate was almost burnt through. In the kitchen, she smiled. *Bless my boy.* At some point during the night Sonny had washed up and cleared everything away. By the end of the evening Richard had been drunk, garrulously so. She'd had to tune out, let Sonny take over. She'd been proud of her son, the competent way he'd eased Richard into his coat, done up the buttons, knotted the scarf, turned him in the direction of the doorway. But then Richard had sunk down onto the floor, laughing. "So sorry," he said. "Sorry, sorry, very sorry! Mrs Gifford, can you text Raoul?" Sonny did the texting. She'd been amazed. A text came back.

"He'll be about fifteen minutes," Sonny said. "Richard, we better make a move."

"Darling, where did you learn how to text?" she'd asked.

"Martin showed me."

Martin! How could she have forgotten Martin? What was the time? Only just after eight. Martin had always slept in. Quickly she made a flask of tea, adding a dash of brandy. Some chocolate biscuits. Looked for a tray. And then she noticed, next to her favourite cup and saucer, a clear-plastic globe. Under it was a cake, covered in pink-and-white marbled icing. On top of the cake, standing on one leg, was a tiny ballerina. Tucked beneath the globe was a hand-painted card: *To Mrs Gifford with love from Shona.* Mrs Gifford stepped back. She didn't know how she felt about this gift. The shawl had been enough. This seemed an encroachment. A reminder of all she'd lost wasn't what she wanted on Christmas morning. She covered it with a tea towel.

Carrying the tray, she let herself out into the corridor. The only sound was the beat of her heart. Quickly, she took the five steps that brought her to Martin's old room. She tapped at the door. Heard nothing. Quietly she said, "Martin, I'm coming in." The room wasn't quite dark. Putting down the tray she switched on the red lamp. Martin had gone. He'd taken the clean clothes she'd left for him: socks, underwear, a sweatshirt and a man's reefer jacket she'd once imagined might be a stylish item for Sonny to wear.

Deflated, she sat heavily down on the edge of the mattress. The evening before she'd carried Richard and Shona's coats and scarves in here. Immediately the smell had hit her. And there was Martin struggling to wake himself up. What a sad sight he'd looked, all the fire gone out of him. And filthy. Absolutely filthy. Mud and dirt, a total absence of soap and water.

"Don't chuck me out," he'd pleaded.

"I wouldn't dream of it. I'll bring you some food and later when I get a chance hot water and a towel. Some clean clothes."

"I'm sorry," he said but he hadn't looked sorry. He'd looked mischievous – the old Martin.

"Nothing to be sorry about. We have guests. I'll pop in when I can. Get some sleep."

She'd come back twice after that. Once with food and wine in a laundry bag. No one noticed her leaving the party or returning and by then Shona was slipping into a world of her own. Carrying in the water was tricky but she managed it at a point when Richard and Sonny were deep in conversation. Towels, clothes, flannel, all that type of thing came out of the store cupboards in the corridor.

He'd left behind his filthy clothes. They weren't worth washing. The tea mug had been used as an ashtray. Where was the plate she'd heaped with food? The wine bottle? She wondered what time he'd left. Probably early morning when she and Shona and her son were asleep. She tugged off the bed covers. There was what looked like blood on the bottom sheet. Quite a lot of blood.

She heard Sonny's voice calling her from out in the corridor. "Ma, where are you?"

Late last night she'd allowed herself a daydream: not quite the same as emerging from the kitchen with a garlanded roast turkey on a silver platter to great applause, but that Martin would agree to stay at least till the new year. As she and Sonny assembled for their Christmas dinner she'd casually say, "I believe we have another guest." Her son would look bewildered and then hope would dawn on his face. Enter Martin, bathed and pristine.

"My gift to you my darling son," she'd say.

49

SHONA

2014

I don't know how I managed the walk back to Canberra Road. I felt nauseous and my head was splitting in two. Once indoors, kicking off my shoes, I turned the central heating to max and carried my rucksack into the kitchen. I checked my phone. There was a text from you, sent around midnight. About the time I passed out.

With Raoul till the new year. Usual rules don't apply at Christmas. Smiley face & love.

Now I texted back, *Enjoy your holiday. Smiley face & love to both.*

Some might be devastated at being alone at Christmas. Not me. I felt nothing but relief. I took two paracetamols with a large glass of red wine. Not the best way to deal with a hangover but almost immediately I began to feel better. I let the unsatisfying evening slip into 'yesterday's news'. I would think about it later, much later.

I took out Mrs Gifford's present: Sainsbury's chocolates: good. A purse made from pink plastic beads: destined for the bin. However, on opening the purse I found a ten-pound note which was more than welcome. 'From Sonny' was written in neat letters on a tiny package wrapped in emerald-green crepe paper. I opened it carefully. Inside was a single diamond stud. I wore earrings but never just the one. I could see this was an expensive present, the diamond was set in eighteen-carat gold. I re-wrapped it. Set it aside. There was nothing from you but then we don't give each other presents. That was agreed when we first began living together. Your decision. "I can afford the best. You won't want that. You can afford crap. I won't want that. Okay?"

I allowed myself a few minutes of resentment, that you were no doubt exchanging expensive gifts with Raoul and enjoying passionate sex. It was still early in the day as I made myself comfortable at the table. I opened the chocolates. They went well with the hangover *and* the red wine. My thoughts were random, ranging from *what constitutes passionate sex?* to musing that this huge space for cooking and entertaining was wasted on us, that the room cried out for a ceiling-height Christmas tree in front of the bi-fold doors. Like the Giffords, I too would enjoy putting my individual stamp on the decoration. To fill the space there should be a family or a group of friends who liked and trusted each other, conversation and music, the smell of something delicious on the hob and in the unused oven. To paraphrase Stevie Wonder, *That's what Christmas is all about, Richard Christopher Maplin,* even though we've never experienced such a Christmas. It wouldn't take much to make a vibrant home here but it would take passion. And that's the bottom line: you and I, we both lack real, gut-wrenching, unavoidable passion. What we have instead is the excitement of being found desirable.

Alcohol was still affecting my emotions and so I allowed

myself to think of Beatrice. Yes, I'd enjoyed what Bea could do for me but I was never that generous in return. Like a sleepy cat my imagination stirred and off I went, creating images, my heart as a pale bloodless thing lying on a white enamel plate. My sex drive – and there was the cat motif again, stretched out in front of a fire, squirming with pleasure as the heat stroked her skin. Always an outside source required, very little coming from the interior. This insight didn't upset me, I was interested.

Last night there'd been passion in Mrs Gifford's living room. She adored her son, had put her life on hold since she was a young woman in her twenties. She'd kill for him, I thought. I doubted he'd do the same for her. You Richard, imagining you love Raoul, but how would you really like it if he told you, 'Richard, I love you with my heart, soul and body.'? I'd lay money on, not much. A plethora of love would be a turn-off. And there we are: you and me, very little lighting our fires.

50

SONNY

Like the eyes of a china doll, Sonny's eyes flip open. He stares up at the ceiling. A memory from the night before has pierced a deep dream. With a groan he rolls out of bed. In the past he has always looked forward to Christmas day: being fussed over by his mother, presents, dinner, wine, warmth and a particular safe feeling he associates with this time of year. The bedroom is cold but that doesn't worry him, but he's late and that does. He'd intended to wake at six. He has much to do. He checks his watch: eight-forty am.

He pulls on the same trousers he wore the previous evening: a long-sleeved t-shirt and then his one pullover. He rejects socks and shoes. He checks the living room. It's empty. No welcoming fire. No mother in the kitchen preparing breakfast. The kettle is hot though. He can see that tea has been made. He tries her bedroom. The bed's unmade. Where can she be? There is nowhere else for her to go. He begins to sweat. Surely, she hasn't gone searching for him. He tears out into the corridor. Shouts, "Ma, where are you?"

She emerges from Martin's old room. "Such a pity he's gone," she says.

"Martin? He left months ago."

"I know, but I still like to go into his old room. Those were nice times. Now then, what would you like for breakfast?"

"You choose," he said. "Is Shona still here?"

She shakes her head. "Pop down and put the batten in place. No more callers."

The corridor is in darkness but within a matter of seconds, his vision attunes. He reaches the lift's safety gate, but the actual lift is stationery down on the ground floor, he will have to take the stairs instead. The anxiety Sonny is experiencing has made him sweat. There is no escape from the situation he alone has created. How he wishes for an adult self: a grown man who drives a car, has college students clamouring for advice.

As he re-enters the room, she's kneeling in front of the fireplace. "You've been gone ages."

"Not that long."

"Where were you?"

"I went outside for a breath of fresh air."

"With bare feet?"

"Don't fuss."

"Never again," she says.

"Never again, what?"

"A party the day before Christmas. I'm exhausted this morning." A small flame flickers. She leans towards it and gently blows. Another flame appears. "Come on my love," she coaxes.

"Happy Christmas," Sonny says.

"Happy Christmas, dear." Stiffly she gets to her feet. "Keep an eye on the fire while I make tea. Biscuit?"

He shakes his head. "We haven't had breakfast."

"Surely we have."

"Surely, we haven't. I'm hungry."

"Make yourself a turkey sandwich. I'm sorry but I'm taking my tea back to bed for an hour or two."

"You're not ill?"

"Just old."

"Don't be melodramatic."

"I'll be fine later on."

He curls up on the daybed. The room is a mess. There's a strong smell of Richard's cigarettes. "You shouldn't have allowed your guest to smoke in here," he calls out to her.

"I'm missing two wine glasses," she says.

"I washed them up."

"They're not in the cupboard."

"Then I must have put them somewhere else. Does it matter?"

She brings in tea, a mug for him, cup and saucer for her. "What time did you go to bed?"

"Don't remember."

"I stayed up for almost an hour after you'd disappeared with Richard."

"I waited with him for Raoul. He'd said fifteen minutes, but it was more like an hour. I don't like him very much. Richard could do better. Can we talk about the evening when we both feel brighter?" He cradles his tea, feeling the warmth of the mug calming the turmoil in his chest.

"Of course. We'll open presents later. As we always do." She edges towards her bedroom door. Hand on doorknob she hesitates: "I'm sorry if I'm not feeling festive. Last night took it out of me."

"You have a snooze." He bends his head over the mug of tea. "I enjoyed the evening." He was smiling.

51

SHONA

2014

On the train into London, I texted Richard. *How's Italy? Guess what, meeting with Beatrice Salmon today! Smiley face and love.*

An hour later, he responded. *All fine here.*

So, no more 'smiley face and love'.

The evening before I'd set out my clothes: jeans, woollen shirt and from my younger glory days, a designer coat by Max Mara. I'd kept it in polythene through all the years I'd been pumped up with prescription drugs and too overweight to even get my arms into the sleeves. Now it fitted perfectly. If anything, the coat was a little loose but that looked good, relaxed, classic vintage. I wore my hair in one long plait. No make-up. I am an artist not a fashion model. My thin face is bony and interesting enough. My reflection told me, I looked okay. Maybe better than okay.

Beatrice Salmon's agency was in an elegant four-storeyed house behind Lamb's Conduit Street. I half expected Joan Vigo to open the door, but it was Beatrice. To me she looked *Parisienne,* more sophisticated than when we'd been together. In her short dark hair there was a streak of grey, but otherwise her face was the same, only her wary expression was unfamiliar.

"I'd forgotten how tall you are," was the first thing she said. "Sorry, that was rude. Good to see you, Shona."

I'd forgotten how small *she* was. I held out my hand to her but she stepped forward and lightly kissed my cheek. She led the way up a wide wooden staircase. I caught glimpses of rooms obviously used as offices. At the second floor we stepped out onto a large landing set up as a reception area. A woman, fiftyish, sat behind a wide leather-topped desk, bare apart from a vintage telephone and a laptop. Even in the early days I'd only ever spoken to Joan Vigo on the phone, but immediately I knew this was her. Before Bea could introduce me, I held out my hand.

"Hi," I said, "You must be Joan?"

Her grip on my hand was firm. "Hello Shona." Her glance moved to Beatrice. "Coffee, tea?"

"Coffee would be good. With milk still Shona?"

I nodded. "Two sugars." I don't take sugar but I was fighting against feeling intimidated by the two of them. Wearing muted shades of grey and tan they both seemed so cool and elegant. I could feel myself disappearing within the Max Mara coat I'd been so pleased with.

"This way." Beatrice touched my elbow and moved ahead of me. We entered a large airy room, the only furniture a couple of leather chairs and a circular glass coffee table. A sheet of oiled plywood balanced on chrome trestles in front of a floor-to-ceiling window. I handed Bea my portfolio.

"Thank you." She laid it on the wood. "Shona, do take off your coat. It's warm in here."

No choice of tea rather than coffee, instructions to remove my coat, this was not how I'd hoped our meeting would go.

She took my coat, draped it quite carelessly in my opinion, over the back of one of the chairs. "Sit," she said and then looked slightly embarrassed. "If you'd like to sit."

"Thank you." I sat.

"May I?" Beatrice tapped my portfolio.

"Of course." Oh, how awkward it all was.

She drew out the three small paintings I'd brought with me and carried them over to the window. My stomach clenched. Two were of Mrs Gifford: a portrait and the one of her as a child-like figure on the beach. The third was the woman in the boat. I hadn't altered the face: it was still Dorothy rowing implacably towards the shore. Each meant so much to me, protecting them meant I was protected. Just like that, I'd handed them over to someone I couldn't trust.

Beatrice took her time studying the detail in each one. The minutes ticked by.

Finally, she said in a low voice, as if speaking to herself, "Shona, I am so sorry."

My heart stopped. She didn't like them.

We were two statues: me hunched in the chair and open-mouthed, Beatrice, body rigid, head bent over the image of the woman in the boat. She straightened up, walked across to the window and pressed her forehead against the glass. I was determined not to break the silence.

Carrying a tray, Joan Vigo entered the room. Her glance went straight to Beatrice. "Everything okay, Bea?"

Beatrice turned. "Yes. We're fine. Just leave the coffees. We'll sort ourselves out." Her smile for Joan was almost apologetic.

The tray was placed on the coffee table: cafetiere, two cups, a jug of milk, no sugar.

"I take sugar," I said.

"I'm afraid we don't have any." Joan's glance was steely. "Can you manage without?"

"If I must." I smiled thinly up at her.

"Good." As she left the room she looked again at Beatrice. "I'm just outside."

Beatrice took the other chair. She poured the coffee. "Help yourself to milk, Shona. You never used to take sugar."

I had no answer.

"My apology just now was involuntary. I love your work. The pictures you brought are extraordinary. Can I set them aside for a moment? Yes, no?"

"Of course."

"The way everything ended between us, for *that* I'm sorry."

I added milk to the coffee. Unprompted I had the random thought that Bea should have more stylish cups, that at home we had Le Creuset from John Lewis. I forced myself back into the present. My voice harsh I said, "After all this time, the way you treated me did have an effect, but I've moved on. I imagine you have too."

"We – I wondered in the circumstances why you contacted the agency? Why not draw a line under your connection with me and try others? Joan said you were persistent."

I sipped the coffee, wiped my mouth on the tiny triangle of paper napkin. "Richard told me that you'd rung him, asking about my work. Perhaps I was mistaken but I took that as a positive sign that you were still interested in what I was doing." I can't quite control the tremor in my voice.

"I didn't ring Richard. He rang me."

"But he said-,"

"If he said I rang him, then he was lying."

"Why would he lie?"

"You know him far better than I do." Her head was turned towards the table where my paintings were spread out and then as if a decision was reached, she faced me. "It was a long time ago but do you remember the telephone call I had on our last day together?"

"Of course."

"It was him. Your friend Richard."

Waiting, I slowly stirred my coffee.

"He told me that for my own safety, there was something I needed to know about your background." Our eyes met. "He told me that you burnt down the house of the couple – the Kirkpatrick's who had adopted you. That they died in the fire. He said you were a psychopath with a talent for deceiving people who tried to get close to you. I was shaken, frightened even."

Richard, you have no idea how I felt listening to Beatrice, as if my stomach had dropped away, that you could have done such a cruel thing, you who know me, have surely guessed a little of what I went through in childhood. And I hated the thought that Beatrice was now contaminated with my unabridged history. I was so very . . . distressed.

"It didn't occur to you to question me? You'd never liked Richard and yet just like that," I clicked my fingers in her face, "you believed him."

"I didn't want to but doubts that I'd always dismissed in the past kept coming back to me. There was so much I didn't know about you, family, childhood. These were subjects you never spoke about. I'd respected your silence.

Anyway, I checked Shona Kirkpatrick out online. There wasn't much, but there was an image; a blurred photograph of you sitting on a bed and the name of a hospital. The girl was young but she was you."

I keep my face averted.

"It was almost a decade earlier but there was a nurse still working at the hospital who agreed to speak to me. We met up at a café."

"Did you pay her for the information?" I have no idea where that question came from.

Immediately Beatrice looked defensive. "Yes. Why wouldn't I? I'm trying to be honest with you, Shona. God, I need a cigarette." She got to her feet and left the room.

I wasn't angry with her or even disappointed. She'd thought she knew me and what I was capable of but I never dared come close to confiding in her. No, it was you I was thinking about, that you could be so duplicitous and uncaring. Whatever our problems, I'd always believed deep down, on some weird level we did both care as much for each other as we were capable of caring.

Holding a lit cigarette and an ashtray, Beatrice sat down again.

"And I assume the nurse came up with her own diagnosis?" I prompted.

She inhaled, breathed out a thin stream of smoke. "The woman had become friendly with the police, apparently, they interviewed you, countless times?"

I didn't bother to even nod.

"She said many abused children hold on to anger. But . . . the consensus, unproven, was that you did murder your parents. Everyone: doctors, nurses, psychologists, even the police had real sympathy for you, how you'd suffered during childhood."

I made no reply. Let her talk herself out and then let me go.

"Several days later Richard rang again. He'd discovered that when you first went to live with the Kirkpatrick's, you'd tried to kill a childhood friend. He didn't know the details but again no charges were brought. You'd actually admitted to him that you had tried to kill her, made a joke of it, he said."

"I didn't."

"You didn't try to kill her?"

In a deadly voice I said, "She was never my friend." What was left of my coffee was tepid but my throat was dry. I drank it down. "It was a childish game that went wrong. I was only eight or nine years old at the time."

"He was so convincing, not exactly nasty about you, Shona. He said you represented family, all he had, that he was a selfish bastard – those were the exact words he used – but he would always look after you, make sure you came to no harm, did no further harm."

"How gallant. So, if I'm such a monster, why agree to see me now?"

Her hands were clasped in her lap, her expression eager, girlish. "Joan persuaded me. I'd never shared our history with her. You were just an artist who used to be on our books. She researched your work. When you sent in the photographs, she was excited. Insisted I look at them."

"And does she know my history now?"

"Yes." She smiled, a secret contemplative smile. "It's not possible to keep a secret from Joan. She advised me to at least see you for myself, make a decision based on my own intuition."

"And now?"

"My intuition tells me that whatever you were guilty

of, you'd been an abused child with no one to turn to. I always understood that the Shona I knew battled with her own demons but I never once felt anything but safe in your company. I warned you about Richard. I believed he was a toxic influence and I was right." She held out her hand.

I couldn't take it.

"Shona, I can only repeat that I'm sorry. No excuses." We sat quietly for some minutes before she stood up. "Shall we discuss your work?"

I wasn't ready to let her off the hook. "But why would we want to do that? At the time you said you loved me, that we should live together. And then on the strength of one phone call from someone you mistrusted you made up your mind that I was dangerous and had to be erased from your life. Paying the woman for information came after." I was so tempted to break the coffee cup, chuck the tray across the room, upend the flimsy designer table, give her even more justification. "You'd already got rid of me!" I was shouting.

"Time to leave, I think." Joan Vigo was in the room.

"Joan, just give us ten more minutes."

"No." Joan's hand was pressing Beatrice shoulder, keeping her in the chair. "I told you there was a chance this wouldn't work. Let's leave things for now. You're upset."

I pulled on my coat. Gathered up my three small paintings. I felt such love for them, such pride, for Mrs Gifford, even my sad damaged mother. What had her childhood been like? As I packed the pictures away, I asked, "So what exactly did Richard say when you spoke recently?"

"Shona, I want you to leave." Joan's voice was pleasant but determined.

"No, let me tell her. She needs to know." There were tears in Bea's eyes. From her sleeve she took a tissue and blew her nose. "He said, I would be wasting my time seeing you. That you were a . . . pill junkie but he couldn't bear to put you out on the street."

Richard, I remembered the argument you and I had at the time. How you insisted that you'd described my work as 'brilliant'. I'd thought there would be a caveat to 'brilliant' but I could never have imagined you being so vile.

Foolish I know but I made a dramatic exit, sweeping past the two women, letting the hem of my coat brush Bea's immaculate grey trousers. In the doorway I turned. "I may always be on medication, but I'm not an addict nor am I a psychopath." And then I rather let myself down by resorting to one of your witticisms: "There will be other fish in the sea for my work, Ms Salmon."

Walking back from Hawksbridge station, I'm chilled right through. It's far colder here than it was in London. Once indoors, I leave my bag, portfolio and coat at the foot of the stairs and head for the kitchen. From the wine rack I choose a bottle of Richard's most expensive red wine. Apart from the steady tick-tick of the kitchen clock and the thermostat, the house is quiet. Tomorrow, weather permitting, I may walk over to the Giffords', share my good news. I retrieve my bag from the hall, take out the long white envelope. Joan Vigo has typed my name on the front. I don't need to re-read the contents; it's a signed and witnessed contract with the Beatrice Salmon Agency. My goal has been achieved and in the end the process was less painful than expected. Objectively I now understand why Beatrice cut me off. I even understand why she chose to believe Richard over me. Sensible move. Look at Richard, look at Shona Blake. Who would put their complete trust in a woman that dangerously flakey?

*

Joan made the decision. Bea has met her match there. Joan Vigo is made of polished steel. She let me get as far as the front door before calling me back. I'd slowed my pace, hearing steps behind me.

"Shona, don't go."

I turned. Joan and I faced each other. I didn't resent her in any way. I admire strength although so often I'm tempted by the weak. Yes Richard, you are the prime example.

"It may be futile after the histrionics upstairs, but Bea – we – still want you back as one of our artists. I don't know if you're in touch with the present art market, but you have a desirable name, your work still sells, prices have risen." She pauses then lightly touches my arm: "The way you look. There is something quite impressive about you, Shona, even some aspects of your history might enhance your market value."

She spooned out exactly the right amount of flattery. I followed her back upstairs. Bea hurried towards us. Something in Joan's expression brought her to a standstill. For the next thirty minutes we talked only of my painting and its future. The conversation was low key, emotions on all sides well under control. Joan left us and went to prepare the contract. Bea and I sat quietly. She apologised again. I said, "That's okay. I'm more upset about Richard."

"I'm sure he cares for you in his weird, warped fashion. But you know that already, don't you and yet here you are years later, still–,

"Bea, enough," Joan snapped.

It's so snug in the kitchen; my bones are loosening with pleasure. Shona time. I've come to love this house. So often now, when Richard is away with Raoul, I wish it were mine. I believe it to be a woman's house, not a man's.

It's the last day of the year. I could never imagine the year ending so well. *You can paint, Shona. You're not just average or good, you are immensely talented. That's what both of them told you.* I had no idea how much I needed praise. I pick up my glass and sort of sashay out into the open space in front of the glass doors. I'm not graceful, I can clearly see how awkwardly I move, but I don't care. All this time I've seen this as a negative, but not today. I am 'impressive'. My awkwardness has paid off.

I raise a glass to my reflection. The entire kitchen is reflected spread out behind me. My gaze focuses on a roll of black bin liners on the kitchen counter. I'd bought them only yesterday, placed them in the drawer. The paper wrapper has been torn into two pieces. The roll has been opened.

52

Standing in the hall I call out your name. The air feels undisturbed, the silence complete. When you're here even if it's just coming in before setting off again, you invariably leave a trail. You never wear the same coat or jacket twice. The smart Crombie you wore to the Gifford's would be draped over the banister. Having spent Christmas with Raoul there would be presents in a heap on the floor, your suitcase.

I push open the living room door. Since the Gifford's party I haven't taken advantage of your 'usual rules apply' and the room is scrupulously neat. Next to the television I recognise a file you often refer to. It contains utility bills marked 'paid' in red felt-tip, receipts dated just before Christmas. Bewildered, I find myself staring at your passport. I flick through the pages. The last date stamp was when you were at a trade fair in Germany over a year ago.

Beneath a copy of The Guardian for the twenty-third of December I discover a small stack of Christmas cards. Ten in all. I read every one. 'Have a great Xmas'. 'See you next year'. 'Don't do anything I wouldn't do.' Hah! Only the final card is of interest and then not much. 'Love forever, Raoul.'

I study the non-festive image for further indication of Raoul's feelings. It's an expensive card, a seascape by Andrew Wyeth, an American landscape artist who died some years ago. I love his work and it surprises me that Raoul might love his work too. The image would be lost on you though. You have a disdain for realistic painters. If it isn't graphic or illustrative or 'contemporary' then 'yeah, yeah' it may be good but just not relevant, Shona.

Upstairs your bedroom appears undisturbed. Pushing the one armchair out of the way, I turn to the fitted wardrobes, slide open the doors. Your clothes are packed tightly together: jackets, then shirts, trousers, then jeans. Two tiers of shoes and boots. I'm amazed. In all the time I've shared this house it has never occurred to me that you love clothes. A good detective would no doubt check the pockets, jacket linings, look inside shoes but I feel so tired and anxious, these tasks are beyond me. I lower myself into your armchair. It is the one incongruous item in here, a fussy Chesterfield style in brown antiqued leather with wide curved arms and back. It's made for relaxation, giving oneself up to sleep or daydreaming. Not for one moment can I imagine you doing either.

From my lower vantage point, I find myself looking directly out of the window. There is a view stretching far across the rooves of the town. Indistinctly in the distance, I realise that I'm staring at the footbridge. I make out a block of dark colour which I'm almost certain must be the upper storeys of the Miller Building. That you might have sat looking at this same view, I find somehow unsettling.

Getting up, I realise that I've left an indentation in the leather seat cushion. It refuses to be smoothed away. I try to lift the cushion. It gives a little. I pull harder. Suddenly with a 'click' the cushion flies upwards hitting my chin hard. My cry of pain is cut short. I'm staring down into a cavity. There is a laptop and a cardboard box. I lift both out. Across the lid of the box, I recognise one of your pastiches of HR Giger's artwork: a woman lies in a position of abandonment on a bed of writhing metallic-bodied snakes. Beneath this image, in swirling calligraphy is written, My Own Sweet Alien.

With care I ease off the lid. The faces of a younger Richard and Shona stare up at me. We are posing in front of the Eiffel Tower. It is the photograph stolen by Mrs Gifford months earlier. Taped to the back of it is the Cosmos flower that Beatrice gave me. The glue from the tape has destroyed the fragile petals. Here are my adoption papers. Clipped to them is a yellowed newspaper cutting from almost twenty years ago, *Devoted Couple Die in Blaze*. Beneath the headline is a small grainy picture of Sheila, Brian and myself taken on my birthday trip to Regent's Park Zoo. There are copies of death certificates; theirs and Dorothy's. An even older scrap from a local newspaper, just a brief paragraph; '*Tragedy Averted*' about an unnamed child who was almost killed when an innocent game went badly wrong. I dig deeper and find photo-copies of police reports, fire and social services, a bulging envelope charts the journey of my mental health through two breakdowns: what I am capable of, a prognosis.

You have gathered together every crime, every mistake I've ever made, every single sad fact. Last of all is a flimsy blue envelope with my name on it, addressed to your flat in Islington, postmarked nine years earlier. I recognise my mother's handwriting. With foreboding I take out the single sheet of paper but it is nothing much. No threats or put-downs. No apologies or remorse – just a paragraph in which Dorothy asks me for money to ease her through the last weeks of her life. I say that 'it is nothing much' but in fact I find the letter painful to read. I've rarely imagined a vulnerable Dorothy. Kneeling on the floor, the worst parts of my life scattered around me, I feel bereft. All the kindnesses I've ever thanked you for, the roof over my head, the garden, the belief that whatever cruelty you showed me, underneath you'd cared, were only ever keeping me safe. They were all a sham. I'd been the Stepford Wife, the dog relied upon to respond to your fake boyish grin, the constant companion to mask your true self.

I set the box aside and opened up the laptop. I know the code. In fact, I know all your codes, each one is a play on SHhOna and my date of birth. You trust me with these, or at least imagine I have no interest in any of your creative work.

Surprisingly few files appear on screen: home, college, personal and projects. No sign of me in the first three but in the last I find: *Shona, Years One to Ten.* There are literally hundreds of images of me, both drawn and photographic, none of which I'm aware of having posed for. Some are naturalistic, others enhanced. In the early years, following your Alien success I am a serpentine female monster. The year you brought me here from the hospital when I'd put on weight, you've shown no pity. I am repugnant, my eyes and mouth made tiny within rolls of glistening flesh. Seated, naked, my veined breasts reach my thighs. You've added a patchwork of scars across my limbs. Chilled I open the file for last year: Year Ten. No photographs, only pastel drawings. You've made me softer, voluptuous. My face is smooth, almost childlike, my eyes clear and innocent and yet – there is a teardrop of red in the corner of my mouth, red on my hands and pooled at my feet. The drawings are painfully good, the best things you've done since that initial project. Is this why you keep me with you? Love, hate, despise, I provide the only impetus for you to access some deep-seated warped talent.

I close all files, switch off the laptop. Leave everything scattered across the floor.

Downstairs, I pour myself another glass of red wine. On the table in front of me is the signed contract. I resist the overpowering urge to sabotage myself, pour wine over the pristine sheets of paper before someone else can spoil it for me.

It is now totally dark outside. Avoiding your room, I make my way through the house drawing blinds, imagining myself as I'd often imagined Mrs Gifford, small shadowy female figure appearing at each window before blotting herself out. I'm nervous still, checking cupboards, behind doors. Double-locking the front door, I remember the one room I haven't checked; the loft room. I tell myself that my anxiety is unnecessary. There is nothing left in the house to fear as back upstairs I go.

That small closed door on the landing has always held a sinister quality. My hand hits the light switch. I climb the narrow wooden staircase, Above, I can see the chair holding the door open. You never came up with an alternative and it soon failed to be an issue. I look straight into an empty room. There is my table, a further chair and the easel. Paintings face the walls. I count them, nine in total – correct. The table top is always an untidy mess of paints, brushes, scraps of paper but it is my known mess.

I decide to text you. *When will you be back?* I place my phone on the table and wait.

Five minutes pass with no response. I'm about to text again when I hear a scraping sound. With horror I watch as the chair holding the door open slides forwards. The door swings shut. Too late I rush across the room. The handle won't turn. Someone is holding it from the other side. And then I hear the turning of the key. My own key is in my bedroom. I've never used it. Picking up my phone, I try to ring emergency service, but the battery is dying. For over a year, I've been free of panic attacks but I recognise the signs of one now. I'm sweating, my breath coming in short gasps. I wedge the chair under the door handle then franticly push open both dormer windows, hold my face up to the cold fresh air. Try not to think too much.

I let an hour go by before trying the door again. This time it opens easily. I'm full of doubt. In my panic, had I imagined the door was locked?

53

SHONA

Six am. New Years Day 2015

I wake from a restless sleep to find it's starting to snow. I shower and dress for outdoors while having no idea where to go so early on the first day of a new year. I need to get out of this house. There are no friends, no kindly neighbors to turn to. I've lived here for more than several years but this morning I feel under threat. The only person I can think of to turn to is Mrs Gifford. In the kitchen I make a list of what I would need were I to make the journey to the Miller Building. The snow on the terrace is now an inch thick and falling in flakes the size of postage stamps. As if preparing for a trek through the Alps I write down: flask of tea, biscuits, thermal gloves, hat, scarf. Check torch batteries – *Shona, it will be daylight*! Waterproof. Tissues. Chocolate. A gift. I can't go without a gift on the first day of the year. *Shona, you can!*

I realise that I've drawn a tiny stick figure beneath the list. It is Sonny as I saw him posing in the doorway of Mrs Gifford's living room. 'Namaste, Shona,' he'd said. I'd liked him in that first instance, imagined that both of us held our strangeness, our destructive shadow selves in common. I start to draw again. Mrs Gifford and her son, same height, same build, same grace. I rough them out as salt and pepper pots. Even as I draw, a different image occurs to me. I begin again. One of Dorothy's few possessions was a Welsh doll, no more than six inches tall, wearing national costume: high hat, dark dress, white apron. The apron predicted the weather, changing from white to blue if it was about to rain. Back to white for a dry spell. It worked, was reliable but even now, remembering is to see the apron as magical. As I draw, I concoct a daydream that while I was with Beatrice in London, the Giffords had let themselves into the house, sat at this same table.

But they didn't have a key, Shona.

But they have so many keys. Perhaps Mrs Gifford made a hot drink, admired the new kitchen, imagined herself living here. And then, happily chattering to each other, they went upstairs. 'Not much to see in Shona's bedroom. Let's take a look at the master. Nice bathroom!'

But why would they?

Curious, bored? There are no shops open for Mrs Gifford and her shopping trolley. Sonny has lost interest in his library books. Or perhaps he's fallen in love with you, Richard. Who knows what makes the Giffords tick?

Suddenly, I've had enough of my own thoughts which are only a distraction from thinking about you, Richard: the whys and how could yous? Suddenly I am eager to be on the move. I pack up my rucksack adding an extra fleece, zip myself into my waterproof, pull on fur-lined boots. Dropping my torch into my coat pocket, I straighten up, unlock the front door. I step out into a still and silent world.

*

I reach the promenade. The Christmas fairy-lights strung between each lamppost glow weakly. It all looks dismal. I turn right heading into darkness. The tide is in. It makes a soothing *ssshhh.* I tell myself that whatever is going wrong at this moment, I am an artist with a contract. There will be money in my bank account. I have a destination to head for on this first day of January. My mood holds. Half an hour later, reaching the wooden beach shelter I'm startled as some small animal dashes across my path and disappears into the flattened marram grass. I can hear its progress as it nuzzles its way beneath the snow. Startled but not fearful.

Turn inland. Mrs Gifford's words run through my mind and there against the lightening sky the building stands, bleak and alien, the perfect setting for a horror story. Every window on the top floor is lit up. The Giffords are usually careful not to show any sign of occupation. This lapse seems significant. And then, one by one, the lights go out.

The snow is around three inches deep. At first, I think I'll have difficulty finding the path but already I can see the paw-prints of small animals. Snow or not, it is obviously their thoroughfare. I add my footprints, stepping carefully over the uneven ground.

54

SONNY

The temperature in the corridor is just above freezing. Seated cross-legged on the floor, the khaki blanket draped around his shoulders, Sonny's breath trails from between his lips in wisps of white. From the other side of the door directly in front of him comes a burst of coughing. Sonny shifts his position, pulls his legs up to his chest and holds his knees. His feet are bare, so pale they glow.

The coughing continues, full of phlegm and from deep in someone's chest. It's a horrible sound. Sonny pulls the blanket up around his head, presses the material hard against his ears. Eventually the noise stops.

"Sonny, I know you're out there."

Sonny freezes but then his face breaks into a smile. The voice is weaker than it was the day before. Surely the time was approaching when he'd be able to take his dear love in his arms and comfort him. Sonny twists and turns his head, imagining warm lips moving against the sensitive carotid pulse point at the base of his neck.

"At least . . . come in . . . and talk to me."

Between each word the voice pauses and Sonny hears the rasp of laboured breathing.

Sonny has entered this room, which he has painstakingly made wonderful, only four times during the last week: to deliver a very little amount of food, water and change the grim toilet bucket. The visits have been terrifying. Sonny remains bewildered: his plan had been perfect. Each step right up till early on Christmas morning had progressed as intended. He had felt euphoric, emotional. He alone had delivered unto himself the best of gifts. The days since have been nightmarish. He has rarely been the receiving end of anger or the threat of violence. Should he open the door will someone furious and of superhuman strength rush towards him? Will the chains hold? Sonny leans his head back against the wall and closes his eyes.

"Sonny?"

As his mother emerges from the stairwell, he scrambles to his feet.

She glides towards him. Her hair is uncombed and sticks up around her head in snow-white peaks, dressing gown hanging open over a creased nightdress. "Is it the drains?" her voice is querulous. "Did this awful smell disturb you too?"

He's grown used to the smell. For a second, he has no idea what she's talking about. "I've no doubt that it's just a blockage," he answers.

"Darling, 'just a blockage' is an understatement."

Her voice is too loud. It hurts his ears. He wants to hush her, take hold of her shoulders and hurry her back down the three flights of stairs.

"Sonny, we can't just ignore this. Something has to be done."

"Be quiet," he whispers fiercely.

She looks confused. "But why?"

"Because I say so."

She grasps one of his hands. "You're freezing. How long have you been sitting up here?"

Sick with fear he can't bear to look at her.

"Don't worry; the two of us can sort this out." Her voice is soothing. "Come downstairs now. It's very early. I'll put a bottle in your bed. Sleep in till nine perhaps?"

He shakes his head. Quite distinctly, on the other side of the door, the coughing begins again and then the choked words, "Mrs Gifford."

Listening, her head tilts to one side.

"Mrs Gifford." The voice is louder now.

"Sonny, who have you got in there?"

He tries to place his hand over her mouth.

She slaps him away. "That's enough. Behave yourself."

Suddenly they are struggling with each other but with no real force. The struggle becomes a dance, both hopping from one foot to the other, their hands flapping ineffectually. Another time, another place, the dance might end in laughter, but Sonny is desperate. He reaches out to grab a hank of her hair. She steps backwards. Sonny lunges forwards. Together they fall against the door. The door swings open.

Performing a clumsy *arabesque,* Mrs Gifford is the first to regain her balance. For a split-second, she stands completely still, hands loosely clasped in front of her as she stares at the creature lying on the bed.

At his mother's party, posed in the doorway trying to impress her bland friend Shona, he'd heard the lift being activated and suddenly felt so happy. But also, disconcertingly he'd glimpsed himself – no more than a shadow on the blistered plaster of the corridor wall, as an enormous spider settled in the centre of a web, quivering with excitement. Leaving the two women: tall statue, small statue, silhouetted against the flames from the fire, he'd run, danced, oh, he could have turned cartwheels on his way to greet Richard and Raoul. Without regret, he'd wished that Martin was with him but he no longer felt that painful conviction that he'd lost a soul mate.

The lift gate had crashed open and there stood Richard. Man and boy (because boyish was how Richard made him feel) appraised each other. Sonny eased open the safety gate. Richard had stepped out.

"Greetings," Richard had said. He was so tall. He'd had to bend forwards to place a kiss on Sonny's cheek. "No Raoul tonight, I'm afraid."

By midnight, the party was over. His mother looked bedraggled and exhausted. Her hair that had seemed so dramatic and extraordinary was a mess, straggling around her face. There was grease on the sleeves of her dress. After several phone calls to and from Raoul, Richard had decided to get silently drunk. Shona curled up on the floor, fell asleep.

"Another ten minutes and then I'll ring Raoul. He's picking me up," Richard said.

His mother fetched Richard's coat from Martin's old room. "You'll take some turkey for Christmas Day?"

"No really, Mrs G," Richard's words were slurred. "We have plans for tomorrow."

"Oh, there's nothing like a turkey sandwich for mopping up alcohol."

Richard took out his phone. Dialled. Frowned. "Wrong number." Tried again. This time it rang and rang. "He's not answering. What's he playing at now?"

"Let me try." There was some element in Sonny's voice, the way his hand arced forwards, that Richard had seemed to find hypnotic.

"But do you know how to use a mobile?"

Gently he'd taken the phone from Richard. "Of course I do."

"Really darling?" his mother said. "Are you sure?"

"*Really mother.*" He'd hated the intimacy in her voice, as if she knew every last thing he was capable of. "Martin. Remember?"

He stood by the window, texting. In the kitchen Richard was filling a glass with cold water. As he came back into the room, Sonny looked up triumphantly. "Raoul's twenty minutes away. Better get you downstairs."

"And Shona?"

All three turned to look at her. It was amazing how she could be so easily forgotten.

"Let her sleep," Richard said.

"If we hurry, I could show you the top floor balcony? There's an incredible view from up there. We'll see the lights of Raoul's car when he arrives."

"I don't know. I'm feeling pretty ropey."

"I promise, the fresh air will do you good."

"Do I seem drunk?"

"A bit."

His mother said, "But darling, I have a surprise for you."

Without looking at her, Sonny answered, "It can wait."

In the open doorway of the seventh-floor apartment Richard hesitated, his gaze panning across the walls and upwards to the ceiling. "Christ, what a state. This place will cost millions to renovate." He now seemed completely sober.

"Come on in. It's warmer than the corridor. I lit the paraffin stove earlier this evening, just in case you and Raoul wanted to take a look."

Richard didn't seem to notice the bed with its pillows, sheets and blanket or the rugs Sonny had scattered on the floor over the previous weeks. He made straight for the balcony doors as if he wanted to get the chore of pleasing Sonny out of the way and leave.

From next to the bed, Sonny retrieved the wine bottle and two glasses, before following Richard outside. "This building is like a fortress," he said cheerfully, "No, a castle. The land surrounding us is our dry moat. We can see anyone approaching from the town, from the sea. We are invincible, or that's how I imagine us to be."

"But you're not." Richard's tone was sharp. "At the most, in a month's time you, this entire area will be overwhelmed by the developers. Then what?"

"No idea. Something. How about one last drink?" He held up the bottle.

"No thanks."

"For the road?"

Richard sighed. "Go on then."

The sigh, Richard's acquiescence marked an alteration in the dynamic between them as if Richard's desire to be elsewhere had abated. In a couple of gulps, he finished his wine and seemed not to notice when Sonny re-filled his glass.

"Let's go inside," Sonny said. "It's freezing out here. Will it snow, I wonder?"

Sonny opened the second bottle. At first as it had been with Martin, they were both self-conscious in each other's company, seated upright at opposite ends of the big bed, but their conversation flowed. Sonny knew how to achieve this: ask questions, appear not just politely interested, be fascinated. Richard began to recount his plans for the coming year, his ambitions to make a short film. "Early stages," he'd said. "Don't want to jinx the project by talking about it."

"Fair enough. But Shona? My mother said the two of you have been together for years." He'd giggled foolishly. "Are you in love with her?" Sonny put everything into that question. It was intimate, he was stepping over a possible boundary.

"For some weird reason I crave her company. She's my lucky talisman. I associate her with success. For months on end she's little more than a disappointing heap of stones and then suddenly I see a flash and she becomes a rare and curious diamond. She's cold, can't be reached, enigmatic. Stop me if I'm talking rubbish."

"No, no. Go on. I don't know her very well but my mother finds her remarkable."

"Your mother's right. If Shona wasn't in my life, *effff*," he grimaced as if in pain. "I don't know if I'd ever recover."

"Oh, I'm sure you would. And your friend Raoul, you like him a lot?"

"Not sure I like him at all. Again, I crave his company. Sonny, I don't take to many people, but when it happens, I keep them close." He laughed. "Whether they want me or not."

Richard held out his glass for Sonny to fill. "Before the new year, take me round the building. I'd love to get some photographs before the developers come in and destroy the history. Will you do that for me, Sonny?" And he'd looked into Sonny's eyes.

It had been close to two am on Christmas morning when Sonny gathered up the empty bottles and their glasses, placing them on the wooden draining board in the bare kitchen.

Going back to the bed he shook Richard's shoulder.

"Go 'way." Richard's eyes were tightly shut, hands tucked between his thighs. "Cold," he said.

Gently Sonny spread a blanket over him before drawing one of the wooden chairs closer. Seated, hands on knees, chin resting on the heels of his hands, he observed Richard's face. Tentatively reaching out he lightly ran his fingers over Richard's light brown hair. It felt silky smooth and clean. He stroked Richard's eyelids. They quivered but didn't open. Tracing down his nose, his index finger stopped at Richard's upper lip. Sonny held his breath before slipping the fingertip into the warm wetness of Richard's mouth. From somewhere in the room, he heard a moan and then realised he had made the sound himself.

Heart thundering, he silently placed the chair back against the wall. He slipped on Richard's Crombie coat. It was huge on him, almost reaching the floor, but the weight of the material and satin lining felt wonderful, smelt wonderful. In a pocket he found Richard's mobile. Good.

From the cupboard under the kitchen sink he retrieved a canvas bag. Returning to Richard, he put the bag down in the space between the iron headboard and the wall. He breathed deeply, checked himself. So far Sonny had done no wrong.

In a low voice he asked, "Richard, are you awake?"

Richard began to snore. He was dead to the world.

Just above the skirting board, two iron rings were embedded into the wall. From the bag, Sonny took a small metal box and two lengths of thick chain, each three metres long. On one end was a padlock, on the other a handcuff. Efficiently and soundlessly Sonny fastened the padlocks to the wall rings. Then he laid the chains on the floor, one each side of the bed. If Richard roused himself right this minute, if Richard sat up on the bed and said, "What the hell are you doing with those chains? Is that my coat you're wearing?" Sonny would answer, "Just a game, Richard. Foolishness, no harm done."

Carefully, Sonny eased the blanket down.

Richard groaned.

Sonny hesitated.

And then as if to a summons, Richard removed his hands from between his thighs and spread out his arms.

Again, Sonny waited. Would Richard's eyelids open? Satisfied that Richard was fast asleep, Sonny took a key from the metal box.

He eased up the sleeves of Richard's sweatshirt.

He rested his fingers on Richard's wrist, felt the beat of Richard's pulse before snapping on the handcuff.

Silently he moved around the bed. Snapped on the second cuff. Really the entire process was so straightforward. But it was now Christmas Day. A present was required. From his pocket, he took out Martin's watch and strapped it around Richard's wrist. Job almost complete, he untied the laces of Richard's leather shoes and slipped them off. Blanket replaced. *Et voila*, Richard transformed to a contentedly sleeping guest.

Weeks ago, he'd brought up a plastic bucket and a pack of toilet rolls from his mother's storeroom. She had enough toilet rolls to last all three of them at least a decade. He placed these next to the bed before stepping back to consider his handiwork. Not perfect. Maybe in the future he would find some form of ankle restraint.

He remembered water. Richard would be dehydrated when he woke up. Sonny filled the wine glasses and one of the bottles from the kitchen tap and left them within reach at the side of the bed. His heart was no longer beating fast. Satisfied that he'd done all he could, Sonny left. He didn't lock the door. There was no need.

55

MRS GIFFORD

In slow motion, Richard turns his head towards her. The hollows of his eyes are so dark that the skin appears bruised. His face is ashen apart from two spots of high colour blooming across his cheekbones. On the soiled sheet the fingers of one hand are turned upwards, like the claw of a bird. And then she notices the handcuff around Richard's wrist, the thick chain winding back under the blanket.

"Sonny," she whispers. "What have you done?"

Ignoring her, Sonny begins to edge crab-like along the wall towards the bed.

"Mrs Gifford, help me. Please." There is no strength to Richard's voice.

Sonny steps around the overflowing bucket, the dried faeces on the floor. He's still fearful of any remaining strength Richard might have, so he keeps just out of reach. Another fit of coughing racks Richard's body. When he falls back against the pillows, he gasps for breath. With increasing confidence Sonny steps closer.

He lays the palm of his hand on Richard's forehead, waits and then nods. It's as if he is a doctor, checking for a raised temperature but reassured that his patient is on the mend. *Hmm, no need for antibiotics.*

Richard's gaze remains fixed on Mrs Gifford.

Her head is spinning. There is too much here to comprehend. Her son's smile is familiar: he seeks her approval. Impassively she appears to assess the situation before saying firmly, "Shame on you. Sonny. You mustn't treat a friend like this. At the very least we need pyjamas, and clean bed sheets."

"I'm so cold," Richard says.

Her focus on her son doesn't waver. "The bucket's full. When did you last empty it or bring the poor man food and water?"

Again, Richard answers, "No food, hardly any water. He sits outside. Refuses to come in here."

"We must remedy that, mustn't we, darling?" She holds out her hand to Sonny. "Will you let Mummy help you?"

Relief washes across Sonny's face. "You're not angry with me?"

"Never angry, darling. Now, why not go downstairs and heat up a tin of chicken soup?" Briskly she crosses the room and closes the French doors. "You'll have to bring up the other paraffin stove."

"But there's no paraffin."

"In my kitchen, under the sink, at the back. There's plenty of paraffin. Silly boy, do you think I'd let us run out in the middle of winter? Take the duvet and pillows from my bed. Sheets, blankets, as much as you can carry. Pile it all in the lift. You'll have to make several journeys."

Mrs Gifford bustles into the kitchen. She finds a second bucket and some cloths, also a glass and another wine bottle. When she turns on the cold tap, it makes a juddering roar. She waits till the brown water clears then fills the bottle.

Returning to the room, Sonny still hovers near the bed. As she offers the water to Richard, he intercepts the bottle. "No, let me."

"I think your friend can manage."

"But I want to."

Richard licks his dry lips. "Please." He is begging.

As Sonny holds the bottle to Richard's mouth, Mrs Gifford is thinking, *if Richard has the strength, now is his chance.* But all Richard wants is water. With difficulty, choking, he tries to drink.

"Put your hand under your friend's head and raise him up a little. Be gentle," she says. If her son was still a child, say nine or ten, *she* would have sent him flying. Water begins to pour out of Richard's mouth.

"That's enough!" She snatches the bottle out of Sonny's hand.

"It's mine," he says, eyes full of hatred.

Richard is choking. She tries to bring his head forward while Sonny struggles to push him back into the pillows.

"Sonny, just stop," she shouts.

Sonny does stop. Over Richard's body they glare at each other. She lets the anger die from her eyes, says gently, "You don't want to hurt your friend, do you?"

"No." He is her own Sonny again. For the time being.

"Look, while I clean up this mess why don't you make a start bringing up supplies?" Her tone is brisk and cheerful. She wants the situation to replicate the old days, when they embarked on an adventure and nothing was impossible or right or wrong. "Perhaps some of the clothes I washed that Martin left behind?"

"He has clothes in his suitcase," Sonny says. "He wouldn't let me undress him."

Reluctantly, he leaves the room. The slap of his bare feet on the corridor floor fades. Not daring to shut the door she waits till she hears the lift arrive and then the drone as it starts its descent.

"Help me," Richard says. His lips are cracked and rimmed with white.

Frowning, she places her index finger against her lips. *Don't speak. It isn't safe.* Picking up the pungent bucket from next to the bed she goes into the bathroom, empties it into the toilet then pulls the old-fashioned chain. With relief she sees water gush into the toilet bowl. On top of the cistern she finds a packet of six desiccated sponges and she washes the bucket as best she can in the filthy bath.

Outside the sky is brightening. The sun will soon be up. There had been a heavy fall of snow first thing but it will clear by lunchtime. Mrs Gifford knows this coastal weather well. Twice now, Richard has attempted to speak to her. He is weak but her presence has revived his spirits.

Finally, having ensured that the corridor is empty and the lift stationary on a lower floor she whispers, "It is in your own interest to ignore me." She squeezes his hand so tightly he winces. "I will do my best for you. Do not annoy my son. Be nice."

Richard starts to cough.

"Stop now!"

Eyes bulging, he manages to take control of the spasm. In silence she proceeds. Richard raises his torso allowing her to slide a towel under him. She is able to remove his trousers and socks but is forced to cut away his sweatshirt with a pair of rusty scissors she finds in a kitchen drawer. Her arthritic hands make this a time consuming and painful task and Sonny is back struggling with the heater and a can of paraffin before she's finished.

"He smells, Mummy."

"Well of course he does. You'd smell if you hadn't washed for days on end. Shall I wash him?"

Sonny doesn't answer immediately. "Okay." He looks at her. "Don't make a meal of it."

He has never spoken to her in such a tone before, as if no emotional tie exists between them. She understands. Her son's life, what's left of it, is in this room. *Their* life together is over. "Now the bedding," she says. "It's most important to keep your friend warm."

With Sonny away again, she's able to wash Richard. The water's cold but he gets used to it.

"Thank you," he says.

Each time Sonny makes a delivery, her list of requirements grows longer: more towels, wet wipes, blankets, body lotion. But she takes care not to overwhelm her son with the demands, to always appear practical, even playful. She does not use Richard's name, referring to him only as 'your friend'. She does nothing that might change Sonny's gratitude into mistrust.

At one point, as she makes up the bed, Richard indicates a need to use the bucket. She doesn't offer help, merely pushes the bucket and toilet roll nearer to him.

"My legs are weak," he says. "I need assistance."

"Hang on till Sonny gets back. He'll have to help you."

"But can't you? I feel safer with you."

At that moment they hear Sonny whistling as he makes his way along the corridor. She recognises the tune, 'Autumn Leaves'.

Her son has changed his clothes. He wears his favourite silk kimono.

"Very nice," she says. "But Sonny, your friend needs to use the bucket. I'll wait in the kitchen while you sort him out."

"No, you sort Richard out." Like a can-can dancer he flaps the folds of silk at them both. "*I'll* wait in the kitchen."

The smell is bad but bearable. Afterwards she takes the bucket and re-washes it. Sonny leans against the door frame of the bathroom and watches her. "You've restored order. I knew you would."

"Now, one more trip and I think we're done. That chicken soup and some sweet tea?"

The room is warming up, and there is a pleasant smell of paraffin from the heater.

"No more trips. We're done," Sonny says.

Richard has been transformed. Some natural colour has returned to his face. Against Mrs Gifford's floral pillowcase, it is possible to see him as a house guest taken ill, forced to remain with his hosts for several extra days. His shoulders are bare. It was impossible to get the pyjama jacket over the chains and cuffs.

Mrs Gifford smooths down the duvet. Sonny can see his mother is satisfied with her industry. And he is satisfied with her. She is no longer the dull, distracted companion she's been since Christmas. He has provided her with a purpose.

"Socks." Sonny waves a pair of thermal socks at Richard. "I expect your feet are frozen."

"No to the socks," Richard says.

"They're clean." Sonny sniffs the socks. "They smell of lavender. A Christmas present from Mummy."

"I said no."

Sonny throws the socks at Richard who tosses them to the floor.

"Please, darling, your friend has a right to decide whether he wants to wear socks or not."

Apart from Richard's breathing there is silence in the room.

"The chicken soup?"

"Fuck the chicken soup." Sonny grins. Never before has he sworn in front of his mother. "There's hummus and some slices of ham. It's a feast. Time for you to go," he tells her. "Richard and I intend to tuck in."

Richard's eyes flicker. "Don't go, Mrs Gifford. You must be famished after all your hard work. What a marvel you are." He can't or won't stop talking to her. "I feel so much better. Honestly you've done wonders in here." On and on he goes, ignoring her son's darkening mood.

Finally, Sonny strides over to the bed and places his hand over Richard's mouth. "Go now, Ma."

Once out in the corridor, the door closed between herself and Sonny, Mrs Gifford slumps against the wall. She is frightened and totally confused. Always there has been a plan. You do this, followed by that and there is the result you hoped for. Or almost the result, beggars can't always be choosers.

"Richard, why won't you eat?" she hears Sonny say. There is an edge to his voice.

She straightens up and sets off towards the lift. Suddenly the darkness gives way to a grainy grey light. Behind her, Sonny must have opened the door of the apartment. She dares not glance back. She walks as fast as she can; there's no strength left in her legs for running. Under normal circumstances she would choose the stairs, but having held her nerve for over two hours, courage has deserted her. Three floors below, the safety of the warm familiar rooms beckon. She could lock herself in, barricade the door. Wait till Sonny becomes her son again. She has almost reached the lift when the corridor is plunged back into darkness. Mrs Gifford stretches out her hands, clasps the icy metal of the lift gate and yanks it open. Something: Sonny's hand? brushes her shoulder. She leaps forward, attempting to turn her body to close the gate and shut him out. There is no floor. Her thin legs kick out as if she is dancing. Like a trapped bird, her body beats against the walls of the lift shaft.

56

SHONA

2015

I jog the last fifty metres. Close to the Miller Building the snow is turning to slush. Ahead of me is the front door. I pray that it's unlocked. As I step out into the open, I hear the purr of a powerful engine, the gear change as a vehicle takes the slip-road off the dual carriageway. Whoever it is, they're approaching from the far side of the block. I jump back onto the path and duck down behind the bank of snow-covered scrub running parallel to the forecourt, as headlights rake the semi-darkness.

A lorry appears, coming to a standstill in front of the entrance. Nobody gets out but a light goes on in the cab. I see two silhouettes. On the side of the lorry is the logo for Hawksbridge Council. Inside the cab someone lights a cigarette. They switch off the engine.

In no more than fifteen minutes it will be full daylight. I will be stuck where I'm hiding with no chance to retrace my steps or move forwards. I have no option. On hands and knees, I begin to crawl forwards. My trousers and gloves are icily sodden, my skin numb. Reaching the back of the lorry, hunched low to avoid being seen in their rear-view mirror, I risk a dash towards the side of the building. I hear another vehicle turning off the road as I plunge into the foliage concealing the underground entrance.

Here, the darkness is palpable. I risk switching the torch on. The huge space is eerily empty. Taking a deep breath, I sprint across the dirt floor towards the one opening – almost resembling a cave entrance set into the crumbling wall. There's a door and then a short passage. Finally, I step out into the derelict hallway of the Miller Building. The wood concealing the narrow fanlight above the front door has been removed letting in a little light. Everywhere else is padlocked and barred against the outside world. I can hear voices. A key is inserted into the lock of the front door.

"Doesn't bloody work," a man shouts. "Or they've changed the lock."

The lift's safety gates are closed, the lift stationary on one of the higher floors. I take the stairs. As I reach the second floor, my torch beam flickers and then goes out. I'm in total darkness. I fight against panic, a horror of the unknown: that I'll stretch out my hand and touch a living creature that wishes me harm. I tell myself that apart from Mrs Gifford and her son, the building is empty, there is nothing to fear. The Giffords are guileless not wicked. I creep upwards. As I emerge at the entrance of the fourth-floor corridor, the darkness lessens. Their door stands open. Like a fugitive I run towards it.

A lamp is switched on. The Christmas tree is still in its tub. Apart from the naked Barbie doll at the very top all the other ornaments have been removed. Mrs Gifford's spectacles lie on the table next to the armchair as if she has only recently left the room. I tap on her bedroom door, then push it open. The drawers of her dressing table have been ransacked; the contents are scattered on the floor. The room is in complete disarray, the bed bare of duvet and pillows. Has she been taken ill during the night?

I retrace my steps through the living room and into the kitchen. The cupboard doors gape, a broken plate in pieces lies in the sink. Order has been replaced with utter chaos. I check the kettle. The remaining water is still warm. On the draining board are several used teabags, a torn slice of ham and a scatter of breadcrumbs. Anxiety makes me hungry but not for the tasteless, cheap biscuits in my rucksack. In her pantry I find a cake tin, some treat left over from Christmas. There is a wedge of Dundee cake. I cram it into my mouth. It's a little dry but to me at that moment, delicious.

"Save some for me."

I swing round. Martin leans against the door frame. A healthier, better-dressed Martin than the one I'd chosen not to recognise several times in the town centre. He wears a parka, clean jeans, good walking boots. Why am I not surprised? The Miller Building, the Giffords' apartment – what better place for Martin to hang out in winter?

"All gone," I say, my mouth full of cake. "I've got biscuits in my bag."

Martin shakes his head. "Nah! I'm okay." He tosses a slice of ham into his mouth. From the fridge he helps himself to a half-full bottle of milk, drains it, wiping his lips on the sleeve of the parka. Sensing my disapproval, he says, "Shona, she doesn't mind. She likes making a fuss of me."

"Are you living here again?"

He shakes his head. "I stayed the night over Christmas Eve. If it had been just the two of us, a week with heat and food would be great." He grins. "She wanted to present me like a roast turkey to her son. Not happening."

"But where is Mrs Gifford? There are men outside trying to break in."

"Yeah, yeah. The council know they're here. They've tried to make contact. Now they've adopted the element of surprise by coming in on a Bank Holiday. It had to happen eventually. The building can't be sold on till all the tenants are out."

"Hang on. How do you know all this?"

"The bloke you live with told me. He's involved in some way."

"Richard?"

Martin nodded. "We've hooked up a couple of times. He was the one who informed the council about the Giffords. He wants the building empty. He and his associates have plans."

Martin begins to gather together food. From the fridge, a pork pie, some bacon, a small carton of orange juice. Suddenly he stops. "Look at this," he says and holds out the small cake I'd left for Mrs Gifford on Christmas Eve. The ballerina remained but the pretty pink and white icing has been chipped away. He takes a bite, pulls a face. "Too sweet. Horrible." He drops it into the pedal bin. From the hook on the back of the kitchen door Martin helps himself to several empty carrier bags and starts to fill them.

I notice that he's limping. "Have you hurt your leg?"

"Fell over in town. Not healing well. Murder climbing over the footbridge now they've covered it in barbed wire." Back to the fridge for butter. Some cutlery off the draining board. "I think you'll find them both on the top floor. Sonny's been carrying stuff up in the lift for about an hour. Maybe they're trying to barricade themselves in. Not a good time for a visit, Shona. If I were you, I'd go home to your comfortable house and boyfriend."

"He's not my boyfriend."

From somewhere above a door opens then slams shut.

"Time to leave." Martin doesn't move. Instead, we both listen. Faintly we hear the sound of someone running.

"Is it Sonny?" For some reason I'm whispering.

Martin doesn't answer.

On an upper floor, the lift's safety gate noisily opens. A second later that sound is followed by a blood-freezing scream. It seems to last for a horribly long time. I hear a chilling thud as if something heavy has landed on a hard surface. Our eyes meet. Martin's face is ashen.

He touches my shoulder, then he's off with his carrier bags, half-running, half-limping, out into the corridor.

Heart racing, I search for a possible weapon. There are rugs and cushions and patterned throws but nothing capable of inflicting physical damage. In front of the fireplace in the living room, I come to a halt. In the grate, sticking out from a heap of ash and partly burnt logs is a steel poker. I pick it up and weigh it in my hand. Perfect.

I slip off my boots. Leaving the door open to shed some light into the corridor, I head for the staircase. Nearing the lift gate, I hear a whimper. It sounds like the cry of an injured dog. I peer through the iron work. The lift is empty. Again, I hear that eerie whimper.

I take the stairs to the next floor. Getting down on my knees next to the lift gate, I try my torch again. It sheds a flickering beam down into the shaft. Mrs Gifford lies on the flat roof of the lift only a few metres below me. Her nightgown is rucked up. One hand is tucked under her right cheek, the other stretched out at an unnatural angle. Likewise, one leg is bent, the other folded under her.

"Mrs. Gifford," I whisper.

Very slowly she turns her head to look up. She is all

eyes. I don't think I'm imagining the bright familiar blue of them.

"It's me, Shona. Hang on," I tell her, although there is nothing I can do. Not caring whether anyone hears me or not, I try to put encouragement, hope into my voice, anything that might keep her life force flickering. But it's no use. Her entire body makes a movement as if it's falling into place. It is so strange to watch.

"Stay with me. Please," I beg.

The blue of her eyes fades. The torch goes out.

Shakily, I get to my feet. My face is wet with tears. Outside I hear more vehicles arriving, men's raised voices. I should leave now, but I can't.

As I step out of the stairwell onto the seventh floor, I distinctly hear someone coughing. That same racking cough you make most winters when your bronchitis kicks in. It goes on for what seems like forever, becoming increasingly painful to listen to. And then I recognise a version of Sonny's voice, childlike and angry, "Will you stop, you stupid fucker? Just stop." And then he and the coughing are drowned out by the shriek of seagulls taking to the sky: disturbed by the activity down on the ground. I pad silently towards the doorway. Some warmth from the room is seeping out into the corridor. I can smell paraffin and a hint of fresh coffee but also and I force myself not to gag, excrement and urine. Several minutes pass before I hear someone moving away across the floor. There is a gust of cold air as if a door or window has been opened. I wait for a sound or an inner signal. I'm rewarded. I hear a stifled sob.

As I push open the door the sun streaming in through the windows renders me momentarily blind. I rub my hand across my eyes: my sight is back. I'm standing to one side of a cast-iron bed, turned to face the doors to the balcony. Over the back of a chair I recognise your sweatshirt, the one you wore on Christmas Eve. It has been jaggedly cut into two pieces. Your smart wheeled suitcase lies open, the contents spilling out across the dirty parquet floor. There is a tray piled with food: cheeses, bread, slices of ham – all apparently untouched, a half-full cafetiere and a saucer of chocolate biscuits. Silently I slip my rucksack from my shoulders and lean it against the chair. The sweatshirt slithers to the ground. On the chair seat, face down, lies a mobile phone: an iPhone 6+ in rose gold and there is your name, Richard Christopher Maplin stamped on the case.

You appear to be asleep. Your eyes are closed. For some reason I feel no sense of shock to find you here. You look older and ill. I can actually feel the heat rising from your body. Richard, you are burning up. Restlessly you push back the pretty flowered duvet. I see your wrists, the open sores where the manacles have rubbed. My foot makes painful contact with the heavy chain beneath the bed and I stifle a cry. Standing stock still, I hold my breath, gaze fixed on the balcony door. No one comes.

I want you to continue to sleep. I need time to think. Calmly I assess the room. It is huge. This may once have been two rooms. Across the ceiling is a supporting beam. The light in here is incredible. I glance into the small sparse kitchen. On the worktop there's a plastic laundry basket and pillow.

You start to cough. Your eyes flicker open.

"Shona?" Your voice is no more than a dry croak.

I shake my head. "Shush," I mouth.

Carrying the poker, I step out onto the balcony. The remaining snow penetrates my socks but there is nothing to be done, I'm pretty much soaked through anyway. A pair of binoculars and a coffee cup lie under a garden chair. Sonny is some distance away, seated on the parapet, his back to me. He's wearing something pale and silky, a dressing gown or maybe a kimono. He appears totally relaxed as if sitting on a park bench in summer, feet planted on solid ground instead of them swinging crazily in mid-air. How can he bear this cold?

I think of Mrs Gifford lying crumpled on the roof of the lift. I think of Brian and Sheila and how I planned their deaths. These were three innocent people, all love and care wasted on their flawed and damaged children. Reluctantly I place the poker on the ground.

Sonny appears unaware of my presence, absorbed in the scene playing out below. The gown slips from his shoulders. Down on the ground, the sound of shouting increases, the tenor of the voices strident, filled with concern for this semi-naked lunatic. He adores the attention. He leans his upper body out into the air. From below, a gasp of horror erupts as he sways dangerously from side to side. And then he becomes still as if considering just what his next move should be. Sonny nods. In a graceful movement he raises his arms above his head. His torso is surprisingly slender and youthful. Sonny salutes the morning sun, bringing the palms of his hands together.

I walk towards him. I note that his shoulders are pale and smooth and lightly muscled. He is in good shape. On the crown of his head is a perfect circle of pink. Sonny is losing his hair but even that process is neatly done.

He arches his back, face tilted towards the sun.

Slowly, he starts to count, "Five, four, three."

I lay my fingertips on the atlas, that first vertebra supporting the globe of Sonny's skull. He makes a fractional movement, a sinking back against my hand as if ceding all responsibility for himself. Once upon a time, his mother would have supported her baby son's head as I do now.

"Two, one," I say and push.

His body jack-knifes forwards. The roar from the audience below is deafening.

57

As I re-enter the room you call out, "Sonny?" and then begin to cough.

"He's gone." I place my hand over your mouth.

You find the strength to shake me off. "I can't help it," you say. "Where has he gone? Will he come back?"

I look at my hand, there's a smear of blood on it. "Sonny's dead."

Your coughing fit is passing. "Water," you croak.

"First, I need to raise you up into a better position. I can't manage on my own. You'll have to help. It will improve your breathing." I slide my hand under your shoulders.

Your cry of pain is chilling.

"My wrists." You are close to tears.

I feel nothing, no pity. All I have is a desire to be efficient, as efficient as Mrs Gifford would have been. "Do you know where Sonny kept the keys?"

"No."

"Then your wrists will have to wait till someone comes." My gaze turns towards the kitchen, the spare pillow tumbling from the laundry basket. It is patterned with circles of pale blue flowers. If only it could fly through the air and into my hands, save me the wearying half-dozen steps across the room to get it. Richard, you have no idea how much I want to draw this stage of my life to a close, leaving no loose ends. What a relief it would be to lay that pillow over your face and press down. Shut you up, once and for all. But there, unbidden, into my head comes that image of Mrs Gifford; such an industrious little person as she was on Christmas Eve. She would have ironed all this bedding. I see her stepping back from the ironing board and looking with approval at the neat piles of pillowcases, sheets and duvet covers. Mrs Gifford would never be like me, just folding everything haphazardly before stuffing them into drawers and cupboards. Her son might destroy but she would mend.

Is this how decisions of life or death are often reached? In this instance, yes. The imagined ghost of Mrs Gifford and an ironing board have saved your life. I shift the paraffin heater nearer to the bed. I fetch the flowered pillow from the kitchen and ease it behind your shoulders so that you're almost sitting upright. Your laboured breathing eases. Half-filling the empty glass with water, I hold it to your cracked lips. "Slowly," I warn when you try to gulp. Four sips and I take the glass away. I can't quite suppress a smile, not at your discomfort, but because the words that spring to mind are so absolutely accurate. "You're a sorry sight."

Your bloodshot eyes glitter. "Am I going to die?"

"I don't think so." I wave my hand to indicate the room. "In a few hours all this will be a distant nightmare."

"Will you wait with me?"

"No."

As you drift into sleep, I check your mobile phone. There are a couple of bars of charge left. I phone Raoul. He answers immediately. "Richard, where the fuck have you been?" he shouts.

"It's Shona. I'm at the Miller Building. Richard is ill. On the top floor. Come now."

"I can't just,"

"I think you can."

58

Ahead of me was the footbridge. I wasn't daunted. Shut me in a small, enclosed space and I panic. In the open air, with the image still fresh in my mind of Sonny spreadeagled on his downward flight some pale angel, I felt invincible, in total control. There were still vans driving in along the slip-road. In the distance I could see the flashing lights of an ambulance. I put on my soaked thermal gloves, their thickness would give me some protection from the barbed wire barrier. Sensing where to lay my hands, where to put my feet, it seemed I swarmed upwards. Unhurt, I hauled myself over the handrail; a dozen more steps and I was up on the bridge.

The jagged cavity stretched right across my path. I pictured myself flying over it like a Valkyrie, maybe brandishing a sword, to land safely on solid ground. I sprinted forwards. I could feel my plait unravelling. I shook out my hair. The wind caught it. Such freedom!

"Shona, stop! Stop now!" Martin's voice was as sharp as a slap.

I did stop, just in time, feet clenched against concrete, body tilting dangerously forwards over the drop, but not quite enough to unbalance me. A police car passed under the bridge. Mesmerised I watched as it disappeared around the side of the Miller Building. All the heightened energy was draining out of my body. It had started to snow again, the flakes swirling around me. Suddenly I was terrified.

"Don't move." Martin stood on the Hawksbridge side of the bridge. "I'm coming up."

I couldn't answer. I was mute, as I'd been that time in the library, as I'd been for over a year while in hospital. I watched as he painfully clambered back across the barbed wire. Finally, he came sauntering towards me, carefree as if we'd spotted each other on the seafront. Blood was oozing through the cloth of his jeans where his wound had re-opened. For a moment I sort of loved him. He looked so young, he could just about be my son. Say, if I'd created a child at sixteen instead of erasing two innocent people?

A two-metre chasm between us, we faced each other.

"I'll fall," I said.

"I'm here to catch you. I'll come halfway round."

Holding the railing he began to edge around the drop.

I see myself awkwardly reaching out, making an issue of my clumsiness so that *I* take hold of his hand rather than him taking mine. Dorothy is in my head, all the times I've wanted to cause her death as if by random accident: under a bus, off the top of a mountain. Down she goes. And there is Lynda Wilson, our eyes locking, fingers intertwined.

"I can't jump," I say.

"Nobody's asking you to jump. Hold the railing with your free hand, follow me back around the edge. What's left of the concrete floor will hold your weight. Don't look down."

I do as I'm told, sidle forwards. My weight is held.

"Almost there," he says. "Two more steps and you're home and dry."

With just those two steps left to reach my own place of safety my fingers move to Martin's bony wrist. As if about to embrace him: *thank you Martin, you have saved my life,* instead, with all my strength I yank him backwards, try to tear him away from the railing. He cries out with pain as his injured leg twists. My grip tightens. "Give in," I tell him. "Let yourself fall."

"No, Shona," he says.

The two of us are joined together but he is stronger. With a groan of pain, he turns sideways, taking me with him. We collapse, me on top of him, both panting on solid concrete. He strokes my hair. I allow myself to be comforted. "I'm sorry," I say.

"It's okay. I expected you to pull some sort of trick ... but not quite that one."

Together we crawl off the bridge. Surprisingly strong, Martin lowers me over the wire and down onto grass. I offer to throw up my gloves for his own descent.

He shakes his head. "I'm good," he says.

Without speaking, we make our way doggedly into Hawksbridge. Almost at Canberra Road, I realise he's no longer with me.

I think, I hope, I'm done now.

59

Richard paid the cab driver with his bank card before pushing a ten-pound note into the man's hand. "If you could carry my case into the hall please, I'm still a little shaky."

When we got inside, I offered to take the case upstairs for him.

"No, leave it here for now, Shona. I'll start unpacking it in the morning. Oh god, I'm so glad to be home. There were times when I thought," For a moment he looked almost tearful.

"Kitchen? Coffee? Sit for a while or would you rather go to bed, maybe stretch out on the sofa?"

"I've done enough lying around but thanks for the thought. One of the things that kept me going was imagining myself back in my own kitchen, warm, clean and drinking coffee. Can you manage the coffee machine?"

I gave him a ridiculous, roguish smile. "In your absence, I've learnt!"

We sat on the bar stools at his beloved marble island. I watched as his face, his entire body, relaxed and somehow softened.

He sipped coffee. "Just the way I like it." There was a tremor in his voice. "Thank you, Shona."

I felt a genuine pang of regret. Actually far more than that. He'd been in hospital for ten days but still looked so thin, so depleted, every bit of stuffing knocked out of him. One hand lay like a dead thing next to his cup. I was sorely tempted to squeeze it gently.

He grinned, a faint shadow of his usual confident grin. "There is a Chinese proverb that says if you save someone's life, you become responsible for that person and their actions forever." The thing that is his hand wasn't dead; it crept across the island towards mine.

"I'd like to put this house in both our names."

"I can't accept that."

"It would afford you some security. Give it some thought."

"Of course, I will." Smoothly, I got to my feet. "Look, I'll leave you to sort yourself out for an hour or two. I'd like to walk down to the seafront and back. Give you some space."

"That's not necessary."

"I want to."

"But you will think about what I've just said? You got well living here. The beautiful unique Shona came back."

I couldn't bear the soft, sentimental way he looked at me. Only minutes earlier I was convinced that all my anger and resentment was erased but suddenly it returned in full force. Whatever mess his own head might be in, he'd destabilised mine for years.

"We'll talk more tomorrow, when you've had a good night's sleep in your own bed." As I passed him, I kissed the top of his head. There was no pink circle of scalp, Richard's hair was thick and shiny. He must have washed it before leaving hospital.

"I'll just sit here for a bit. Make a few calls. You've kept the house wonderfully, Shona. Everything looks amazing. I love the flowers." He stretched across the island and touched one of the pale pink blossoms. "Where would you get these at this time of year?"

"Oh, you can buy anything online."

"What are they called?"

"Cosmos. Back soon."

Pulling on my coat as I walked, nothing to carry but a shoulder bag containing money, bank card and a set of keys, I kept expecting to hear your footsteps behind me, a shout: "Hey Shona, what's happening? Where are you going? Come back!" The road remained silent: not a car or a person, only me. Once I reached the seafront my pace slowed. I found a bench. As cold as it was, I sat down and allowed myself some time to daydream. Did you pour yourself another cup of coffee? Were you smiling as you carried it back to the central island, congratulating yourself on completing a normal task after so many days of abnormality? Did you decide it was far too early to go to bed, that instead you'd watch a film? Check on the living room and reassure yourself that the precious world you'd created was still intact?

Opening the living room door, did you step into the centre of the room, where once the contemporary Perspex chandelier hung and look around and around and around with disbelief? And then suddenly, shock, horror, did you realise that this might not be the only completely empty room? Despite your fragile health and gasping for breath, did you take the stairs two at a time? Fighting the desperate need to start coughing, did you push open the spare room door, my bedroom door, your bedroom door to find . . . emptiness? Only a lightbulb left on the landing so you could see the absence of everything. Nothing left.

Ah, but I'm forgetting, not quite nothing. The overstuffed leather armchair remained, its cushion removed so you could see the space where you'd concealed your laptop and box of Shona Blake ephemera. You probably have copies but still I took them with me. Also, my paints and paintings from the loft room. That was fair, wasn't it? After all, I saved your life.

60

SHONA

2016

It is mid-summer and I'm walking along a busy London street. I'm early for a dinner engagement. Who would have thought that Shona Blake would have such a thing? I stop at a wine bar and seat myself in the shade of an umbrella. I order a glass of house white. "Very cold." I give the waiter a steely look but then I smile. He smiles back. I've lived in this area for almost six months. He and I are new friends. The wine arrives and also a small saucer of olives. I take out my beloved sketchbook and pencil. I begin to draw Mrs Gifford as I remember her best.

In January of last year on the day of her funeral, it was bitterly cold but the sun shone: weather she would have approved of. There was a smaller turnout than for her son but still quite a crowd. Sonny had been buried on the Friday of the previous week. His funeral made the national news. In death Sonny Gifford had become a household name: the probable killer responsible for kidnapping award-winning film and graphics designer Richard Christopher Maplin. The Miller Building carpark had been dug up and the bodies found of two men and a young woman. On the screen, there'd been an image of the actual building squatting like a gross animal imprisoned within a cage of scaffolding. I hadn't attended Sonny's funeral but Richard and Raoul had gone. Seeing Richard on the television, he'd seemed healthy and tanned, oozing confidence and swagger.

"How are you feeling after your experience?" an interviewer asked him.

"Great to be alive. I thank my lucky stars." He'd looked not into the woman's face, but directly at the camera, as if he was directing his words at me.

Mrs Gifford's service was held in the small church tucked behind Hawksbridge library. I'd had no idea of its existence but as soon as I entered it felt right: simple wooden pews with tapestry cushions, one stained glass window behind the altar and solid stone walls. I could imagine her, were she a mourner rather than the deceased, wrapped in her winter coat, the tilted beret, the fur she'd deemed as 'cat' around her neck. I'd be aware of the effort she'd be making to keep her shoulders straight, head held high – no elderly stooping for an ex-prima ballerina. I'd have taken her woolly gloved hand in mine. The pain I felt ever since knowing she was dead was still very real. Mrs Gifford had meant far more to me than any emotion I'd ever felt for Beatrice Salmon.

Richard was at the service but no Raoul. He made a move to join me but I held up my hand, my palm flat to indicate, 'no entry' and he'd stepped back, entered a pew on the other side of the aisle. Unlike his TV persona from the previous week, he looked haggard, older than his age. I almost softened but at that moment, several other mourners arrived, men in smart suits. Later I learnt that they were estate agents. Mrs Gifford had been a favourite of theirs. The hum of voices ceased. From somewhere near the altar, I recognised the music I'd been allowed to choose; the Black Swan's 'Pas de Deux' from Tchaikovsky's *Swan Lake.* Mrs Gifford's coffin, so small that it could have been made for a child, was carried into the church.

I pay for the wine and olives. Ahead of me is a short walk. I'm nervous so I slow my pace. I come bearing no gifts, only myself. This is a residential road. On each side stand tall Victorian houses. Flights of stone steps lead up to each ornate front door. They have glass skylights depicting a different flower: Anemone, Foxglove, no fragile cosmos. I arrive at number sixty. I'm curious. What flower will I see? The door opens. A woman emerges. She stands in the doorway shielding her eyes from the sun. The fanlight is obscured. I take a guess. It will surely be something perfect in shape and colour, an orchid perhaps?

Self-consciously I mount the steps. "No Beatrice today?" I ask.

"Just you and me."

Without glancing up at the skylight, I follow Joan Vigo into the cool gloom of a spacious hall.

Acknowledgements

I'd like to thank Matthew Bates who believed in my writing long before I was able to. Without Matt's encouragement, I would never have finished this book. Thanks to Kate and Sarah Beal at Muswell Press who have been endlessly patient and a pleasure to work with. Finally, to my own Shadow Self: I've finally allowed her out of the darkness and onto the page.